SCOT &
SODA

To Lisa,

— A LAST DITCH MYSTERY —

CATRIONA McPHERSON

Cheers!

SCOT & SODA

[signature: Catriona McPherson]

MIDNIGHT INK
WOODBURY, MINNESOTA

MIDNIGHT INK

FIRST EDITION
First Printing, 2019

Cover design by Shira Atakpu
Editing by Nicole Nugent

Midnight Ink, an imprint of Llewellyn Worldwide Ltd.

Library of Congress Cataloging-in-Publication Data
Names: McPherson, Catriona, author.
Title: Scot and soda / Catriona McPherson.
Description: First edition. | Woodbury, Minnesota : Midnight Ink, [2019] | Series: A last ditch mystery ; #2.
Identifiers: LCCN 2018041399 (print) | LCCN 2018042600 (ebook) | ISBN 9780738755540 (ebook) | ISBN 9780738754123 (alk. paper)
Subjects: | GSAFD: Mystery fiction.
Classification: LCC PR6113.C586 (ebook) | LCC PR6113.C586 S35 2019 (print) | DDC 823/.92—dc23
LC record available at https://lccn.loc.gov/2018041399

Midnight Ink
Llewellyn Worldwide Ltd.
2143 Wooddale Drive
Woodbury, MN 55125-2989
www.midnightinkbooks.com

Printed in the United States of America

This is for Eileen Rendahl and Andy Wallace,
dear friends and interpreters of California. Thank you.

One

The gaping wound in my chest made it hard to bend over, so I did a sort of a sideways limbo instead and dragged the severed fingers away from the flames before they burned. I was just in time. They were blistered and tight, charred here and there but not quite smoking. I slid them into place between the skewered eyeballs and the cold sick, then turned carefully so's not to bump the axe handle protruding from my chest as I navigated the doorway and made my way to where the screams were coming from.

"Hot sausages, lychee kebabs, chilled cheddar soup," I said, "and I think we're done."

"Best. Halloween. Buffet. Ever," Todd said. "I'll just die if I don't get your infected toenail recipe. What do you think of the soundtrack?" The soundtrack was a wonder. Screams raged and gurgled, curdling blood and raising hackles. "And what do you think of my costume?"

He had come as a character he called Pray Away, and, truth be told, it was hard to look at him. He was in beige chinos, white sports socks, and Keens, a flannel shirt open over a vee-neck t-shirt—"Target's finest," he'd told me, "pilled polyester"—and a phone holster. He had

1

washed his hair with floor soap to dull it down, taken his earrings out, and let his beard grow for a week before threading it with food scraps. He'd had a MAGA cap on too, but Noleen put her foot down.

"It's just under-baked corn chips dipped in mustard," I said. "For the toenails. With some green food colouring marbled in."

"And the phlegm cups?"

"Egg drop soup with a bit of raw, salty meringue for the foam."

"Genius," Todd said. "How did you make the hens' feet?"

"They're hens' feet," I said. "From the Asian deli. Try one."

"Ew," said Todd. "Heave, puke, splat, Lexy. Every time I think you've finally assimilated, you pull something like this and disappoint me."

I opened my mouth to argue, but the sight of Noleen coming through the door stilled the breath in my throat. I'd thought she'd nixed the MAGA cap because it wasn't funny. Turned out she didn't want Todd stealing her thunder. She had dyed her hair the colour of listeria and she was wearing a terrible blue trouser suit and a long red paper-clipped tie. She'd bound her breasts and added a fake paunch. And that wasn't all.

"Wh—What have you done to your skin?" I said. It wasn't just orange; it was puckered and puffy in a way that made me want to pat my pockets, hoping to find a forgotten EpiPen.

"I painted on Krazy Glue and kept my mouth wide open and my eyebrows up while it dried," Noleen said. "It was a hunch, but it worked pretty good, huh? Then I slapped on some gravy powder."

"It's … unbelievable," I said. "Can you do the voice?"

"Nope," said Noleen.

"Thank God," said Todd. "It would be a shame to let Lexy's buffet go to waste. Have a severed polar bear claw, Nolly. White marshmallow fingers and cherry jam. They're yummy."

"They're tampons," I said. "But thank you."

"You are one sick puppy," said Todd.

"I stuck to the rules," I reminded him. "No insects."

That was because Todd had the worst case of cleptoparasitosis I had ever encountered in all my years as a clinical psychologist in Scotland, plus my nine months as a generic therapist here in California. He was an anesthesiologist, married to a paediatrician (in other words, not short of change), and yet he was living in a room in the Last Ditch Motel because it was the only place bug-free enough for him to bear.

And the Last Ditch Motel was bug-free because Noleen's wife, Kathi Muntz, had the worst case of germaphobia I had ever seen in all my years plus my nine months, and her cousin in Costa Rica sent her up drums of heavy-duty insecticide, hidden in gift hampers, that were totally illegal here in greener-than-green, sustainably sourced, hand-knitted, home-sprouted Californ-aye-eh. Actually, the Costa Rican insecticide was so effective it was even banned in Nevada.

In between sprayings, Kathi ran the Skweeky Kleen launderette attached to the Last Ditch while Noleen ran the motel itself, Todd ran the lives of everyone he met from the moment he met them (more of which soon), and Roger, Todd's husband, looked after sick children, despaired of ever moving home again, and moaned to me every chance he got. Which was lots of chances, because we were neighbours.

Me? What was *I* doing at the Last Ditch? Funny story. I emigrated from Scotland to marry my sweetheart. Or so it said in the trailer. Only, he turned out to be heartless and sour. Then I inherited a houseboat from a client—you know, that way you do—and since the Last Ditch is named after the slough that runs along behind it and there's nowhere else in this dusty pancake of a town with enough water to float even a candle on … here I am.

The permits were what salty Americans call "a mother." A Queen Mother. Norman Bates's mother. Getting permission to moor a houseboat in the Last Ditch Slough, live in it, and set up a business there was a mother to rival *my* mother. And my mother is the reason I went into psychology.

I couldn't have done it without Noleen behind me. She's not exactly a high-pressure jet of the milk of human kindness as a general rule, but boy-oh-boy does she hate the department of works in this fair city! Most recently because they put the kibosh on a firepit Noleen reckoned could be the start of happy hours and wine tastings, bringing in a better class of client. Tourist trade, she would say and get misty-eyed.

Ignoring the mist in Noleen's eyes, the best real news the Last Ditch had had recently was when Devin, the skinny kid in Room 101, turned out not to be a meth addict or rentboy as suspected—hence his placement next to the office where Noleen could keep an eye on him—but just a community college student whose roommates had bullied him out of their shared house and who reckoned he could afford the Last Ditch rates if he filled up at the continental breakfast in the front office every morning and cooked noodles in a kettle in his room the rest of the time. Noleen had gone from threatening to kick him out for tying up a bed she could make her fortune with, to delivering tomato soup and grilled cheese when she heard him coughing through the interconnecting wall.

Anyway, since there's no other businesses here on the wrong side of Cuento's tracks (except a drive-through coffee stand, a self-storage facility, and the police station), the impact assessment on a tiny houseboat hidden in the bushes—with a state-of-the-art eco-toilet and a greywater recycling system—defanged the kiboshes like another mother.

Whatever kiboshes are. Blunted them, maybe. Unplugged them and powered them down.

So the back room of my beautiful little houseboat was now an oasis of cream-coloured upholstery, fluffy knee blankets, plump cushions, peach lightbulbs, and several handily placed boxes of top-of-the-range Kleenex. It was my consultation room, all set for people to curl up and weep in. Without getting snotters on the upholstery. And business was booming. (More of which soon too.)

I had locked that room up tonight, not wanting the Halloween party to spill over and leave fake bloodstains because there was a nine o'clock booking in the morning and I knew I had time to eat away my hangover *or* tidy up my consulting room. Not both.

Losing a room wasn't a problem. I mean, don't get me wrong, Creek House is so tiny that one window A/C unit at the back keeps the whole place cool as long as I leave the doors open. And thank God for that. My whole life, the challenge was to keep cosy in spite of cold: extra blankets and hot water bottles in bed at night, and my breath pluming; letting the shower run hot before I took my jammies off in a frigid bathroom where the condensation lasted round the clock; the kitchen only being warm when I was cooking. This was my first year in California and I still hadn't really got the memo that cold is one thing and you can always put more socks on. Heat's the bitch and there's nothing you can do.

I tried. I put fans in strategic corners. I put screens on the windows. I hugged a cool pack like a teddy bear. It was when I found myself getting my nightie out of the freezer and going to bed with four buckets of ice in my bedroom, that's when I caved. Two dollars a bag for ice at four bags a night would soon rack up to the price of a window unit anyway.

Jesus, it was ugly. And Mary mother of God, it was loud. But Joseph the best ever step-dad, it was cold.

Tiny as the houseboat is, most of the space-saving is in the kitchen, natty and well-organised but truly miniscule; the only bathroom, even teensier—nowhere to hang a towel to keep it dry while you're showering; and the two bedrooms with their built-in cabin beds and hanging space for one coat and two dresses—unless shoulder pads ever come back, in which case I'll be struggling.

This room, tonight's party room, usually my living room, was plenty spacious for a single woman with only seven friends. Add the front porch that stretches right along the landward side and it was quite a spread. So even when all the friends had arrived, there was room to spare: Roger, dressed as a nun, needed some wimple clearance; Todd's mother, Barbara, dressed as Dolly Parton (whom she in no way resembled), had a wide-ish turning circle, obviously; Kathi, dressed a bit more successfully as Kenny Rogers, had possibly overdone the fake paunch, which rivalled Noleen's Trump-flump. Della and Diego, though, long-time Last Ditch residents, were dressed adorably as a teddy bear and his owner, so they took up basically no space at all. Della's costume was just her own striped flannel PJs and slippers, and Diego, the teddy bear, was three.

"Trick or treeeeeeeeat," he squealed at me, at a pitch that told me he was full of sugar already and needed no more.

"*De hecho no!*" I told him. "*De ninguna manera, mi pequeño amigo.*"

"Huh?" he said.

"Speak English!" said Della.

"I need to practise my Spanish," I told her.

"That's not Spanish," Della and Todd said in chorus. Then Todd said, "Snap, jinx, I own you."

"Eh?" I said. "Snap *what*?"

6

"You're a terrible immigrant," Della said. "You cram Scottish Halloween down our throats and you don't learn any local customs."

"Don't learn … ?" I said. "What do you think that is on the step out there? I've carved a pumpkin, instead of a turnip—swede—rutabaga. I've made savoury toenails instead of treacle buns, I've even chilled the beer. And I'm calling it 'beer,' even though it's lager. Which isn't beer. Just because I want Diego to sing for his Reese's instead of demanding money with menaces … "

"Give it up," said Della. "Do you see me insisting on *Dia de los Muertos*?"

Roger was sucking his teeth and shaking his head. "Children carve rutabagas?" he said. "With knives? Do any Scottish children have all their fingers?"

I waved all ten of mine at him. "Calm down, Sister," I said. "Have you got a name, by the way? Or are you just a generic nun?"

"Sister Maria Stiletto," he said, lifting the hem of his habit to show me a pair of six-inch spike heels and just a flash of fishnet above them.

"Did you mention cold beer?" Todd said. "And can I get a round of applause, please, for dedication to my costume? Pretending to give a damn about beer when my husband has stockings on under his nun outfit? How straight *am* I?"

"Todd," said Della in a voice that could train a dog to stop chewing. "Do not corrupt my son."

"How did I corrupt—" Todd began.

"Not all straight men love beer, *papi*," Della said.

"No, *mamá*," Diego said, very solemn and helpful. "Straight men love girls."

"What makes you assume he's—" Todd began.

"Straight men love big girls and I love little girls," Diego said. "And some big ones."

7

"And sweeties? I mean, candy?" I said.

"Trick or treeeeeeeat!" said Diego, which is where we came in.

I gave him a bag of the utterly bowfing dried toe jam known as candy corn and he seemed happy. He gave me a smacking kiss and batted his eyelashes, making me wonder if I was one of the big girls he held a torch for.

"Ahem, cold beer?" Todd said again. "Does this mean you've gotten yourself a decent-sized refrigerator?"

"I've already *got* a decent-sized refrigerator," I said. "I am one person and I live in a town where the supermarkets never close. Why does everyone think they need to buy up half of Costco and pay PG&E a king's ransom to keep it all fresh? My fridge is fine."

In truth, my fridge was titchy, like everything else in my kitchen, but it fitted under the bunker—worktop—counter and I didn't want to wreck the doll's house perchinkiness of it all by cramming in a bigger one. To my American friends, of course, a fridge as short as a dishwasher and slightly slimmer was basically camping.

"So ... is it one beer each and then you'll put the kettle on?" Noleen said. "Because I've cleared my morning for recovery time and I planned on getting shit-fa—Sorry, Della—hammered tonight."

"It's not in the fridge," I said.

"Oh!" said Kathi. "You got the Yeti Tundra?" Her germaphobia manifested itself mostly in terms of touch, not taste. She was happy to eat a burrito from the wagon on E Street so long as she picked up the hot-sauce bottle with a napkin over her hand, but the level of angst about my housekeeping in general meant that she'd tried quite hard to make me expand my refrigeration options with the purchase of an outrageously expensive add-on.

"That's right," I said. "I spent four hundred dollars on a plastic box. In fact, I got two. How did you guess?"

"Cadillac of coolers!" Kathi said.

"It would have to get better mileage than a Cadillac for four hundred dollars," I told her. "One guess left," I added. "Look around."

All of them, except Diego who was poking candy corn niblets under his lip to make them look like teeth, cast their eyes around my porch but no one noticed the rope, tied in a loop and lashed to the railing.

"Old-school," I said, sidling towards it carefully. I was getting mightily sick of having an axe sticking out of my chest and I hoped the trick-or-treaters would all come early so I could prise it off and put my jammies on. Della had the right idea when it came to costumes, I reckoned.

In fact, it had taken some soul-searching before I'd been able to embrace the gore of this holiday the way I knew I was supposed to. I'd seen a real dead body earlier in the year, during those few torrid days when I met all these fine people and cleaved to them for keepsies. I wasn't a fan. Didn't like viewing corpses, didn't care for the morgue much, didn't relish brushing up against murder, manslaughter, suicide, or sudden violent death of any kind, was heartily glad that the case was over and my short career as dealer with death and catcher of baddies was behind me.

"You've put the beer in the slough?" Kathi said as I started hauling on the rope. "You expect me to wrap my lips round the neck of a bottle that's been stewing in slough water?"

"Chilling," I said. "Not stewing. And of course not. *Yours* is in the fridge. Yours and yours alone."

Kathi beamed at me, her Kenny Rogers beard rippling. "Thanks, Lexy."

I would have blown her a kiss, but I needed both hands. This seventy-two pack of Blue Moon seemed much heavier coming back up than it had when I was letting it down at tea-time. My muscles were starting to judder.

"Is it a keg?" Todd said, coming and taking hold of the rope with me.

"A box of bottles," I said.

"It weighs more than a box of bottles." Todd pushed his flannel sleeves up and took a better grip. "Sister Mary, get in here and pull."

Roger fitted himself in behind Todd and put his big hands on the rope in front of mine.

"The cardboard will be waterlogged," I said between gasps. "That's a bit of extra weight right there."

"No way," Todd said, straining. "It must be stuck on something."

"I don't think so," said Roger, "it's moving. It's just. So. Heavy. Let's rest a moment."

"Can we help?" said Kathi.

"Not with these babies," said Barb, patting her Dolly falsies.

"And I don't want to break a sweat and melt my complexion," said Noleen.

"We've got it," Todd said. "Here it comes. I can see ... "

He went silent. And he stopped pulling. I leaned over to see what the problem was, buckling my axe and dislodging it from my chest wound. Under the water, floating just deep enough to be semi-visible in the murky water was ... not a box of beer bottles. Not a box of anything. It wasn't square. It wasn't squat. It was long and rounded and waving at one end. Literally, it was waving at one end, because it was a human arm, with a human hand wafting back and forward in the water, its chunky ring glinting.

"Happy Halloween!" Noleen shouted, looking over the side at my elbow.

"Oh!" I said, all my breath leaving me in a huge rush of relief. "Good one! Did you put that down there? It's horribly realistic."

Todd and Roger were heaving again, working at it like a couple of old seadogs on a pirate ship, except for the chinos and the wimple.

"Not me," said Noleen. "And not Kathi. Barb?"

"Not my style," said Barb. "I hate pranks, to be honest."

"Della?" I said.

"I honour the dead today," Della told me. "I don't make jokes." She gave me a sheepish smile. "I am a bad immigrant too."

"Well, whoever it was has excelled," I said. It was more than just the arm now; the head was coming up to the surface and the mask was horrendously real looking. The hair was a bit of a let-down—bright orange fun-fur with a tartan tammy on top—but the face was perfect. It was mottled and bloated, the eyes dull and the mouth opening to show two rows of teeth, fillings and everything, and a tongue waving in the water just like the hand had.

He was on the surface now. Todd and Roger were panting but managing to keep him steady. All those hours in the gym had made them a fine pair of physical specimens. Todd leaned even further back to take more of the strain and said, "Look and see how he's attached, Roger. Let's see if we can let him down really gently so he doesn't float off downstream."

Roger nodded. "But first," he said. "Barb? Della? Why don't you take Diego trick-or-treating up in The Oaks? You can borrow my car."

"You think Barb's neighbors will welcome Diego on their front stoops?" Della said. Barb's house was in the ritziest bit of Cuento, and some people there can be mucho mean to little kids from down near the slough.

"No way," said Barb. "We've come for a party."

"And it's a school night," Della added. "We'll stick close to home."

"Get him *out* of here, Mom," Todd hissed. "This isn't a prank. It's a … It's not a prank."

11

"*Dios mio*," Della said, under her breath, looking over the railing at the floating shape. "Diego, *papi*, let's go, go, go! Ice cream! Chocolate ice cream! Extra sprinkles! Let's roll."

"That's that for Halloween then," I said, as we watched Diego scamper down the houseboat steps on his little teddy bear paws and jump onto dry land. "It's the day of the dead after all."

Two

What do you want to do with the beer?" It was the uniformed cop I knew as Mills of God. He wasn't the brightest candle-stub in the pumpkin, but he was basically decent in a clueless kind of way and he looked genuinely pained at the sight of the seventy-two pack disintegrating on my porch, still with a soggy rope tied round it.

"Isn't it evidence?" I said, thinking that whether the dead guy had washed downstream or plopped in where we found him, he had ended up folded round the rope like a hairpin, hugging the beer with all four of his sodden limbs.

He was gone now, thank God. The twenty minutes he'd spent on my porch after a pair of police divers got him up had been enough to make me rethink every item in my Halloween buffet. There was nothing cute about severed fingers and skewered eyeballs, because death was no joke, and there was nothing much about infected toenails or loaded tampons to soothe our lurching stomachs either.

"Of course it's evidence," snapped the detective in charge. Molly "Mike" Rankinson had been no fan of mine before tonight, and Dead Beer Guy wasn't helping. "Write a receipt and load it," she spat at Mills of God, then she stamped off into the corridor leading to the back of the boat. "Follow me, Ms. Campbell," she threw over her shoulder.

I followed her. She was headed into my consultation room, squelching over my pale carpet in her mud-splattered boots, and dropping down onto my plushy sofa in her slough-scummed trousers.

"Oh come on!" I said. "Can I at least put a cover under you? Jeez!"

"Business that bad?" Mike said. "Can't afford a little dry cleaning?"

Business, as I was sure she knew very well, was far from bad. My counselling practice had started huge (more of which very soon) and was still expanding. Like one of those home-science doo-berries where you pour a cup of stuff on a heap of other stuff and it swells into a discoloured, misshapen mountain of foaming sludge the size of Texas.

"So," Mike said, flicking open her notebook and letting the elastic go with a crack like a rifle shot. "When did you put the beer down?"

"Three o'clock," I said. "And it hit the bottom. He wasn't in there then."

"Thank you, Nancy Drew." I said nothing. "And then you were on the boat from then till you hauled him up again?"

"Yes, and there's no way *he* was on the boat."

My little floating kingdom was a quiet place to live if you didn't count the symphony made up of the motel A/C wind section, the thumping bass from the generator, the jazzy percussion of toilet flushes, and the inevitable profanity-strewn arias that accompany family road trips on the kind of budget that leads to nights at the Last Ditch Motel.

So not that quiet, really. But I didn't need to worry about marauders creeping up on me and me not hearing them, because I could feel them. I felt the dip and surge on deck whenever anyone stepped onto my boat. Noleen, who was solidly built and not light on her tippy-

14

toes, caused enough backwash to spill a cup of coffee. Nor could Kathi, slight and stealthy, hope to surprise me. Even Diego, playing at spies with his midget trench coat and outsize spyglass, telegraphed his approach. And the one time a possum got cocky and reckoned my deck-edge herb garden looked snackable, he lived to regret it. I had told Mike that already. She didn't believe me, but when she tested me—stepping on and off at both ends while I stood, sat, and lay all over the house, not looking—I passed with a perfect score.

"And you're sure you don't recognise him?"

I sighed.

"Sometimes the shock gets in the way and then, hours later, witnesses think it over and realize it's their lawn guy. Or the trainer from their gym. Or the valet from their parking garage."

I opened my mouth to say *I haven't got a lawn and even if I did I wouldn't have a lawn guy, and I don't belong to a gym and even if I did I wouldn't have a trainer, and I haven't got a garage and even if I did I wouldn't have a valet parker. And if I had a dog I wouldn't have a walker, and if I had any money I wouldn't have a financial adviser, and if I played golf I wouldn't have a caddy, and, basically, I might be the European around here but I wasn't the one with a bevy of minions to rival the court of the Sun King.*

What I said was: "Positive. Never seen that face before in my puff."

That face. It was still stamped on the inside of my eyelids two hours after they'd zipped him into his bin bag and taken him away. It was a nice face. More laugh lines than frown lines. Exuberant eyebrows left to go wild instead of being Quintoed till they looked like slugs instead of caterpillars. A gap between his two front teeth that probably signalled devil worship to the dentition-sticklers of these parts but which struck me as friendly.

"Poor guy," I said. "He was probably drunk, eh? How do you drown in a slough this shallow unless you're bladdered? And why else would you wear a Jimmy wig?"

"A what?"

"The tartan bunnet and orange rug combo. Jimmy wig. No sober person has ever worn one of those things."

"The Tam O'Shanter, you mean? The hat?"

"Although, I suppose it's Halloween. But he didn't have a costume on otherwise." He'd been wearing jeans and a blue sweatshirt with Asic trainers. Mr. Generic America.

"So this hat," said Mike. "This 'Jimmy wig.' It's significant to you?"

"It's … " I shrugged. "I suppose so. Football—*soccer* fans wear them to internationals. It's the fan uniform. It's like shorthand for 'Scottish.' He didn't look Scottish to me, though. Too tall. Too fit. And plus the white socks, you know? If he hadn't been wearing the old 'See You, Jimmy,' I'd never put him down as a compatriot."

"He wasn't," said Mike. I frowned. "He wasn't wearing the hat." I frowned harder. "It was attached to his scalp with a staple gun."

"Ow!" I said, helplessly wincing.

"Post-mortem."

"Oh!" I said, my shoulders dropping again. "Hang on. What? How could someone attach it post-mortem? He, what? He drowned and someone hauled him to the surface and put a hat on him then let him sink again?"

Mike could not have looked more thrilled to deliver the next bit of news if she'd hired a pair of oiled hunks to flank her and set off confetti guns. "Oh no," she purred. "He didn't drown, Lexy. He didn't fall in the slough and drown. He was shot before he hit the water."

I gulped like a fish. I knew it even though I couldn't see myself. I couldn't see myself because mirrors don't have any place in counselling consultation rooms, because if clients could see themselves ugly crying, they'd even-uglier cry.

"Why didn't I see the bullet hole?" I asked when I finally got a lungful of air to use up on stupid questions.

"Because the gun was pressed against his belly, under his clothes," Mike said.

"Belly?" I said. "Murder?"

"Bingo," said Mike.

"Poor guy," I said again. "What's his name?" She hesitated. "I won't tell anyone. Before you inform his family, I mean." She hesitated some more. "But yes, you're probably right to do it by the book."

"I don't need your blessing," said Mike. She truly could wring an insult out of anything. "I'm not telling you his name because we don't know his name. Why else would I ask if you knew him but not *give* you his name? He's got no ID on him."

"A mugging gone wrong?" I said.

"Not so many muggers these days travel with their own staple gun and novelty hat."

"Duh," I said. "Sorry."

"So," said Mike, snapping her notebook closed again. We were done, it seemed. "You moving into the motel for the night? We can put you on a thirty-minute drive-by. Or, if you're staying here, I can get a uni to sleep over."

"What?" I said. *Thirty-minute drive-by* sounded illegal. "Is 'uni' another word for co-ed?"

"What?" said Mike, quirking an eyebrow at me.

"Don't quirk your eyebrow at me," I said. "I don't see why you need a word for a student who happens to be female anyway. *Co-ed!* It's like the fifties."

"A uniformed officer. I was trying to offer some protection," Mike said. "For all the thanks I get."

"Protection ... for me?"

"Seemed like a good plan," said Mike. "That guy has been dead four days at least, to my untrained but experienced eye. Then someone staples an ethnic headdress to him and winds him around the beer rope of the only member of that ethnic group in town. You think this isn't about you, Lexy? Really?"

I felt my blood drain. Mike leapt up and cupped the back of my head gently in her hand. I thought she was going to kiss me.

"Put your head between your knees," she said, shoving me down. "If you faint, I'll have to bring you to the ER. And I cannot face the ER on Halloween."

"It never even occurred to me," I said, talking to my kneecaps. "I'm so used to seeing Jimmy wigs! They're everywhere in the tourist-tat shops in Edinburgh. It never struck me that seeing one in Cuento was weird."

"But you're sure you didn't know the guy?" said Mike. "Even though it looks way personal that he ended up right in your back-yard?"

"Didn't recognise his face, his hair, his teeth with the gap, his clothes, his ring, his—"

"What ring?"

"The ring," I said, sitting up again. "His finger ring. A big ugly clunky thing. Middle finger of his ... " I screwed up my eyes and tried to picture it " ... right hand. You must have noticed the ring."

"There was no ring on the body," Mike said. "Maybe it was a bottle-cap on the slough bed? Or a reflection on the water."

"It was a ring," I said. "On his finger. Ask Roger and Todd. They must have seen it too. It must have dropped off as he was coming out.

It'll be on the riverbed. You could put a magnet on a bit of string and fish it back up again."

"We'll tell the diver to look out for a ring when he goes back down to sweep the scene in the morning," Mike said. Then she glared at me. "Do *not* put a magnet on a piece of string and go fishing." I blushed. "And what do you want to do about protection?"

"I'll sleep here," I said. "With a uni. Thank you. If I go to the motel, the press'll be crawling all over this place and me not here to stop them. They have atrocious boat etiquette at the *Cuento Voyager*, you know. No way they'd stroll into some landlubber's home, but I couldn't keep them off when—well, you know. *Then*."

"Oh, I know," Mike said. "But I can't believe you're complaining. You should have paid them commission."

I didn't know where to begin to explain it to her. Anytime I'd tried to tell anyone that there's more to business than turnover, they scoffed. I spent half an hour once telling Noleen that work wasn't just money, that there was personal satisfaction and professional pride too, and she snorted so hard she hurt her uvula.

The thing is that, at the close of my last adventure—the one that brought me to Creek House—I had a certain amount of press attention. I'd helped to solve a murder, kind of, and I'd inherited a historic property. And then I'd been fined by the police department and the fire marshall and the zoning board for all kinds of misdemeanours and shenanigans, none of which were my fault.

So I was feeling pretty goddam hard-done-by when the *Voyager* reporter came sniffing round, and I'd had a small glass of sherry or two and he seemed like a nice guy and I'd never spoken to journos in real life before, as opposed to watching Robert Redford and Dustin Hoffman being them in films. Turns out they're much more Nixon than Bernstein, the scumbags, and this one stitched me up and hung me out to dry.

The interview was finished by the time all the juicy stuff came out. At least I thought so. We were having a drink, and he was having a smoke, and we were just talking. I was talking about the long con that keeps thriving populations of therapists in business year after year and keep the self-help shelves of Barnes and Noble groaning.

"We've all got room for growth!" I remember saying very clearly, because most of the sounds were nice and soft. "It takes two to sink a partnership!" I slurred, much less successfully, what with all the esses. "Pile o' shite!" I shouted. "We *don't* all have room for growth. Some of us are fine as we *are*. It takes two to keep a marriage *afloat*. If one of you stops, if just one of you starts cheating or lying or gambling or throwing punches…doesn't much matter what the other one does, does it? And it's not innocent. Oh no! It's not an unfortunate error, all these battalions of MFTs—or is that the ultimate street-fighting thing? No? Right. All these battalions of MFTs saying 'work on communicating,' 'meet halfway,' 'learn to express your needs.'"

I should have shut up at that point. When I saw that the reporter was scribbling notes, I really should have buttoned it.

"It's built-in complexity to stop it working and stop you noticing it doesn't work. Like the tax code. See? Keeping all the CPAs off the streets? Say your scumbag of a husband is banging his ex-wife, just for instance. You can say, 'infidelity is the effect of unhappiness; not the cause' and 'let's explore where trust began to fray' and three years later at eighty bucks an hour twice a week you can still be poring over all your needs and how to express them and whether you've identified the halfway meeting point and what's getting in the way of communication, can't you? Eh? Can't you?"

The reporter looked up and nodded.

20

"Thank you," I said. "You're right. I agree. But if all these MFTs were to can the crap once and for all and say, 'Ho! Shitbag! Stop banging your ex-wife.' And then the next week say, 'Ho! Shitbag! Banged your ex-wife again?' it's much more clear cut, eh no? And then the honest MFT could turn to the wife and say, 'Lexy, pal, this one's a dud. Just nail the coffin lid down and walk away.'"

"Interesting," the reporter said. "A fresh approach. And this would be Branston Lancer? And his ex-wife is ...?"

"She's his ex-ex-wife now," I said. "He remarried her after he divorced me. Brandeeee, with four Es."

"Four?"

"No," I said. "Three. I'm just being bitchy."

The next morning, my recall was hazy, but the worst I thought might happen was names being named and faces going red. I knew Bran and Brandeee wouldn't sue me, because of the truth defence, and I didn't care what they said about me to their friends.

But when that day's *Cuento Voyager* hit the newsstands—or driveways anyway, Cuento hasn't got newsstands—the headline screamed THE BLAME GAME and the first line read *Maverick marriage and family therapist Lexy Campbell sets out her controversial imported therapeutic technique for our reporter in an exclusive interview this week.*

And I didn't read any further because my phone was ringing. It was a wife who needed me to straighten out her scumbag husband, in accordance with my imported therapeutic technique. She was in a major huff because he'd suggested she get a job, or as she put it "a job outside the home" when she *had* a job, or as she put it "a full-time job parenting my fifteen-year-old son," and as I put it "a cushy succession of Buzzfeed and yoga since her son left the house at eight in the morning and worked after school in the yoghurt shop."

I didn't know that that first morning, of course. I gave her an appointment and then switched to the call waiting, which was a man in his forties wanting me to straighten out his deadbeat wife who'd had the nerve to get fat giving birth to his three children and was on his case for having a girlfriend *and* refused to go to the gym, even when he offered to drive her.

Long story short, I had a client list full of the most selfish, thoughtless, lazy, shallow, entitled, unappealing, impossible to sympathise with, impossible to help, well-heeled, high-spending, gullible individuals I'd ever shoved a posh box of tissues at when they started snivelling. And every other therapist in Cuento despised me.

Even before Todd and Kathi piled on. (More of which still pending and coming soon.)

"No luck on the uniformed officer," Mike was saying when I zoned back into the here and now. She holstered her phone and let out a sigh. "You either sleep in the motel or put up with me."

"You?" I said. "You? Staying here overnight? To protect me?"

"It's my job," she said. "I'm no happier about it than you are."

"I'll sleep in the motel," I said. "Not becau—" But her face had shut like a man-trap on a bare ankle. "Just that you'd be better off IDing the dead guy and finding the ring and solving the case. Than babysitting. I'll be okay."

Three

I love Creek House. Truly, I do. It's the first house I've ever loved, the first place I've ever lived that I've given two hoots about, but still. Stretching out on the Cali-King bed in Room 112 in the Last Ditch was bliss. I rolled over and then over again and then a third time, just because I could. I slid off the end onto the floor instead of getting out on one side or the other, just because I could. And I danced around in the shower doing the Funky Chicken, just to luxuriate in not bashing my elbows on both bathroom walls or accidentally flushing the toilet with my knee.

Only Della pounding on the connecting wall and telling me to stop jumping around in case I woke Diego made me simmer down and end my space salutation. I washed the fake blood out of my hair and scrubbed the slough water off my feet and tried not to think about the dead guy wrapped round my beer rope, or who might have killed him, or why, or what the Jimmy wig was supposed to signal.

Todd was lying propped up on my bed when I came out of the bathroom. Of course he was. But I was used to it and I was swathed in a bath sheet.

"You stopped praying then," I said. He was back in diamonds and linen again, cashmere at the throat. "How have you got that scarf tied?" I added, taking a closer look. "Every time I think I've learned all there is!"

"Are you changing your mind?" Todd said. "It's about time." I started to protest, but he shushed me and kept talking. "What did the good detective tell you when she had you on your own? Because the uniforms wouldn't tell the rest of us anything."

"Not much," I said. "He had no ID on him. He's been dead for four days. GSW to the stoma—"

Todd was cackling. "'Gee Ess Double-Ewe' has two syllables more than 'gunshot wound,' Lexy, and it makes you sound like a dork."

"—to the stomach," I carried on, "and the Jimmy wig was stapled to his head post-mortem."

"Why?" Todd said.

"Dunno. Mike didn't share her theories."

"Don't say *Mike*," said Todd. "So she doesn't believe in pooling resources to build a whole greater than the sum of its parts? Can you believe it? Some people have no vision."

I rolled my eyes, refusing to open the tomb of the forbidden subject. We had agreed to have the Halloween weekend off bickering. "I don't say it to her face," I said. "Did she ask you about the ring?"

"What ring?"

"He had a ring on. Dead Guy. On the hand that was waving as he came up, he had a great big ugly lump of a ring. But it fell off as they were getting him out."

"I didn't see it," Todd said. "I saw his head and the start of his sweatshirt but no ring. What kind?"

I shrugged. "A bog-awful big barnacle of a hideous ring. Looked like it came free with coupons, or maybe had a cyanide compartment in it. Did Roger see it? Get him in here and let's ask him."

Todd plucked his phone out of his back pocket and speed-dialled Roger.

"Better get dressed," he said once he had hung up again. He waved a languid hand at my bath sheet, which had unravelled to the Renaissance nymph stage, leaving a lot of thigh and shoulder on show. "Roger's not numb to it all, the way I am."

"You're not exactly convincing me to let you loose on clients at vulnerable stages of recovery."

"I thought we weren't talking about it till Monday?" Todd said. He really was the most infuriating individual I had ever dealt with. And I've dealt with undiagnosed sociopaths and my mother.

Roger let himself in and grinned at me. He was also back in the slouchy linen shirt and trousers Todd and he favoured for evenings at home, the pale pink shirt open over his perfect mahogany chest and the pale lemon trousers rolled up above his perfect mahogany ankles. He was the most beautiful human being I had ever seen. Well, Todd was beautiful too, but Roger was much less annoying.

"Blotchy neck, clenched jaw, beady eyes," Roger said, looking me over. "What's Todd done to drive you to the edge of reason now, Lexy?"

"Oh, nothing out of the ordinary," I said. "One of the daily specials from his weekly menu. I'm okay. Listen, never mind that now. The guy in the slough—did you see the ring he was wearing when we were hauling him up? It dropped off and it'll be tomorrow before they can get a diver down to retrieve it."

"And?" Roger said.

"They couldn't ID him," I said. "And this thing was quite distinctive. The size of a quail's egg and butt-ugly."

"Don't say *butt*," Todd told me. "You sound dumb."

"Okay, plug-ugly. I was just thinking we could..."

"Interfere in a police investigation and risk prosecution?" said Roger. "Again?"

"Was it metal?" said Todd. "It wasn't jade or onyx or anything?"

"Mike told me specifically not to go fishing with a magnet on a bit of string," I said.

"Shame," said Todd. "Although gold, silver, and copper aren't magnetic anyway. Who wears an iron ring, when you think about it?"

"Nazis?" said Roger. "No, that's an iron cross."

"And it wasn't a spiky design," I said. "The impression I got, through the water, was of ... bubbles."

"Duh," said Todd.

"No, not water bubbles. The design itself was ... bulbous."

"Could you draw it?" said Todd.

"Why?" said Roger. "To what end? They'll dredge it up in the morning. What's the point of trying to get ahead of the cops on this?"

"Well," I said, "there's the fact that Mike reckons he was dumped in the slough by my boat in a Jimmy wig as a message to me." Their faces were gratifyingly horror-struck. "Or a warning maybe." Tears gathered in Todd's eyes and Roger's mouth dropped open. Bless them. "So there's that."

"Dead four days?" Todd said, leaping to his feet and cracking his knuckles. "He must have been reported missing, don't you think? It'll be on the police blotter at the *Voyager*."

"And I can lean on all my contacts at the Senior Center." Roger was on his feet too, squeezing his hands into fists until his muscles popped all the way up to his shoulders.

"Senior Center?" I said.

"You know," Roger said. "The Gimme A Grandma Initiative." It was the joint brainchild of Roger at the hospital, the nursing manager of the attached children's convalescent home, the head teacher of the kindergarten wing of the Beteo County Foster Home network, and the Residents' Activities Manager at the biggest of the three old folks' homes. There wasn't a single white-haired little old lady or baldy old codger in Cuento without at least one adopted grandkid now, and there wasn't a single at-risk little scrap of lisping humanity anywhere in the county system without someone to read stories, comb and re-make neglected cornrows, and shake a tripod walking stick at their care-workers if their assigned moppet heard so much as a cross word.

"Of course," I said. "How could I forget?" Todd was campaigning like a member of the Academy at Oscar time to get Roger nominated as Cuento's man of the year. "But I mean, why the Senior Center?"

"Because even if he doesn't live there, someone who does live there is going to know him from silver-top yoga or chair-cercize, or even bingo."

"But he's not old, is he?" I said. "He didn't look old to me. I'd have put him in his forties."

Roger gave an uneasy little smile.

"Ew," said Todd.

"What?" I said.

"Bloating," said Roger. "His face wrinkles were puffed out from post-mortem bloat. It's been mild. And it was four days, like you said. I'd put him in his seventies. So if he's local, the seniors in town will know him."

"It shouldn't be worse," I said, "for someone to kill an old man. It totally bloody is though. A sweet old man who should have died in his bed with his family around him."

"Huh?" said Todd. "Maybe he was a complete dick. Maybe he was handsy old slimewad who made everyone's life hell for miles around."

"No way," I said. "Not with that adorable gap between his two front teeth."

"Another reason we know he's old," Roger said. "No one young would have a mouth like that."

"Adorable?" said Todd. "Wait, you think British teeth are *attractive*? I knew you could tolerate them, but I had no idea you actually looked at all those rows of condemned tenements and thought they were *pretty*! Huh."

"It's like dog lovers," I said. "I always wondered how they could stand the smell. Then I found out they like it. They actually *like* the stink of dog."

"Or cats," said Roger, who loved dogs.

"Cats don't smell," I said. I loved cats.

"Cats stink!" said Roger. "Why do you think Della and Diego have that Rube Goldberg contraption to let the kittens out of their room to go potty in the bushes?"

"Because cat litter is expensive and Della thinks it's a waste of money."

"No, because the smell of the litter box was making everyone in the whole motel—"

"The smell of cat shit in a box of gravel doesn't mean cats smell," I said. "If *you* shit in a box of gravel in the corner of the room, I wouldn't be dabbing it behind my ears. It's not cats' fault."

"Aren't you paying the kittens' expenses anyway?" Todd said.

"Yes, and cat litter is a drop in the ocean."

"Oh, I know," Todd said. He couldn't have looked more thrilled if he'd been Mike telling me about a gunshot wound in an old man's belly. "How are you getting on with a solution?"

"Fine," I lied.

"Because Trinity—"

"Out!" I said. "Out you go. Go and Google missing persons. Go and bug the seniors. You've crossed the line now, Todd. So go on with yourself and just go."

∞

Trinity. I seethed every time I thought about it. When my client list exploded, Todd was there by my side, like an unpaid intern, taking all sorts of things off my hands and not making a peep of complaint about it. He registered my domain name, set up a website, took out adverts in the *Voyager,* and made me a thousand business cards. And I was so slammed, I'd handed out about twenty-five of the things before I read one.

"Trinity?" I had said, leaning in the doorway to Todd's room. He was patrolling a free-standing rack of large women's dresses with a clipboard in his hand. "Kind of God-sy, isn't it? Won't people be expecting Bible stuff? Faith-based?"

I was bending over backwards so far I could have hired myself out as a hula hoop. Because what I wanted to say to him was *What the frilly hat gave you the right to decide my practice name, Téodor? My business is called Lexy Campbell, Caring and Confidential Counselling. Where the limited-edition, embossed and authenticated fuckity-fuck did* Trinity *come from?*

"We didn't think so," Todd said. "We thought it just said 'three' with a dash of *Matrix.*"

"Who's 'we'?" I said.

He pushed his reading glasses up onto his forehead and gave me a look of incredulity. "Kathi and me," he said. "The other two of the three."

"What?"

"Have you even looked at our website?" Todd said. "I worked hard on it."

"*Our* website?" I echoed, reaching for my phone and scrolling. "'Trinity Life Solutions,'" I read aloud. "'Our team of experts offer counseling for relationships and family upsets, wardrobe and grooming makeovers for personal positivity, and decluttering and deep-cleansing for healing and a happy home.'

"You have got to be joking," I said.

"We even put you first."

"Upsets?" I said. "*Upsets*? You provide personal positivity, Kathi does healing and happiness, and I fix UPSETS?"

"You're the one that always said there was too much psychologizing everything."

I pointed at the rack of clothes. "Do those belong to one of my clients?" My finger was shaking. So was my voice.

"One of *our* clients," Todd said. "You betcha. Oline? With the credit card debt and the bossy sister? I've sent her to a spa in Calistoga while I write up a diet sheet and torch these muumuus."

"Yeah, she had her second session scheduled tomorrow," I said, nodding, "but she cancelled. She said she was sick."

"All those toxins coming out in the mud bath," Todd said. "She probably is. But nothing to worry about. She's posted on Instag—"

Oblivious as he usually is, he stopped talking when he saw the look on my face and left his phone in his back pocket. We agreed to leave it until after Halloween because the buffet food was already ordered, then I turned on my heel and swept away.

So when Della told me, the day before my party, that Flynn and Florian needed to be groomed, I couldn't turn the problem over to Todd and his contact list, or to Kathi and her can-do attitude. I needed to deal with it myself.

Why? Because I'd bought Diego the kittens. And the rabbit. And the seahorse. When I was supposed to be buying him a goldfish to make up for persuading him to put his tadpoles back in the slough. Noleen and Kathi bent their NO PETS policy for the menagerie, and their NO STRUCTURAL MODIFICATIONS policy for the tunnel leading out of the back window into the bushes now designated as Pussycat Pottyland. They also had a NO HYDROPONICS policy, which was nothing to do with the illegality of pot, it turned out, and everything to do with how it hiked their electricity bill if everyone was growing under heat lamps. They dropped that for Diego too, even though the heat and lamps and oxygenation pump for a seahorse and a modest shoal of clown and angel fish was enough to make Noleen drop her duct tape in the middle of her monthly maintenance initiative.

If it was anyone *but* Diego—mop-haired, dimpled, piping-voiced angel that he was, with eyes bigger than his cheeks and cheeks as round as his chubby knees and those chubby little knees with more dimples than his sweet face—the whole zoo would have been in the pound quicker than Noleen could say, "Who cares if it's a kill shelter?" But Diego hugged her round her sturdy calves and told her he loved her every day on his way to preschool. So I had two Persian kittens with knots in all eight armpits to try to find an emergency groomer for.

At least it would take my mind off murder.

I had tried to do it myself the morning of Halloween, thinking if I could just cut the lumps of matted hair off them and then start a daily brushing habit to stop them building up again, all would be well. But even the smallest nail scissors looked like chainsaws when they got close to the fondant-pink skin and feather-white fluff on the underside of those two kittens, and I couldn't bring myself to make the first snip. The kitten between my knees was crying like an orphan in Dickens and the other one was matching it peal for peal as well as hiding in terror down the side of the chair, where I could feel it trembling. And Diego was watching out of his window doing that Disney-tear-brimthing that he could take on the road.

I opened my knees, let the trapped kitten go, fished the squashed kitten out from beside the seat cushion, and watched them scamper off back to Diego, moving like some film student's first try at animation, because the knots in their pits stopped their legs from working.

But the morning *after* Halloween, when I went out on an early coffee run as an excuse to stop at the cop shop and ask if they'd made any progress overnight (which they hadn't, or at least if they had, the night shift dispatcher wasn't willing to tell me), the solution was right there staring me in the face at the Swiss Sisters drive-through queue. The car in front belonged to a cat groomer! There was a decal in the back window: a white line drawing of a sleek cat washing its paw, a verse of badly scanning guff about velvet coats and satin paws and the stroke of serenity and peace. Which, if a Facebook friend of mine had posted it over a photo of a sunset, meadow or—I suppose—cat, would have made me unfollow at least, if not unfriend, if not block, if not anonymously harass online for crimes against poetry. And a phone number.

Of sorts.

Far be it from me to complain about any aspect of America that's been serving Americans perfectly well for generations and only strikes me as a tiny bit awkward because it's so unfamiliar. Well, not that far. If I'm honest, I bitch and whine about everything from the colour of the mailboxes—because dusty blue merges into the shadows and is functionally invisible and mailboxes should be red, so you can see them—to the way no one ever tells you how much anything is going to cost, but instead says a random price stripped of all mention of tax, like it's a secret, and then whacks you with the truth at the register, which is as off-pissing to me as if a waiter brought me a plate of big juicy prawns, put it down on the table, said, "Bon Appetit," and then ate one. And speaking of waiters, why—if you agree to another drink—do they whisk away the one you're drinking that's still got two good mouthfuls left in it? Even if the last two mouthfuls are kind of watery because of the truly insane mountains of ice in absolutely everything, scamming everyone out of stuff they've paid for in a way that hasn't been seen in civilised circles since Georgian reformers stopped traders putting brick dust in sacks of flour at the London corn market.

And then there's the phone numbers. Which are not numbers at all! Oh, they're numbers at the start, but then they're slogans that are supposed to help you remember the number. 1-800-GOOD LUCK WITH THAT, SUCKER. Because by the time you've located the G number and the O number, you've completely forgotten whether the end of the aide-memoire was *doofus, sweet-cheeks, sucker,* or *ma'am.*

The car groomer decal was a case in point: six digits, randomly broken up with dashes to make them harder to use, and then TABI instead of 8224, which is tons easier to remember.

I keyed in the number anyway, using every scrap of my pre-caffeine mental capacity, and listened to it ringing, only thinking about the fact that the groomer was currently juggling coffee and payment for coffee through her car window when it went to voicemail.

"Speak!" said the message.

I stared at my phone. That was a bit basic for an outgoing phone message on a business line, wasn't it? "Hi," I said, anyway. "Sorry to bother you when you're on the road. I'm actually right behind you right now. I'd honk but you might spill and burn yourself. Anyway, I'll get back to you soon. It's a cutting job I need. Too much for me to tackle. Cheers, then. Bye."

The car in front was moving away. I gave a bit of a bibb in the end, since I thought the coffee was safely stowed, and I waved like a loon at the tinted back window. Then I pulled up to the window and started reciting my morning prayer.

Four

The divers had arrived by the time I got back to Creek House, coffee half gone already. Mike was standing on the bank in waders and two frogmen in full wetsuits, with tanks and masks, were standing chest-deep in the slough just off to the side of my porch.

"Move along," Mike said.

"Absolutely," I said. "Have you IDed him yet? Did the missing persons list turn anything up? When's the autopsy? Was the bullet still in him?"

"I'm not answering questions," Mike said. Then she raised her voice. "Anytime you feel like starting, guys! Let's get done here." I was sure she wrinkled her nose. But then she was standing plank in the middle of the kittens' favourite patch of undergrowth. I really didn't live in a very salubrious neighbourhood in any way at all.

"Will you answer this question, though?" I said. "Should I cancel my list of clients for the day? Is it okay to have people traipsing in and out? What with the crime scene and everything?" I waved at the two ribbons of yellow tape running from the side rail of the boat to the opposite bank, carving out a wedge.

"This isn't a crime scene," Mike said. "The tape's only there for the dive."

"Not a crime scene?" I echoed. "*What?*"

"I'm not answering questions," Mike said.

"I'll cancel," I said. "It's not exactly conducive to good therapy, is it?" Then I pulled my *Voyager* from the box nailed to the post at the bottom of the steps and climbed aboard.

She scowled at me when I settled on the porch, at the riparian side, to finish my coffee and pretend to read my paper. But what could she do? I was on my property. It just so happened that my property had an excellent close-up view.

One frogman jumped up, jack-knifed, showed me his black rubber bottom and disappeared with a flick of his flippers. "You have my sympathies," I said to the other one, who was treading water above the surface. I couldn't see much face inside the mask, but I thought he looked puzzled. "Slough water," I said. "With a bit of corpse juice still."

He spat out his breathing apparatus to answer me. "Good money."

"Where there's muck there's brass," I said. "Never mind," I added when he pursed his lips to start asking what the hell I was on about. It didn't happen every day anymore, but often enough for it still to be tiring.

"And you're supposed to be working for it!" Mike shouted from the shallows. "Not hitting on bystanders."

The bits of the frogman's face that I could see round the edge of the mask went deep magenta and he turned away. I shook my head slowly in Mike's direction and opened my paper.

I started on the back page, as ever. It was soothing to read of sports I'd never seen and couldn't understand, like whale music for the eyes. *Sophomore's fine defense yielded only two touchdowns*, I read. *Ommmm*, I thought.

The small ads were the usual carnival of weirdness. Spray-on bed-liners for sale, Soroptimists' Crab Grabs coming up, Mandala planned at dawn. None of it meant a damn thing to me.

At my side the frogmen changed over, the first one coming up and the blushing one—who had absolutely not been hitting on me and even if he had, I wasn't interested—going down. I watched out of the corner of my eye. Yip, no interest. Whose bum and thighs *wouldn't* look good in black rubber?

I turned back to my newspaper. Ah, the letters page. Feuds were simmering, snowflakes being triggered, and sheeple calling wahmbu-lances. In the Community section, where the feathers ruffled in the letters were smoothed again, I saw that the Name of the Month was open for entries. I loved the Name of the Month thing. All the shops and small businesses took it in turns to offer free stuff to people with a certain name. And once a month the person with the most free stuff won a big prize. So the florist would offer boutonnieres to Sarahs on Thursday morning, and then the petrol station would give an oil change to all Josés over one lunchtime. The downtown independent cinema gave matinee tickets and popcorns to Daves one Sunday. I imagine more Daves saw more Iranian film in Cuento that day than in the rest of California all year.

I always entered my personal total to the prize draw, just to make a point: L-E-A-G-S-A-I-D-H, I texted, and then ZERO. It had been the same my whole life. I'd never had a key-ring or Coke can with my name on it. Not once. But I was convinced that, one of these months, someone in this town would take pity on me and realise if they put a sign out on the street with Free Pedicures for Every LEAGSAIDH, it would cost them at most one pedicure. It made good business sense as well as being a nice gesture to a recent immigrant, just what Lady Liberty would do.

The frogmen, once more, were swapping places. This was a very thorough search of the slough bed and the air on my porch was no longer its usual blend of washing powder, leaf litter, and a whiff of kitten. There was an unmistakable eggy top-note now. I recognised it from when I had churned up the slough running cable out to Creek House and driving in a pole to lash the propane tank to in case of earthquakes, in accordance with many city ordinances. I felt sorry for the blushing frogman, who was adjusting his rubber suit at the waist as he surfaced. If there was a gap in the middle and the slough was seeping in, his drive home wasn't going to be much fun.

I put my phone away again, took a draught of my coffee, and turned another page, ready now for the hard news—for whatever the *Voyager* had made of the corpse in the slough and for however they were going to stick it to me for finding the body.

But the front page wasn't a grainy shot of the back of the Last Ditch, or a blurry shot of the pathologist's van speeding away with the body bag on board. The dead guy wrapped round my beer rope had quite a write-up. Of course he did. This was Cuento, and a corpse was big news. But, on the other hand, this was Cuento, and even bigger news was animal cruelty. Cuento had a duck crossing staffed by volunteers during fledging, and a designated turkey advocate to represent the rights of the local wild flock at city council meetings. Cuento had protective orders slapped on wasps' nests and anthills.

And so the photograph on the front page of its news organ today was a picture of a horse, staring straight into the camera, and a rider, dismounted and standing by its head, managing to pull the longer face of the two somehow and holding up a mystifying handful of … What the hell was that? Dead grass?

I ignored the splash of the frogman coming up at my side and bent over to read the story.

Veterinary Science student Kimberly Voorheft (20) had her evening ride cut short yesterday when a vicious attack on her pony, Agnetha, left both horse and rider in shock. "I was headed home, just crossing the pedestrian bridge near the stables on the east side of town, when Aggie pulled up short and made sounds of distress. I dismounted and tried to lead her over the bridge, but she showed great reluctance. If I didn't know her and if I didn't follow this route twice a week, I'd have said she was spooked. But there was nothing to spook her." An experienced horsewoman, Ms. Voorheft decided to turn back and take an alternate route. "It was when we turned that I realized what had happened. I skidded on something slippery. At first I thought it was a patch of oil that I hadn't noticed on the way up the approach. Then I looked back at Aggie to see if she was all right. And that's when I saw that her tail was gone."

I coughed up an inhalation of coffee. Did I really just read that?

"Her tail had been chopped off, leaving only six inches still attached, and the hairs were spilled all over the path. That's what I had skidded on." This bizarre attack on an innocent animal has left Ms. Voorheft mystified. "Someone crept up behind us and took a pair of shears to Aggie's tail," Ms. Voorheft confirmed. "It was the feeling of suddenly having her tail hairs removed that spooked my poor pony. I just don't get what would make anyone do such a weird and sick thing to such a sweet creature. She didn't deserve this." If anyone has information that might shed light on the mystery, we invite you to call the Voyager at 530-752-HELP.

"Mi—olly," I said, standing up and waving the paper at her. "Have you seen this?"

"We're busy here, Ms. Campbell," Mike said, rolling her eyes. I couldn't tell if she was rolling them at my slip or my save. She was in the slough up to her knees now, bagging items as one of the frogmen handed them over.

"Have you found the ring?" I said, even though it looked like Dorito bags and crushed water bottles she was currently handling. She ignored me. "Did you see this about the horse?" She tried to ignore me, but it's hard not to react to someone saying something wildly unexpected. And among the many occupational hazards of being a cop, one of the worst ones is how they're incapable of not being interested in unexpected stuff. They're professional noticers. Must be exhausting.

"Horse?" said Mike.

"A horse had its tail cut off crossing a bridge last night. It's in the paper."

"What?"

"I don't think the Jimmy wig's got anything to do with me after all."

"*What*? What bridge?"

"The wotchermacallit call it—the overpass. The footbridge over the railway line out near the stables over there." I waved my paper in the vague direction of the east side of town where the railway line cut through the suburbs.

"That's miles away," Mike said. "What are you talking about? Please stop interrupting me while I'm trying to work."

"I'm trying to help you," I said. "Forget what I said about the hat. No one here calls it a Jimmy wig except me. It's what you call it that matters."

"Ms. Campbell, if you continue to obstruct the progress of this enquiry, you will be charged."

"Was there any aggro at the cemetery last night?"

"Are you high?" said Mike. "Hat, horse, cemetery ... it's word salad!"

"Was there?"

"We had a detail up there," Mike unbent so far as to say. "Halloween, better to not take chances."

"Hmph," I said. "Right."

As the second frogman came to the surface, brandishing a rotted tennis shoe in one hand and a bike wheel sans tyre in the other, I skipped down the steps to go and assemble my posse. "Just do me one favour," I said to Mike as I swept by her. "At some point, google *Tam O'Shanter* and read the poem."

"Poem?"

"Poem."

"Word salad," she said again, shaking her head and laughing at me. She'd be laughing on the other side of her face once she'd put in a little Wikipedia time.

I had no idea where Todd might be, but the chances were good that Kathi would be on duty in the Skweeky Kleen, so it was Skweeky Kleen–ward I trotted, Googling on the fly. The page was loaded by the time I burst in through the door into the delicious fragrant warmth of Kathi's domain. She was ironing shirts, a crumpled pile of them in a basket beside her and a sheaf of cardboard inserts waiting on the folding table. And Todd was there too.

"What are you doing?" I said. He was hunched over a sewing machine set up in the window.

"Saving my bacon," Kathi said. "Did you know the Wash-n-Dry started offering alterations?"

"Okay," I said.

"So, when one of my best sweaty but fussy customers cancelled her standing order and told me why, I opened my piehole and said *we* were doing alterations too."

"Can you sew?"

"Nope."

41

"Can *you* sew?" I said to Todd. His phone was propped up in front of him with what looked suspiciously like a Wiki-how page on threading a machine needle open on it.

"Yes," Todd said. "For Kathi, my good friend, in these uncertain times, I'm sure I can."

"Oh, change the record!" I said. "And get out the way, will you? What is it you're trying to do?"

"Replace a zipper," said Todd standing up and letting me slide into his place. "Wait. Can *you* sew?"

"Like an extra in *The Pajama Game*." I threaded the needle, checked the tension, and grabbed Kathi's pin-cushion to start fixing the new zip into place in the dress that was sitting in a heap on the floor. "Did you read about the horse?"

"That poor horse!" said Todd.

"Yeah, well now you can read off my phone and tell me what you think."

"What?"

"Humour me," I said. "Go on. Start reading."

Todd cleared his throat. "'*Tam O'Shanter*,'" he declaimed. "'*A tale*.' But not that sort of tail."

"We'll see," I said, my mouthful of pins making my voice even grimmer than the grim idea forming in my mind.

"'*When chapman billies leave the street*,'" Todd began. "What's a chapman billy?"

"No clue," I said. "Keep reading."

"'*And drouthy neebors neebors meet*.' What is this garbage?"

"Good point," I said. "Google an English version and read that. Sorry."

It only took a moment. "'When peddler people leave the street and thirsty neighbors neighbors meet,'" he began again. "This is a very long drinking song, Lexy. Even for Scotland."

"It's not a drinking song," I said. "It's a ghost story. Set at Halloween. Keep reading."

He kept reading, breaking off every so often to editorialise. "So Tam O'Shanter's a guy's name? Not a hat?"

"Typical unreliable alcoholic husband," Kathi said, when Todd got to the bit about Tam's wife waiting at home with his dinner drying out.

"No way he's fit to ride a horse," she added when Tam set off at last. "This guy's a jerk, Lexy."

She snorted when Tam stopped at the churchyard wall to watch the dance of the witches, salivating over the comely wench in her short shift. "When was this written? Nothing ever changes, does it?"

But when the witches gave chase to Tam on his trusty mare, hounding him to the bridge, trapped on its one side (since devils and demons cannot cross running water), catching poor Maggie by her tail, pulling it off at its roots, Kathi grew quiet again. And, by the time Todd finished, she was standing gazing at him, her iron steaming away neglected on its stand. I had abandoned pinning the zip too.

"So … Tam O'Shanter is the story of a man who sees witches dance in a graveyard at Halloween and has his horse's tail pulled off while he's escaping across a bridge," said Todd.

"And last night," I added, "at Halloween, a man with a Tam O'Shanter stapled to his head was tipped into a river and a horse crossing a bridge had her tail cut off. I asked Mike if there was any trouble at the cemetery, but she said they watched it like a hawk last night of all nights."

"The cemetery, I bet they do," Kathi said. "But what about the old burial ground?"

I shivered. Who wouldn't? Then I realised the sudden cold draught was because Mike had opened the launderette door.

"We're done," she said.

"That was quick," I said.

"You're welcome," she told me. "When we find the scene of the death, we'll have more to do, but the slough was just the dump site."

"Did you find the ring?"

"There was no ring," Mike told me. "Dr. Kroger here didn't see it. Dr. Roger Kroger didn't see it. No one saw it except you. And let's be honest, you didn't see it. You were partying pretty hard, weren't you? A seventy-two pack of beer is not tea with the vicar. You saw a reflection."

With that she was gone.

"A seventy-two pack of beer that we hadn't started yet!" I yelled after her. "I didn't imagine that ring any more than Tam imagined the dancing witches. I wonder if he got this much crap from the authorities the next day."

"So where's this burial ground?" Todd said.

"Noleen knows the way," said Kathi. "Let's ask Della if she'll do a stint on the desk when she gets in from work tonight and we can go see if there's anything to see."

"Won't it be getting dark by then?" I asked her.

"We can wear our head lamps," said Kathi.

"I am not wearing a flashlight strapped to my head," said Todd.

"Also," I said, "how can we get in touch with the vet student kid?" I said. "I bet she's got more to say than got written up in the paper."

"You think?" said Kathi. "I'd have thought they'd stretch it out instead of cutting it down."

"That's just my cover story," I said. "Actually, I was wondering if she knew him."

"Who?" said Todd.

"Dead Guy," I said. "Who else?"

"We can't keep calling him Dead Guy," said Kathi. "It's disrespectful."

"Jimmy?" I said. "Mr. James Wigg?"

"You said that was a red herring," Todd pointed out.

"And it's nearly as bad as Dead Guy," Kathi added.

"Okay," I said. "Till the cops find out his real name, let's just call him Tam."

Five

Just as well Mike and the divers were finished at the slough because I had completely forgotten to cancel my clients. My eleven o'clock was waiting on the porch when I picked my way round the side of the motel at ten past the hour and hopped over the bank.

"Sorry!" I said.

She beamed at me. "Don't be. I think it's a great idea and it wouldn't work if you told me in advance." Hoping to snag a clue, I cast my mind over our first two sessions, during which she had complained relentlessly about her hard-working sweetheart of a husband and her two high-achieving drug-free teenagers. My mind slid off without catching anything. Luckily she kept talking. "Dr. Kroger said increasing in five minute increments was fast enough, but I'm delighted you stretched it to ten. I need to be ready by next September."

I threw my mind at it even harder but, once again, nothing.

"September," I said. "You've set a clear goal then? That's wonderful."

She gave me a puzzled look as I ushered her into the corridor and followed her to the consultation room.

"When Buster goes to Purdue," she said, mystifyingly.

I gestured her into a seat, settled myself in the chair opposite, and motioned for her to go on.

"I did what Kathi suggested in the garage too," she said.

"Great!" It came out one notch too hearty, and she leaned forward to look at me like I was a specimen of something. "I mean, good," I said, thinking it was nice for Kathi to have made a useful suggestion at the end of her life. Because I was going to kill her. "We ... haven't had a case meeting since your last session with me," I said, "because I didn't get you to sign the consents. So maybe you could just catch me up. With the increments. And the garage."

"Oh," she said, rooting in the backpack at her feet. "I signed the consents with Dr. Kroger. Should I give them back to him or can I leave them with you to pass on?"

I swiftly replanned Kathi's funeral, edging her coffin to one side of the altar to make room for Todd's too. "I'll take them," I said, managing not to snatch the sheaf of papers out of her hand, shred them into confetti, and stamp on them. "Now then ... ?"

"I do want to work on the causes of my abandonment issues with you, as we planned," she said. Abandonment issues? News to me. I hadn't got any further than suggesting that she couldn't keep asking her husband to pack in his good job and move to Indiana for no reason. "But clearing out the garage so the car fits in has made a surprising difference."

I agreed. *Surprising* was exactly the word for it.

"Our street is long," she said. "So when I turn in at the east end, I don't know whether or not Marty's home. And I've put up hanging bike racks for Buster and Tooty too." Buster was her kid! Finally my brain was working. Purdue, I was almost sure, was a university, probably in Indiana, and this woman wanted the family to move there when her son started college next September! Because of her abandonment

47

issues … as diagnosed either by an anesthetist or a dry cleaner. I wasn't quite ready to cancel the funerals yet.

"But I just walk and breathe," she was saying. "And sure enough, by the time I put my key in the door, the panic has passed. It's true what the doc says about panic. You can't sustain it for long. It fades."

Especially if you're under a general anesthetic, I thought, *which was "the doc's" speciality.*

"It's really working," she said. "Waiting here for you for ten minutes would have sent me into a spin if I hadn't been practicing every day walking home."

"I'm very glad," I said, although it just about choked me. If I had sprung an unannounced ten-minute wait on her as a test of her recovery, I'd lose my licence to practise counselling and probably have to get a job in Target to pay the fines. "So what else has been happening?"

∞

She was the worst. Todd and Kathi hadn't managed to plant quite as many flags all over the three clients that came after her, but two of them had different hairdos and were in suspiciously new-looking work-out gear. The other one was a recent widower in his late seventies who'd been hounded into counselling by his kids, but who didn't need anything except permission to grieve.

"They want me to take up ballroom dancing," he said. "Wednesdays at the Oddfellows' Hall." He mopped his tears with a hanky the size of a picnic tablecloth. "I haven't danced with anyone except Maddy since VK day. I can't go weeping over nice little old ladies every Wednesday."

"Of course not," I said. "Ignore the kids. You just go home and curl up on your recliner with your photograph albums and remember the happy days. If they want someone in the family to dance, they can go dancing themselves. Tell them that from me, and if they give you any crap you just send them my way."

"You're a good girl, Lexy," he said. "You remind me of Maddy when I first met her. Did I tell you that? If you backcombed your hair and put stockings on, you'd be Maddy to a tee."

"Tell me how you proposed," I said. "I bet you've got a story about that, haven't you?"

∞

Todd and Kathi were waiting in the motel's front office when I got there at sundown.

"I'm glad you're here," I said. "I'd hate you to kick up any *abandonment issues* in me."

They looked back at me with faces as innocent and eyes as round as a pair of kittens when Fancy Feast tins are being opened.

"Della's just dropping off Diego at his little friend's house," Noleen said, coming in from the back office. She was wearing a sweatshirt that said *You're welcome to try*. Vague but somehow no less aggressive for all that. "When she gets back here we'll have a good two hours and then we'll pick him up on the way home. Home from what, is the question. What is it that's stuck in your grille this time, Lex?"

"Humour me," I said. "Todd, did you find Kimberly Voorheft?"

"Yep," he said. "She wasn't hard to track down. She's meeting us at the stables in the morning to see if she can ID Tam."

"ID him from what?" I said. "Have you made a sketch?"

Todd's eyes couldn't get any rounder, but he dimpled his lips in a little smile that upped the innocent look from Shirley Temple to Bambi. My radar started humming.

"No!" I said. Bambi got bumped for the pink butterfly that lands on Bambi's nose and makes him sneeze. "When did you take a photo of him, for God's sake?"

"One while Roger had him near the surface," Todd said. "And one with zoom once the cops hauled him on deck."

"But you can't show the kid that!" I said. "She'll be scarred for life."

"I've Photoshopped it," said Todd. Of course he had. "She'll be fine."

I shook my head. "How did Roger get on with missing persons?" I said. "Anything?"

"He delegated that to me," Kathi said. "And there was nothing in Beteo County. Not in the last week anyway."

"And nothing doing at the Senior Center either," Noleen said. "Except the good news that it's a hotbed of hookups. Roger didn't tell them the guy was dead and five old broads want his number."

"How is that good news?" I asked.

"Because some of them are in shared rooms," said Todd. "*Awkward*! So Noleen was thinking about discounting motel rooms on hourly rates."

"Plus a shuttle," Noleen said.

On the whole, I'd rather think about corpses. "Hey, Todd," I said, "does the photo from when he was still in the slough have his hand in it?"

"No, Gollum, it doesn't," Todd said.

"Hey!"

"Frodo, then."

"Better."

"But we've had an idea about the ring, actually."

"Great," I said.

"You're not going to like it," he added.

"Which would ... what? You're saying that would stop you? If I'm not happy about something, you'll take it into account?"

"Quit bitching," Noleen said. "Della's here."

∞

As we were leaving, Della rapped on the window of Todd's Jeep and held out her closed fist to me.

"Here," she said. "For you." She let something small and soft drop onto my open palm.

I squinted in the low light. "What is it?" I said. "A talisman? Good luck charm? Is it a rabbit's foot." I squeezed it, but it didn't feel solid enough to be a foot.

"It's a hairball," Della said. "Florian coughed it up and I kept it for you. Get. A. Groomer."

I dropped the hairball at my feet but Kathi whimpered and pulled her feet up so her knees were round her ears, so I scrabbled it into my hand again and pinged it out the window.

"I'll pick it up and dispose of it when we get back," I said, to reassure her. I spoiled it by reaching out to pat her knee though.

"Don't touch me!" she said. "Todd! Hand sanitizer! Now!"

"Groomer!" Della shouted through the window as we peeled away.

"I'm trying!" I shouted back to her. Then Kathi started squirting me from a gallon bottle of industrial strength chemicals and I had to shut my mouth in case I choked.

We were all out of our gourds on the stuff by the time Noleen pulled off the county road ten minutes later.

"Anyone want to sniff my Sharpie for a chaser?" I offered.

"Leave the windows down," Kathi told Noleen. "There's no one to steal a car here anyway."

That was true. We were only just out of town, but Cuento's a town that shuts with a bang. Once you're across the southerly drainage canal that connects to the Last Ditch slough, there's nothing but flat dusty fields, empty this late in the year with the last of the tomatoes gone and the first lettuce not due till after Christmas. Live oaks, half dead from drought and irony, stuck up here and there at worrying angles, like drunks without lampposts, and above it all the sky soared like the backdrop of a dream sequence, gold bruising to purple as the first stars came shyly winking.

"Where is it?" I said, turning round on the spot. I was looking for a stone wall with a lychgate and rows of headstones, stupidly.

"Just there," said Noleen, pointing to one of the saddest sights you'll ever see in California, a sight that never makes it onto a postcard or a tourist board trailer. Well, to be fair, nothing from Beteo County gets onto the postcards and tourist trailers. Beteo County isn't that bit of California. I tried to explain that to Alison, my old pal from home, when she announced she was saving up for a holiday. "It's not Hollywood," I told her. "It's not even San Francisco. Have you ever seen that film *Erin Brockovich*? Well, that was California too, remember. What? Yes, the beaches are lovely but the sea's bloody freezing."

The sad sight Noleen was pointing at wouldn't even make it into a Chamber of Commerce montage playing on a loop at the bank. Fifty yards to our left, just visible as the gold gave up and the purple darkened, was a withered orange tree, a withered grapefruit tree, a couple of spindly oleanders just about surviving, and a prickly pear cactus going from strength to strength, except that it had missed a fair few essential prunings to keep the weight balanced and several big lumps of it had dropped off to lie rotting around its base.

The house was long gone, lost to termites and storms, and the paths were long gone, submerged somewhere under the star thistle and stinkweed, but this was undeniably an abandoned homestead, chewed up by the agricultural behemoth that had finished delivering tomatoes to the Campbell's factory for the year and would be cutting its first three-packs of Romaine hearts come Valentine's Day.

The rest of them had started walking. I hop-skipped to catch up with them.

"I remember this place from when the family lived here," Noleen said. "We used to help with the harvest. Mrs. Armour made pink lemonade."

"Where's the burial ground?" said Todd.

"The Armour place was built on top of it," Noleen said. "It was … oh sometime in the late thirties it was discovered. They were replacing their furnace and Mr. Armour dug up an artefact. It's in the museum in Sacramento now. Anyway, they got some archeologists to come from the university. It was Christmas morning for the ancient archeology department. It pretty much put UCC Archeology on the map. And it turned out that what Mrs. Armour had always thought was a decorative hill that someone had scraped up to give the yard some character was actually a burial mound."

She stopped walking and pointed. Just ahead of us, part hidden by the collapsing prickly pear cactus, was a sort of half-hemispherical hillock sticking up out of the star thistle. In Dundee I'd have thought it was an air-raid shelter, still submerged, with its door on the far side. The gardens round where my granny lived were littered with them. This was much more glamorous. I stood and stared, with Noleen on one side and Todd on the other. Kathi clicked on her headlamp and then swung her head back and forth like a cow to light the hill up for us all.

"But how can it just be sitting here abandoned?" I said. "Shouldn't the local native council—whatever they're called—have jurisdiction over it? Isn't it sacred or at least protected or something? And how come the artefact's in the museum? Shouldn't it belong to the descendants of the people who're buried here? Oh my God, *are* they still buried here? I don't know what's worse. Them still being here, neglected, or them being dug up and moved. What are you doing?"

This last was because I had heard a crackle and seen a folded note pass from Todd to Noleen.

"I told him you'd been here too long to just swallow an Indian Burial Ground story," Noleen said. "He wouldn't listen." She stretched the fifty-dollar note and flicked it, making a noise like a snare drum.

"So it's not real?" I said. "You're winding me up?"

"Kinda," Noleen said. "It was a tale Mrs. Armour told. They'd moved out by then, into a nice little ranch in the new subdivision. But every Halloween she'd light a fire and we'd gather round and she'd tell us the story of the lost princess and her trusty attendants and how they walked above ground once a year."

"They walked at Halloween?" I said. "*Would* they? The ... who would this be?"

"Patwin people," said Noleen. "Nope. But we didn't know that fifty years ago. Hell, we were still playing cowboys and Indians fifty years ago, feathers in our hair and everything."

I winced.

"We were kids," Noleen said. "And the Armours meant no harm either. She was a princess, the one Mrs. Armour told the tales about. Not a savage. No one got scalped."

"Jesus," said Kathi. "Nolly, we've talked about this before. If you wouldn't say it in front of a native person, you shouldn't say it at all."

"Standing right here," said Todd. "Hello! Native American standing right beside you!"

"What?" said Noleen. "You're Mexican."

54

"Mexico was in North America last time I looked and, no matter what Lexy thought when she first met me, this—"

"Not again!" I said.

"—this is not *a tan*."

"I wish you would stop dredging that up," I said. "I said I was sorry. I am sorry. So maybe this could be my last punishment? I've proved myself too assimilated to swallow this lot."

"'Kay," Todd said.

"And now you've had your fun," I said, "can we go? Della shouldn't be stuck in the office for two hours after a double shift just so you can mess with me."

Kathi had climbed the little hill while I was talking. Standing on top with her headlamp shining down she looked vaguely *First Encounter*-ish.

"Wrong again, Lexy," she called back. "We're not wasting your time and we can't go till the cops secure the scene. There's a cutty sark here, unless I'm seeing things."

Todd gasped and surged forward. I gasped and surged forward. Noleen came trotting after us. "A what?" she said. "A cut what?"

"A mini dress," said Kathi. That's not usually how it's translated from Burns's eighteenth-century Scots, but that's what it means. I clambered up the mound and took hold of Kathi's arm for balance. The beam of her headlamp shone down on where the gossamer light little shirt lay carefully draped over the stinkweed, so that it floated like ground mist on a winter's morning.

Todd reached out towards it, but I laid a hand on his arm.

"Best not," I said. "Look. Kathi, can you shine your light on the collar there?"

Kathi bent over to train the beam more directly and we all got a better look at what I was sure I had seen. There was a dark red mark on the back of the neckline, seeping a little way into the white linen and turning it rusty.

"Some girl's been hurt here, hasn't she?" Noleen's voice was shaking with suppressed emotion. "Some sick fuck's done something bad, hasn't he?"

I didn't always agree with Noleen about the rights and wrongs of this world. I didn't believe that all women were gentle angels and all men were monstrous devils. Well, neither did she, really. She knew it was muddier than that. And we'd both agreed it was sick that someone killed a man and stapled a novelty wig to his dead head. This little smear of blood didn't strike me as in that league, not nearly.

But there was something about it. The way it floated there, six inches above the ground. And the way it had been placed there and left there, as if it was waiting for us to find it. Above us the sky was full dark now, ink black, the stars piercing and cold, but the cutty sark only seemed to grow more luminous as night fell and thickened. Even when Kathi switched off her headlamp, it still glowed as it lay there.

Six

Mike wasn't on duty. There was an upside. The guy who came out to look at the cutty sark and listen to us tying it to the horse tail and the corpse in the slough wasn't already sick of Todd, Kathi, Noleen, and me giving him the run-around from earlier in the year.

But there was a downside. The guy who stood there in the wreckage of the Armour farmstead and listened to us tying a discarded mini dress on the southwest edge of town tonight to an assault on a horse over on the east side last night and a guy who'd been shot who knows where days on end ago didn't know we'd helped to catch a killer earlier in the year, kinda.

"A poem," he said, snapping on a pair of those blue latex gloves. He would have been played by Kevin Costner in the movie version, sparkling white shirt, crew-cut, moisturiser emergency.

"A famous—Yeah, a poem," I said.

"And some girl gets attacked in this poem?"

"No," I said. "The woman is a witch who chases the drunk."

"So because a witch in a poem chases a drunk, you think a shirt in a field is evidence of an assault," he said, bending to lift the flimsy garment up between finger and thumb. "This is why you dragged me out here?"

"There's blood on it," I pointed out.

"It was Halloween last night," the detective said. "There's fake blood on costumes dumped all over town."

"Fake?" I said.

"Probably not even the good stuff," said the detective. He stripped off one of his gloves and scratched at the bloodstain with a thumbnail, sending flakes of it spiraling to the ground. Kevin Costner wouldn't have taken his glove off and contaminated evidence like that. Not unless he was in on it and trying to tank the prosecution's case before it got started. "Dollar store, I reckon."

"Hmph," I said.

"But the wig was fake too," said Todd. "And yet the guy was really dead. Just because the blood is fake doesn't mean the girl this dress belongs to wasn't in real trouble when she lost it."

"I suppose the case is still open?" said Noleen. "The dead guy?"

The detective said nothing, but he said it so grumpily we got our answer anyway.

"Where's the dress from? " I said, thinking if it was handstitched by a local tailor, or if it was a genuine eighteenth-century linen slip from an antiques shop, or even if it had come from one of the pricey little boutiques in downtown Cuento, someone might remember who'd bought it.

"Where's it *from*?" said the detective. "What, in case it's from some frou-frou little boutique and the owner remembers who bought it?" Kevin Costner would never have spoken to a crucial witness that way.

58

He squinted inside the neck. "Evangeline's Costume Mansion," he said. "Like I said. Halloween."

"Look," I said, taking a step towards him.

Todd laid a hand on my arm. "Sorry to trouble you, Officer," he said. "We were spooked. We're not trained to assess threat. We panicked."

I thought he was laying the grovelling on a bit thick, but Kevin-Costner-cast-against-his-wholesome-type-as-a-total-plonker just gave a gruff sort of nod and turned back to his car, the cutty sark still dangling from one hand.

"We can throw that in the trash for you," Todd said.

"Be my guest," Kevin-Costner-wouldn't-touch-this-role-if-Fellini-came-back said and let the garment drop to the ground as he strode away. We waited until he had disappeared in a puff of dust from under his back wheels and then Kathi switched her light back on and we all gathered round the little pile of white linen.

"Mike's gonna have his ass on a cracker when she hears about this," Noleen said.

"How can anyone be so dumb?" I said. "Of course it's a Halloween costume. The whole thing hinges on Halloween."

"Yeah, what a twat," Todd said.

"Don't say *twat*," I told him. "You sound like an arse. Has anyone got a baggie?"

"Don't say *baggie*," Todd told me. "You sound like a douche."

"But has anyone got one?" I insisted.

Noleen patted her pockets. It took a while. She had breast pockets on her shirt; front, back, and leg pockets on her cargo shorts; and seven compartments in her bum bag. "Nope," she said. "Kathi?"

Kathi tried to look innocent then shrugged and took a pair of blue latex gloves out of her jeans pocket and snapped on one, just like a real detective. "Don't look at me like that," she said. "They're for pressing the buttons on crosswalks and opening bathroom doors. It's common sense."

It wasn't common sense, in my professional opinion. In my professional opinion, it was out of control. But it would be rude to nag her while we benefitted from it. When she took out a folded pad of clingfilm, though, and used it to parcel up the shift, I had to say something.

"For ... toilet seats?" I said.

"Have we met?" said Kathi. "I would have to touch a toilet seat to Saran Wrap it."

"So ... ?"

"Touchscreens," she said. "You never know."

"I never know what?" I said. "I never know if I'll need to touch a screen with a finger I could then wash by entering a bathroom, whose door I opened with a glove on?"

"I don't open the door through a glove on the way in!" said Kathi. "The outside of my glove would get contaminated. I wear the glove on the way out. When my hands are clean."

"At least you use public loos," I said. "I've heard of some poor souls giving themselves kidney infections refusing to pee."

"I'm prepared for emergencies," Kathi said. "But I haven't used a public bathroom since 1997, and that was on an international flight. Now stop badgering me and let me wrap this thing up before it turns to compost."

∞

"You know what troubles me," said Todd. Noleen wasn't willing to switch on the NO VACANCIES sign when there was that one tantalising room still free, but she didn't want to miss out on the summit meeting either. So instead of lounging in comfort on my porch or in even greater comfort in Todd and Roger's room, where Todd had ditched the standard-issue motel furniture in favour of goose down and mole-skin, we were crammed into the front office. Noleen was behind the duct-taped counter in her Barcalounger; Todd, Kathi, and Roger, just off his shift and still in his scrubs, were in front of the counter sitting on three of the four excruciatingly uncomfortable wrought-iron breakfast chairs. I was perched on the counter itself because it was nice and high and I found it weird to have a conversation with people I couldn't see.

Kathi had shaken out the cutty sark to show Roger and he'd taken a long close look at it.

"Before you folded this to wrap it, did it have signs of being worn?" he said. "Creases at the elbow? Anything?"

"What troubles me," said Todd, "is that the blood is fake—according to a detective, who should know—and the wig was fake, but the horse really had its tailed chopped off. Doesn't that trouble anyone else?"

"No," I said. "The bullet was real enough."

"Yes, but the bullet was necessary," said Todd. "You can't kill a guy with a fake bullet."

"Ohhhhh!" said Noleen. "I see."

"I don't," I said. I stared down to one side at Noleen in her lounger and then down to the other side at the three of them on their lumpy bistro chairs.

"The blood wasn't needed," Todd said. He was scrolling on his phone. "The witch in the micro-mini doesn't bleed, does she?"

"Someone bleeds," Kathi said. She was scrolling too. "Translate this part, Lexy,"

I took the phone from her hands. "'A murderer's bones in gibbet irons ... a thief cut down from his hanging rope ...' Here we go: 'five tomahawks with blood red-rusted, five scimitars with murder crusted.'"

"Tomahawks?" said Noleen.

"Yadda yadda yadda," I said, scanning forward. "'A knife a father's throat had mangled ... grey hairs still stuck to the shaft.'"

"Yucko," said Todd. "But stuck with blood probably, wouldn't you say?"

"What *is* this that's going on in this poem?" said Roger.

"The devil's playing the bagpipes in a cemetery and all the coffins have opened up like cupboards to show who's inside them," I said.

"Doesn't anyone just die of old age in Scotland?" Roger said. "Sounds worse than Stockton."

"It's only a story," I said. "But you're right, Todd. The dancing witch doesn't bleed. That's significant. I suppose that dumbo detective is right, is he? It's really not blood. Because if it is, it's from a throat wound."

"One of the five tomahawks?" said Noleen. "Why would there be a tomahawk in a Scottish coffin?"

"Or a scimitar?" said Kathi.

"I don't know if it's fake," Roger said. "But no one's ever worn this costume."

"Did you just sniff the armpits?" Kathi said. "You ... You ... Lexy, what's that expression?"

"Clarty besom?" I said.

"You clarty besom!" Kathi said.

"So someone bought this from Evangeline's Costume Mansion," Roger went on, "put fake blood on the neck, and left it at a fake burial ground."

"But cut a horse's tail off for real," Todd said. "Which, like I said, is still bothering me."

"The ring's bothering *me*," I said. A look passed around the three of them on the public side of the counter. "What?" I whipped my head round to look at Noleen. She gave me a sheepish smile. "What?" I asked her.

"Todd's had an idea," she said.

"Oh?"

"You're not going to like it."

"Try me."

"I think you should draw the ring and then we can take the drawing to Mike," Todd said.

"Why wouldn't I like that idea? It makes sense. I should have done it already."

"Well," Todd said, "you suck at drawing and your recall is a testament to the amount of hard drinking you did in college."

"None taken," I said.

"So I want to hypnotise you."

"No way, José."

"Racist."

"Bullshit."

"Bully."

"Todd, you are not hypnotising me."

He was just about managing to keep a straight face, but Roger was nose laughing and Kathi and Noleen were openly tittering.

"Why?" said Todd. "Don't you think it'll work?"

"Sod off."

"Racist."

"How is *sod off* racist?"

"It's anti-Irish. It's telling Irish peasants to leave the land of their fathers."

"Bollocks it is. It's short for *sodomise*. It means go away and bugger yourself up the arse." Which didn't put me on the strongest moral ground, I suppose. And I didn't have strong grounds for refusing to be hypnotised either, only just that when we had gone out to a stage hypnotist on Todd's birthday, they had all enjoyed the show and I had come away with a black hole in my memory. But Kathi filmed it. I could have got to the end of my life quite happily without seeing myself as Rocky Balboa, wearing nerf boxing gloves and sparring to the knockout with a piñata, shouting "Yo, Adrian!" and "Cut me, Mick!" in my very own Dundee accent.

"I'll draw it without any hypnosis, thank you very much," I said. "Nolly, fling me up a pen." I turned over a flyer that was lying on the counter, trying to pretend I hadn't read the front of it—*Trinity solutions: turning your life around is as easy as one, two three*—clicked up the pen nib, and drew.

I drew a lump, with some swirls, and a squiggle.

Then I gave it a long hard look.

"Okay," I said, "hypnotise me."

"When Noleen locks up for the night," Todd said. "Over at your place."

"Why does Noleen have to be there?" I said. "No offence, Nolly, but it's not a spectator sport. Why are you giggling? Todd, if you want to be part of a therapeutic trio, you've got to aspire to higher ethical standards than making me eat raw onions and filming it on your phone."

"Deal," said Todd.

"Wait," I said. "What deal?"

"If I stick to helping you sketch one ring tonight, Kathi and I will finally be accepted as full participants in our company."

"I didn't—" I began.

"Everyone heard you," said Kathi.

"Roger?" I said, turning to the usual source of all sanity in the face of Todd's whackadoodalitis.

"Tag, you're it," he said. "You shouldn't have spent so long telling me how I could manage him with just a little effort."

"You did?" said Todd. "Well, don't mind me, I'm sure."

"Time to put your money where your mouth is," Roger said.

"And how does Kathi get grandfathered in on a full ride?" I said.

"You have no idea what either of those two expressions mean, do you?" Kathi said.

"We need the Trinity income," Noleen said. "We've got two rooms permanently sidelined in quite a small motel to start with." She gave me a hard look. Stony hard, that is. Not hard to interpret. I knew Noleen wanted me to therapy away Kathi's germaphobia so that they could move back into the Last Ditch owners' quarters. At the moment—a moment that had lasted two years and counting—Kathi cleaned the empty owner's flat and they slept in one of the renting rooms, with another renting room held in antiseptic readiness in case the first one somehow got unexpectedly dirty. We had never said it out loud, but I knew the only reason Noleen put up with a houseboat moored off her property and a succession of mentally fragile clients battering their way through her oleanders to counselling appointments all day every day was because I was supposed to be curing Kathi.

∞

Hypnosis is lovely, if I'm honest. I sat back in my comfiest chair, with Kathi, Noleen, and Roger crammed in a row on the couch, beers in hand and chips in laps.

Todd stood behind my head. "Listen to my voice," he said. Already I could feel my arms getting heavy, lolling at my sides like two unbaked baguettes. "Let your mind unhook from all your cares and drift up into the gentle world of dreams."

Someone crunched a chip. Someone giggled. Todd tutted.

"Feel your feet sink against the floor," he said. I could do better than that. I felt my feet melt through the floor and dangle in the cool water of the slough underneath us. "Feel your back resting against the cushion behind you. Become aware of your hips settling into the cushion beneath you. When you feel ready, let your head fall gently—Jesus!"

My head had thwacked back against the armchair as if someone had cut my throat. I knew it. I could feel it. But it didn't bother me. Someone crunched another chip but no one giggled this time.

"When you feel ready," Todd went on, "close your ey—Oh."

My eyes were glued shut already. I could tell I was drooling but I didn't care.

"Now, Lexy," Todd said. "It's Halloween. You are looking over the side of the boat, through the water. You are looking at a waving hand. The hand is wearing a ring. Tell me about the ring."

"It's got engraving at the top," I said. "Four letters. Numbers. Letters. Numbers."

"Can you read them?" Todd said.

"BC545," I said. At least, I might have said it. It didn't feel like me anymore.

"What's underneath the engraving?" Todd said.

"A finger," said the voice that might have been me. Far away on the couch someone giggled and someone hushed them.

"What's lower down the face of the ring than the engraving?" Todd said.

"A stone," said the voice. "A blue and yellow stone. A marble. A stone. A marble. Glass. A glass stone."

"Anything else?" The voice was strained.

"Three bubbles. Circles. Bubbles. Three balls. Bubbles."

"You're feeling refreshed and calm. You're coming back. You're waking up. You're alert and awake. You're a freaking maniac when you're hypnotised, Lexy."

I sat up blinking. Todd was flushed and breathing fast. The three on the couch were clutching each other, gnawing knuckles and stuffing shirttails into mouths to smother helpless laughter. One of the bowls of chips was spilled all over the floor.

"Did it work?" I said.

Todd thrust a pad of paper and a Sharpie into my hands. "Draw it before you forget," he commanded.

I took the pen and sketched a pretty skillful drawing of a big ugly lumpen ring with the legend BC545 across the top, a yin-yang swirl of a stone in the middle and three little circles underneath. One on the left and two on the right.

"You're sure those three bubbles were laid out like that?" Todd said. "It looks unbalanced."

"That's what I saw," I said.

"Never mind that!" said Kathi, coming to stand behind me and look at the sketch. "BC545? Maybe that's why it disappeared!"

"Why?" I said.

"One of the frogmen stole it," she said.

"Why?"

"To sell, of course," Kathi said. "To sell on the black market and fund his kids' college careers."

"How come?" I said. "What does BC545 mean?"

Kathi gave me the kind of look you'd give to an idiot. "You're an idiot," she said. "It means it's over two and a half thousand years old!"

"If the bronze age jeweller who made it happened to know when Christ was going to be born," I pointed out.

"Oh yeah," said Kathi, rubbing her nose.

I noticed that nobody spilled their chips laughing at her, even though that was dumber than anything I'd ever said by far.

"But you're right about what must have happened to it," Noleen said. "That was smart thinking, Kath."

I felt a little slump inside. I didn't mind being single and I loved my friends, but it would be nice to have a partner sometimes. Someone to soothe my pride after I'd made a complete fool of myself. That must be sweet.

"You think one of the divers pocketed it?" I said. "So even if it's not an ancient artifact, you think it might be valuable?"

"What stones are blue and yellow?" said Roger.

"Sapphire with the gold of the setting sun showing through?" said Todd. "A sapphire that size would be worth a decent chunk."

"But aren't the frogmen actual police?" I said.

"Maybe in New Orleans they are," said Roger. "Or San Francisco. Somewhere with water. What's the bet they're hired by the hour from the local diving club here in Cuento?"

"Something else to check out," said Todd. "Along with the vet student."

"And the pet groomer," I said. "Before Della takes out a contract on me."

Seven

Cuento is at its best early on a November morning. For a Scot any-way. It's still t-shirt weather but the ground fog tamps the dust down and the low sunlight burnishes the dying leaves on the walnut trees turning them briefly picturesque. What a disappointment wal-nut trees are! Their blossom isn't a blossom for a start. It's little grey-green wormy things, that look like diseased leaves unless you put your reading specs on. And in autumn they turn a uniform shade of don-key brown, curl up like crumpled lunch bags, and let go at the first puff of wind. And as for the walnuts? Well, okay, the walnuts are gor-geous but they're ten dollars a carrier bag at the fruit stand, so it's hardly worth going out gleaning like some nineteenth-century peas-ant. And they're a bugger if you step on one when you're bladdered.

But this morning, as Todd and I skirted the south end of town headed round to the stables at mucking out time, Cuento was doing its Brigadoon impersonation and doing it beautifully too.

Todd was kitted out in an L.L.Bean-looking red puffy waistcoat with a beanie on.

"Aren't you hot?" I said.

"It's winter," said Todd. "In fact, let's stop at Daivz for hot chocolate, in case we end up standing around talking to Kimberly and get chilly."

"Unless she's hanging her horse for butcher meat and won't come out of the cold store, it doesn't seem likely," I said. "But I could go for an iced Americano. We could get her something too as a sweetener."

Daivz, the cool coffeeshop in the downtown as opposed to the drive-through out by the self-storage, did make the best cocoa, it was true. If the temperature ever dropped low enough for me to put a cardigan on, I might even order one.

"You sure you want iced?" said Todd. "Is this the beginning of the menopause?"

"Sod off back to Ireland and plant your potatoes," I said. I leaned out of the window as he was crossing the street. "Get pastries!"

He didn't answer unless you count the extra wiggle he gave, like his bum was winking at me. I was still watching him when something more interesting than an out-of-bounds (although undeniably pretty) bum crossed my field of view. It was the cat groomer again.

I'd have said it was a different car, but then I don't really care about cars enough to notice them properly, and it was definitely the same decal: line drawing of a cat, emetic poem about a cat, and six numbers followed by FELIX. 10-23-17 FELIX. I keyed it in and waited.

"Yup?" said the voice that answered my call.

"Hi again," I said. "This is Lexy Campbell. I called a couple of days ago. Maybe it was only yesterday. There's a lot going on. About booking an appointment."

"For?"

"Grooming. Two kittens. Pretty urgent. They might need sedation."

"Who is this?" the voice said.

"Lexy Campbell?" I said. "But they're not my kittens. I'm calling for a friend. Oh! But it's my money. You'd be sending the bill to me."

"Oh it's your money? You're helping out a friend?" She didn't sound like a cat groomer. Cat groomers should be friendly and a bit mental.

"Flynn and Florian," I said. "The kittens. The friend is Diego. But you wouldn't be dealing with him. He's—"

"Oh I wouldn't be dealing with Diego, huh?" She sounded … like someone who didn't work in any job where customer relations had a part to play.

"Or maybe I'll try again at a better time," I said. "It's early."

I clicked the phone off and then stared at it. Truth is, I was beginning to get used to the insane levels of courtesy and service in California. I was beginning to like getting smiled at and greeted like a long-lost cousin in shops. I was beginning to love knowing my waiter's name so I could call him over and ask for another substitution on top of the five I'd already described while I was ordering.

"'Sup?" said Todd, arriving back with the coffees.

"Nowt," I said. The day I admitted I liked friendly waiters and helpful shop assistants was the day I would have to eat crow like the Beteo County all-star crow-eating champion at the state fair. And the day I admitted I liked the eating competitions at the state fair, I might as well give up and buy a Tesla.

∞

Early as it was, the stables were hopping. Muck was being raked, concrete hosed, and enormous bags of hay lugged around, making the stable girls look like dung beetles. There was even a class returning from a riding lesson. Americans—and I'd never get used to this, no

72

matter what drive-through, boxed-to-go, download-the-free-app weirdness I managed to wrap my head round—didn't half get up early. School started before eight. The lunch rush was over by one. Blue plate specials kicked in at half four, and late-night telly got going before the sun went down. That probably wasn't even the first riding lesson of the day.

Kimberly didn't take much finding, despite being identical to every other girl in the stables, not to mention the horses. Long limbs, good hair, great teeth, ton of expensive kit. She was standing picturesquely framed against the morning light rising over the distant mountains, pummelling a pony's behind with two brushes, like a shoeshine man. The pony was steaming gently in the cool air and its breath was shot through with sunbeams. Kimberly herself—in long boots, tight jodhpurs, and a skimpy little thing that looked like a stab-vest (but couldn't be)—looked like a Hollister catalogue made flesh. Not much flesh either. She accepted the cocoa and cinnamon roll Todd offered and inhaled both without blinking.

"I'm carb-loading," she said, ruining it. "Cardio day today."

Todd chatted knowledgably with her for a minute or two about ketogenics and fascia breakdown. I wasn't quite sure enough that they were kinds of dressage steps to join in, so I waited, patting the pony on her steaming rump and trying not to notice the stump of her tail, sticking out like a spoon in a pudding.

"Agnetha, right?" I said, when Todd ran out of small talk. "Poor baby."

Kimberly turned her mouth down and nodded.

"Will it grow back?"

"Eventually," she said. "In a year or two."

"What do you think it was about?" I said. "Have you ever heard of someone doing that before?"

"No way," said Kimberly. "Freaky." Maybe it was unconscious, but as she spoke, she took the scrunchie off her own lustrous, coppery tail of hair and ran her fingers through it. I must have imagined the pony giving her a look that said *Bitch, please.*

"And it wasn't for the hair itself, was it?" I said. "I mean, you said it was dropped all over the path, so you skidded in it. Right?"

"Right," Kimberly said. She pulled her own hair halfway through the scrunchie again and left it in a messy hank on top of her head. The pony rolled her eyes, I swear to God.

"Unless it was just a few hairs left on the path," said Todd, "and the assailant took most of it away?"

"No," said Kimberly. "It was a lot. All of it, I think."

"And you didn't see anyone?" I said. "Stealthy, eh?"

"Quick anyway," Kimberly said.

"And you didn't hear anything either?" said Todd. "That's the thing that's troubling me. I mean, if it was quick enough to not spook the horse, how'd the guy—let's say it was a guy—manage to cut through all this really strong, thick hair?" He was brushing his hand over the raw ends of Agnetha's tail stump as he spoke. She looked round, affronted, and the skin on her enormous bum twitched and flinched.

"Sorry," Todd said and took his hand away. "But you see what I mean? He'd need shears to do it quickly and you'd hear the blades. Wouldn't you?"

"Did you have a riding helmet on?" I said. I couldn't remember the picture in the paper. "Do they cover your ears?

"So many questions!" Kimberly said. She was looking more uncomfortable than I could account for. Even more uncomfortable than Agnetha.

"I don't think it's a guy behind this," I said, barely aware of deciding to speak. Kimberly gave me a frozen look. "Seriously. That doesn't strike me as something a guy would do. Chopping off a ponytail is girl's stuff."

"Delilah?" said Todd.

"Right, Kimberly?" I said, ignoring him. Kimberly stared at me, horrorstruck. "You know who it was, don't you?" I said. "You suspect someone, anyway. Someone jealous of you, or of Agnetha? Someone you've had run-ins with? I don't know what stables are like for intrigue. Anything like gyms? More like schools?"

"You—you mean you think someone did this because they think Agnetha is pretty and they're jealous? That they wanted to make her ugly? Someone who doesn't—doesn't—doesn't *like* me?"

"Not necessarily," I said, alarmed by how hard the notion had hit her. She surely had had a pretty golden life so far. "It might have been more like a threat."

Kimberly had been raking through her long hair again. Maybe it was how she comforted herself. But when she caught my meaning, she wound her mane into a rope and tucked it down inside the neck of her stab vest.

"It's only a theory," Todd said. "And it might be nothing to do with you. Or Agnetha. You might just have been in the wrong place at the wrong time. In fact, because of some other incidents that took place in town, we think that's probably the most likely scenario, don't we Lexy?" He glared at me. I had spooked our witness good and proper and we hadn't even done what we came here to do yet.

"We do," I said. "We think this was set up to play out and you two, Agnetha and you, got mixed up in it for reasons that are nothing to do with either of you. I don't think you've got anything to worry about. You could safely take that same route—if it's your favourite ride or whatever. That spot is nothing significant."

I thought I was ladling out tip-top comfort, but Kimberly was looking frozen again.

"That place is nothing significant?" she said. "What do you mean?"

"I just mean the incidents that unfolded at Halloween have their source elsewhere and else ... when."

"You mean," she said, her eyes huge and her voice so taut that she was unnerving the pony. Agnetha shifted restlessly and threw her head up. "You mean I'm not safe anywhere? Even if I avoid the bridge?"

"No, no, no," said Todd. "That's not what she meant at all. It's a language thing, Kimberly. Brits are hard to decipher, you know. *Else-when* isn't even a word in American."

I opened my mouth to say something, but Todd kicked me. Well, not really, but he moved his foot so it pressed against mine and his meaning was clear.

"And, look, we don't want to take up any more of your day," he went on. "We've just got one more favor to ask you. We want you to look at a photograph and see if you recognize someone."

"Okay," Kimberly said. Maybe she had spent her whole life around horses and it was rubbing off, but I swear *her* skin was twitching now and she was paddling her feet in her shiny boots just the same way Agnetha paddled her shiny hooves.

Todd gave her a kind smile and drew his phone out of his back pocket. He had set it up so the modified picture of Tam was right there when he swiped it open. He showed the screen to Kimberly, who immediately started nodding.

"Yes," she said. "I think so. I couldn't swear to it, in a court of law, but yes, I think that's the man who cut off Agnetha's tail. I'm sure I've seen him hanging around the stables. I think he used to sit on the bus bench at the edge of the pavement. He never talked to me, but he always looked. You know that way some guys look at you. Yes, that's him. Tell the police I said so."

"Thank you," Todd said. "That's all we needed to know. We'll let you get on with your day."

Back in the car, we both tried talking over each other.

"What the hell?" was my brilliant contribution. "It *can't* have been Tam!"

"You screwed that up royally," was what Todd went for.

"What? What did *I* do? Tam was days dead!"

"You freaked her out saying it was some master plan and she can't put it behind her. You made her lie to us."

"I *would* have freaked her out, if I'd said that," I admitted. "But I didn't say that. I didn't say anything like that. And anyway …"

Todd said nothing for a while as he navigated one of Cuento's hairiest four-way stops—the one with a bike rack too close to the roadway, a tree with too many squirrels, and sudden swerving from pedestrians when they saw the smiling chump with the SPLC clipboard.

"And anyway what?" he snapped once we were past it all and headed under the tracks again.

"There's something off about the whole thing, don't you think?" I said. "The pony stops dead and won't cross the bridge. While it's stopped, someone—not Tam—jumps out from the bushes—"

"*Are* there bushes?"

"Let's go and see. And this person manages either to chop off a major chunk of pretty sturdy horse hair quickly but silently or manages to snip away until the job's done without the horse realising anything's happening? It doesn't make any sense."

"And why was the pony scared of going over the bridge?" said Todd. "If anything, she'd be trying to get away from the maniac giving her ass a buzz cut, wouldn't she?"

"That's certainly what happens with Maggie in the poem," I said. "She's running away and the witch grabs her tail. This is just like the cutty sark. It's close but no coconut."

"Banana," said Todd, like it mattered. But he was turning the car round in an illegal U-ey to take us to the overpass, so I let it go.

Eight

There were no bushes.

Todd and I stood on the rising slope at the town side of the canal and stared around.

"Sniper's paradise," Todd said. "She's lucky it was just horse hair he was after, whoever he was. I agree, by the way: not Tam."

I nodded. There were a few trees near the path, trunks too skinny for anyone to hide behind, and no actual cover for fifty yards in both directions. What there was—still—was a few of the shiny black hairs from Agnetha's tail, blown to the edges of the path and caught in the weeds there.

"So we know this is the right spot," I said, toeing a few of them up into a clump and then kicking them.

"Don't do that!" Todd said. "That's as nasty as the hairball."

"Is there any point looking for footprints?" I said. "Seeing if some-one hid in those shrubs over there then ran this way?"

"Ants," Todd said. "Roly-polys. And no-see-ums too. What kind of God creates insects so tiny they can be called no-see-ums and then gives them teeth to bite you?"

He was walking away from the weedy path and the distant bushes even as he spoke and it was pointless to try and stop him. I could see that reflexive shrugging gesture he makes to flick imaginary beasties off him and I knew the way he was moving, stamping like an ogre in a fairytale, was mean to squash the seething creatures under his feet before they could jump up past his shoes and start climbing. He didn't stop until he was at the summit of the foot bridge, high up in the windy November air where no insect would make the effort to come and stage an attack.

I gave him a fierce hug and a smackeroo on the cheekbone.

"What's that for?" he demanded, unconvincingly.

"I love you," I said. And I loved California too. Imagine saying that in Dundee to a pal you'd met nine months previously! Sober, I mean. You'd get carted off for an overnight evaluation. Todd nodded distractedly but he was looking out over the rooftops of Cuento, eyes narrowed like Clint Eastwood when the cheroot smoke's bothering him.

"Cutty sark over there," he said, pointing westwards. "Horse's tail here. Tam in the slough over there." He waved a hand to the south side of town. "That can't be everything."

"What are you thinking?"

"There's something missing," said Todd. "Nearly half the poem, for a start. All the drinking in the pub before the journey begins."

"Seventy-two bottles of Blue Moon that Tam was wrapped round?" I said. "That's plenty booze, isn't it?"

"I dunno," Todd said. "It went on and on and *on* and on about the pub on market day and the camaraderie. If we're right that the poem's the thing, what about all that?"

"But are we?" I said. "*Are* we right? That detective that came out had a point maybe. The minidress on the fake burial mound is weird, but Halloween is Weird Central round here. The pony tail … you saw

Kimberly, Todd. She's just the sort of girl that lesser mortals get obsessed by. And when I suggested it, she lost her mind. Like she knew I was right. And the hat's the only thing about that poor dead guy that's got the slightest connection."

"Dead Guy again, eh?" Todd said. "Not Tam anymore?"

"Not if it's going to lead us astray," I said. "I think the ring's the thing."

"Okay, Fr—" said Todd.

"Don't call me Fr—" I cut in.

"—odo," we said in chorus.

"Snap, jinx, I own you," Todd added. "I thought *Frodo* was okay."

"I changed my mind. And I think you'll find *I* own *you*. And if I own you, I demand that you drive me to the SPCA Thrift Store. Their notice board is bound to have cat groomer business cards, eh no?"

"As you wish," said Todd. "I kinda love that place but it's too sad to go alone, Roger would rather die, and it's not Kathi-compliant. Let's go."

I kinda love the place too. Where else does one go to find Sesame Street spatula sets and platform flip-flops under the same roof? Today, of course, the Thrift was only just hauling itself back together after Halloween, packing away the unsold fangs and neck-bolts and still trying to offload the polyester wedding dresses and zoot suits by slashing the price to the bone. I had a bit of a rub on a fake bloodstain on one of the wedding dresses. It didn't flake like the blood on the cutty sark. Maybe this was the good stuff.

Despite the mess on the shop floor, I managed to snag a pair of floral flannel granny nightgowns that looked just the ticket for winter nights at Creek House.

"What's with the Mother Hubbards?" Todd said. He was leafing through a stack of framed paintings.

"What's a Mother Hubbard?" I said.

"Are you going to use the fabric to make pillow covers?" Todd's voice was stern.

"No, I'm going to wear them."

"God help us," Todd said. "Oh!" He had found a picture of a little girl with a kitten on her shoulder. "Hold this while I see if they've got the others," he said.

"Are you buying this for the frame?" I said.

"Who cares about the frame, Lexy! This is one of the Northern Paper Mills toilet paper babies. There are twelve and I've only got five of them." He gasped and drew another picture out of the pile. "Oh my God! It's the orange-haired hatless boy. I can't believe it."

"Me neither," I said. "At least when I curl up in bed in my tartan flannel there's nobody there to see me. If you put that on your wall, you'll never live it down."

"Roger loves them too," Todd said.

"No," I told him. "Roger loves you. Oh, how Roger loves you, to give you a free hand with decoration."

"Really?" said Todd. "*My* taste? *You're* going after *my* taste? Did you ever think, Lexy, that if you didn't curl up in plaid flannel, you wouldn't be doing it alone?"

I put his stupid ugly print down on the floor before it gave me diabetes and flounced off to pay for my nighties. He was right. I knew he was right. I was thirty-two and hadn't ruled out kids, but I hadn't had a date since the spring when I found Bran and Brandeee going at it like porn stars and left him. And even though I was proud of myself for how psychologically healthy I'd been, cutting bait immediately and moving on, I knew I'd only taken the first step. The easy one. I knew I had to take the next step some time. The hard one.

And speaking of psychological health, if I was honest, I'd been avoiding speaking to my mum for two months because I knew she'd raise the subject and I wouldn't be able to argue. She'd regaled me with her take on the situation when I rang her up on her birthday and I was still recovering.

"I had to carry quite a big bouquet when I married your dad, Lexy, but I must say it stopped me shilly-shallying."

"Mum?" I said. "Are you telling me you were pregnant at your wedding?"

"Sick as a dog," she said. "Waste of a honeymoon."

"You never told me."

"I'm telling you now. I'm not getting any younger, Lexy. Nor your dad neither and we didn't want you to get a shock when you're clearing out the house."

She was right too. It *was* better to find out I was the shotgun at the wedding while she was still here to be judged, without me feeling mean. And she was right about Bran too. It was a pity I'd been so scrupulous about contraception while I was with him. His personality, morals, and dress sense left a lot to be desired, but his genes were second to none.

I looked down at my nighties while I was shuffling forward in the queue to pay for them and I let myself wonder if Todd was right too. Then I sniffed and stuck my chin in the air. Men get laid all the time in flannel pyjamas. I was sticking it to the patriarchy buying these. It's like I used to tell my ex-boyfriend when he bought me another birthday, Christmas, Valentine's, or anniversary present made of satin ribbon and marabou. Any day he wore a G-string, I'd wear a G-string. And the same went for corsets.

Remembering chucking all those unworn sets of sleazy underwear in the bin when he dumped me cheered me up again, and I smiled a laidback smile at the shop assistant over the head of the old man in front of me who was taking his sweet time counting out the right money. He had tipped his change onto the counter and was searching for one last quarter in the heap of nickels and dimes.

He was stirring it round with a gnarled index finger. The other three fingers were tucked into a fist. And that threw the blue and yellow stone on his ring into relief so the light shone through it. I leaned forward. He'd found a quarter. He pushed it over the counter and then spread his hand on top of the pile of coins to scoop them up.

It was! It was the same ring. Gold and lumpy with letters and numbers set all around in crude engraving and that same stone in the middle. How the hell had he got it? How could I even begin to ask him? I couldn't ask him. He might be dangerous. But if I managed to get a picture to show to Mike, maybe this case would break at last.

I manhandled my phone out of my pocket and doinked the buttons like a starving pigeon, but here's the thing about fishing out the right money to pay for goods in a shop with a no-return policy. There's no waiting for a receipt or change. The old man in front was done. He turned on his heel and stumped out of the shop.

"I'll be back," I said to the assistant, dropping my nighties on the counter. I swerved back to where Todd was still feverishly looking for more bogging pictures, grabbed the two out of his hands, jammed them back into the pile and dragged him, protesting, out into the carpark.

"I've seen the ring," I said. "A man—Oh where is he? Look, over there! That man. He's wearing the ring."

"For real?" said Todd. "You're sure?"

"I was hypnotised into being sure," I reminded him. "Shit, he's getting in a car. Sir! Si-ir?"

The old man, one leg in his Saturn and one still on the ground, twisted to see if I was talking to him.

"Sir," I said, galloping to his side, "sorry to bother you but—"

Todd overtook me and got there first. "We need to ask you something," he said.

The man looked expectantly between Todd and me. He was holding onto the inside of the door with his right hand, hiding the ring completely. Todd looked at me. I shrugged.

We could ask him, but if he was mixed up in the murder, asking him wasn't such a great idea. And we could just grab him, but if he wasn't mixed up in the murder, if he was just a frail old gentleman, that didn't seem like a winning plan either.

"We kind of wanted what you bought in there," I said. "I laid it down for a minute and I think you picked it up."

"Fair and square," the old man said. "Wunt no reserved ticket on it."

"Oh no, no, no, no," said Todd. "We're not complaining. We were just hoping you might be willing to sell it to us."

"Sell it?" the man said. He looked into his car towards the passenger seat. I squinted but couldn't see anything.

"Sell it," I said firmly. "We'll give you double what you just paid."

"Twenty dollars," he said.

"You never just paid ten dollars in quarters!" I said.

"I paid twenty dollars," the old man said. "You owe me forty."

"Wow," said Todd under his breath, but at least he was getting his wallet out. I would have but I wanted to make sure and snap a clear picture of the ring while the old man was handing over his forty dollars' worth of mystery item. Which he now was. He reached into the car and lifted a tattered paperback biography of Ronald Reagan with its 50¢ price sticker plain as day on the jacket.

"Well worth it," said the old man.

"I'm not complaining," said Todd. "This transaction is completely aboveboard. There's no book-sales embargo on this parking lot, is there?"

I had no idea what he was on about, but it pissed the old man off for sure. He poked his finger at Todd's chest, the same finger he'd used to sort out his change, meaning that I got some great close-ups of the ring while he was at it. "You read that book, sonny, and you'll see the country I love," he said. "Not this wasteland." He lifted his chin at the neat thrift-store car park, the kindergarten across the road, and the back fence enclosing the timber and gravel section of the DIY place. As wastelands go, it was pretty spiffy. Then he got into his car and slammed the door.

"I hope those pics worked out," Todd said. "Because I forgot to look at the goddam ring!"

"Feast your eyes," I said, starfishing the best shot into an even better one and handing the phone to Todd.

He starred down at it. "You're kidding," he said.

"What? It's the same ring."

"Oh, I'm sure it is. You misunderstand me. Lexy, this is a class ring from Beteo County Senior High School. Half the old geezers in Cuento probably wear one."

"BCSHS!" I said. "Not BC545! And what about the bubbles? The three bubbles at the bottom." I grabbed the phone back from him and peered at the picture. "Five three," I said. "It's a number!"

"Of course it's a bloody number," said Todd. "It's a bloody class ring. The top part is the name of the school and the bottom part is the graduating year."

"Don't say *bloody*," I told him. "You sound daft."

"It's a freaking class ring!" Todd said, very loud.

"Better," I said. "How was I supposed to know it was a class ring? We don't do class rings. We haven't got class rings, lockers, drivers' ed, proms—wait, they might have proms now—valedictorians, letter jackets."

"Nobody has letter jackets anymore," Todd said.

"Home room, homecoming, home schools—"

"I just spent forty dollars on nothing," Todd said. "You owe me twenty."

"Nothing?" I said. "What are you talking about? Can you really not see what this means? Guess what else we don't have that you've got, Todd. What else have you lot got that us poor deprived Brits have to stagger along without?"

"Guns?"

"At school," I reminded him.

"Guns? Sorry. Mouth guards?"

"In the library," I hinted. But he was stumped. "Yearbooks! If Tam came by that ring honestly, he'll be in the Beteo County Senior High School Yearbook for us to ID!"

"Ah, but what year?" said Todd.

"Three bubbles," I reminded him. "Six eight, sixty-eight. I just didn't notice the straight bit."

"Sonofabitch!" Todd shouted, but not in a celebratory way. He jabbed his finger at the door of the thrift where someone was edging out, her arms full of square things that looked exactly the size and shape of Northern Paper Mills toilet paper baby prints. It was hard to tell since she had wrapped them in flannel nighties to carry them home.

Nine

If I'd known I'd be putting in so much busybody time, I would have cleared my schedule. As it was, I went back to the Last Ditch to start chipping away at the hang-ups and melt-downs of another day's worth of affluent navel-gazers with the library trip waiting as a treat at the end, like a biscuit placed just beyond the nose of a dog while you brush it. I had no idea how groomers played it with cats. Flynn and Florian were far from feral and weren't yet fully grown, but they'd just smack the brush away with their claws out, snaffle the treat, and then climb the curtains to get away.

"Your eleven, your noon, and your three are booked in with me afterwards," Todd said, as we drove home. "Kathi's out at your eleven o'clock now, decluttering."

I said nothing. For nearly thirty seconds I managed to say nothing at all, then the words shot out around my clenched teeth anyway. "Booked in for what?"

"Huh," said Todd. "You've never sounded like Sean Connery before, Lexy. But you sounded way like him then. Say some more."

This time I said nothing and stuck to it.

Todd sighed, then started counting off on his fingers and talking in a sing-song voice: "Basic wardrobe advice for Marcie at noon. A bit of bitch training for Helen at one, and a massage for Ron at four."

"You're massaging that Ron guy with the—" I said, before I remembered that my clients' difficulties were confidential.

"I know!" said Todd, wiggling his eyebrows. "Who'da thunk it?"

"Also," I said. "Bitch training?"

"Oh yeah," said Todd. "All that woman needs is a few put-downs to get Mommy Dearest off her back and she'll be sailing into the sunset on her honeymoon."

Helen was a twenty-five-year-old medical receptionist who had cancelled her wedding twice already and was beginning to check the refund dates on flowers and chair skirts for her third one. All to the same guy, let me say. I had met her twice and covered commitment versus contingency, contentment versus happiness, and the end of the patriarchy. She hadn't mentioned her mum.

"Right," I said as we parked at the Last Ditch. "Well, I think I'll nip up to the Skweek and finish sewing that zip in. I've got twenty minutes."

"We're like a 1970s Coke ad," said Todd, heading towards his room. "Go us."

Finding Noleen behind the counter of the launderette seemed like more evidence of the general love-in. But one look at her face told me she thought the same as I did regarding the Last Ditch turning commune.

"There's a sign on the door of my office sending check-ins up here," she said. "No way to stop them moving on to La Quinta instead, though, if they don't want to climb the stairs. And all so Kathi can go stick Q-tips in a stranger's keyholes and pretend it's for them. It's for her. She's getting worse, Lexy."

"I'm no happier about it than you are," I said. "And I'm sorry to hear Kathi's having a dip."

"I do my best with her," Noleen said. "Keep her spirits up. Keep her outlook sunny."

I knew my expression was growing fixed, but thankfully Noleen was staring at the floor while she shook her head in sorrow like a basset hound. She loved Kathi. I'm sure she did, but she was no cheerleader. This very day, she was wearing a t-shirt bearing the legend *We're all going to die* across the chest. It wasn't a set-up for a cute punchline; there was nothing written on the back. That was the whole message and it was one of Noleen's favourites. She had it in four colours.

I sat down and pulled the cover off the sewing machine. "Maybe," I said, checking the tension and wrangling the pinned edge of the zip under the foot, "just maybe, this could be the way in. If I was to give in on the Trinity thing."

"You spat when you said that," Noleen said. "Don't spit on the alterations."

I unclenched my teeth and tried again. "If I give in on the Trinity thing and start agreeing that a bit of a tidy round and a new scarf are essential components in therapy … " At least that made Noleen smile. She did love to hear some sneering. " … Kathi won't have a leg to stand on if I ask her to submit to my bit of the three-way."

"Don't say *three-way*," said Noleen. "But you're right, Lexy. If you embrace them—Todd too, not just Kathi—they'll have to embrace you back or look like wankers."

"Don't say *wanker*," I told her, but I spoke without any real conviction. I was looking deep down inside myself, proctology-deep (only down, not up), and wondering if I could really bring myself to embrace Trinity Solutions. But then, if my plan worked, I wouldn't be embracing it for long. If I cured Todd's cleptoparasitosis, he would go back to being an anaesthetist, and if I cured Kathi's germaphobia, she'd no longer want to go around pulling out other people's drain hair. At which point it would be goodbye Trinity and hello sanity.

"Right," I said. "I've finished the zip. Will I press it or should we dry clean it? Did I really spit?"

"Press it and bring me up to speed with the case," Noleen said. "What happened at the stables?"

I told her about the stables, the Thrift, and the upcoming library visit, and she regaled me with the perfect 100 percent negative response to Tam's picture at the two smaller senior centers when Roger had flashed it around.

"And you know they'd do anything for him," she finished up. "They love him more than the kids love him. And the kids love him nearly as much as the mommies love him."

"How could anyone not love him?" I said.

"I don't love him," said Noleen, rearing back as if I'd waved smelling salts under her nose. "He's been tying up one of my rooms, make that two of my rooms, for a year and a half and he comes with a built-in Todd."

She was doing her best. She was shaking her head like a basset hound again, but her eyes were sparkling. She loved him. Hell, she loved both of them.

So I was overflowing with love as I began my professional day. And talking Trinity up was much easier than pretending it wasn't happening.

"She is a terminator of filth," said Marcie. "She can find dirt I never even imagined. Have you any idea how much dirt collects in the overflow of a kitchen sink? It was like an eel! I took a photograph of it. Look, Lexy."

"Wow," I said. It was the first overflow eel I had ever seen so I didn't know if it was a whopper or a tiddler, but *wow* summed up the sight overall.

"And she's so organized! She explained her household systems analysis to me so clearly I'll never forget. It's all so straightforward."

I had never asked Kathi about the internal workings of her mammoth cleanliness obsession, I was ashamed to say. I didn't want to give it oxygen. But Marcie, with the zeal of the convert, was waxing unstoppably.

"There's shelter," she said. "And clothing and sustenance. Every bit of housekeeping falls into one of those three areas. Then there's management, which is different."

"Mkay," I said.

"Shelter!" Marci said. "You have to clean your house: mop, scrub, wipe, sweep, dust, vacuum, and declutter. Clothing! You need to sort, mend, wash, dry, fold, and stow your clothes. And sustenance! You need to buy, store, cook, and clean up after your meals. And that is how a household runs. Like a machine."

"And management?" I said, intrigued in spite of myself.

"Running the calendar, running the white board, birthdays, bills, invitations, and thank yous."

"And separating these systems lets you ...?" I said.

"Lets me see how much I do without anyone asking me and lets me see how little *he* does unless it's all set out for him. I've told him I'll take over the barbecuing next year if he does carpooling and bathrooms."

"How did that go down?" I said, taking a wild guess.

"He couldn't argue," she told me. "I showed him the spreadsheet of weekly and monthly totals that Kathi and I worked up together. He takes out the trash—forty minutes per calendar month; I fold the laundry—forty minutes every two days. Every two days!"

I nodded. I wanted to ask about fitted sheets but I stopped myself.

"Interesting," I said. "So if you think about your life—over time—the way you think about a snapshot of your house in the course of a week, what would *that* spreadsheet look like?"

Marcie frowned at me.

"Like you said, your husband reckons putting the bins out and grilling a few burgers is a significant contribution. What looms largest in your mind when you think about your life?"

"My first marriage," she said, every cell of the spreadsheet falling away, taking Marcie's smile with it.

"And how long did it last?"

"Eighteen months."

"And you're how old?"

"Forty-four."

"So that's forty-four times twelve … which is eighty-eight times six … that's five hundred and twenty-eight months. Other than that marriage, there's five hundred and ten months of adult life we need to account for. What else you got?"

"Is that how it works?" Marcie said.

What could I tell her?

"Yip," I said. "Unless you've got PTSD from those eighteen months, that is exactly how it works. The childhood years are extra … Well, we could say the first five years counts triple, the next five double, one and a half up to fifteen, and then the cake—that's you—is baked."

"Is that true?"

What would I say now?

"Yip. So tell me about your first five years. What do you remember? Let's fill in this spreadsheet, eh?"

I was going to have to buy Kathi a bunch of flowers to say thank you, because Marcie took a leisurely stroll down memory lane and recalled her mother making penny soup, her father teaching her to trim his cigars, and her baby sister grabbing her finger and laughing. When she looked at her watch, told me Todd was waiting, and went off practically skipping, I emailed the florist—Name of the Day: As-sussena, a money-saving option disguised as diversity; sneaky—and ordered a pot of chrysanthemums and eucalyptus, remembering just in time that Kathi doesn't like flowers that are too pretty.

$$\infty$$

Balance, I found myself thinking as I pedalled up to the north end of town at the end of the day. The library was open for another two hours and I needed this. Even a great day of clients like today left me fogged with their worries and knotted with their stresses. Cycling in the crisp air of a November evening, with my hair flying back and my muscles pumping, would blow the whole day away. As the wind ruffled my do up into a nest, I thought of Tam on his trusty mare, racing away across the bridge with the devil chasing him, and I thought of Kimberly on Agnetha, stopped dead on the overpass with the shears snipping. As my clothes flew back like flags, I thought of the dancing witch in her cutty sark and that white shift resting on the stinkweed at the old Armour place. And, as I slowed at the library bike stand, losing momentum and starting to wobble, I thought of the first Tam, lucky Tam, away home to Kate and his hangover; and our Tam, our poor unfortunate Tam, dead as a doornail and his corpse made into a bad joke.

Inside the sliding doors, the librarian on duty just about managed not to cry or punch me when I asked for the 1968 yearbook. No doubt it was far, far from the front desk, deep, deep in some dusty warren and she was counting down the minutes till she could get out of here.

"1968?" she said. "Senior high school yearbook?" As if I might smack myself in the head and say *Silly me, I meant the new David Sedaris on disc.*

I grimaced my apologies at her and, with a sigh, she went plodding off, picking over a monster bunch of keys.

The book she plunked down on the desk in front of me five minutes later was not at all what I was expecting. It wasn't some stapled-together kids' project, full of Tippex and typos. It was a serious hardback tome, big as an Ikea catalogue but hardback bound, its nubbly cover lavishly embossed in gold and its upward of two hundred glossy pages telling me I hadn't had time to cycle up here after all.

I found the seniors easily and felt proud of myself for knowing that *seniors* was what you called the graduating year, then I settled down to find Tam.

Wow, they looked old. That was the first thing that struck me. All the Pattis and Suzies and Sandys and Bettys, with their beehives and horn-rims and their little black dresses. Did they really all have identical black dresses? Or did the photographer just put the same bolt of black cloth on all of them. And where were their bra straps?

But I didn't need to be looking at the girls. I turned my eye instead to the Glenns, Johnnys, Howies, and Steves in their black jackets, starched shirts, and skinny ties. My God, they were white. Clean-cut, short-haired, clear-eyed, and stubble-free, they started to freak me out after a page or two. Where were the bad boys? I'd seen *Grease*. Where was Kenickie? Some of this lot looked the same age as Kenickie—in other words, about thirty-eight—but there was nary a snarl and certainly not a leather jacket to be seen.

But that was all to the good. Every single one of these Midwich cuckoos was grinning like a maniac, so finding Tam's gap-toothed gob would be a skoosh.

Except I scrutinised every single one from Larry Abbott to Bobby Zane and he wasn't there. There was one boy with a space in his teeth, but his name was Luis Estrada and there was no way his crisp black curls and big brown eyes could have faded to what I had hauled up out the slough. There was one boy with a set of braces so sturdy they obscured his teeth, but then they'd have been torqueing the gap together, wouldn't they?

Maybe he bought the ring secondhand, because he liked it. I considered the possibility for roughly three seconds. For one thing, the ring was too ugly. That wasn't my opinion. It was a statement of objective fact. The BCSHS class ring was ugly like Cuento was flat. No one would wear one if they didn't have to. And also everyone else in Cuento except me would know it was a class ring. And Cuento-ites of … I did a quick calculation … fifty years' standing, would see it and ask him about it and know he had no right to it.

I was leafing desultorily through the rest of the yearbook as my mind wandered over the possibilities. Cheerleaders, Junior Red Cross, Varsity Band, Sophomore Metro League Champs. It was like reading the fifth book in a fantasy series that had no helpful website explaining anything. The pictures were clear though. Page after page of beehives and skinny ties ranged on benches, some smiling, some sombre. Some very sombre. The Future Homemakers of America looked properly like their soufflés had sunk. I turned the page to the smiling faces of the Future Farmers of America, much cheerier, then my hand stopped leafing, my eyes stopped seeing, and my lungs, briefly but completely, stopped breathing.

I let the page fall back and looked at the Homemakers again.

He was there.

Tam—our Tam—was there in the back row, between a girl in a fur-trimmed overcoat and a girl in a jacket with a big embroidered *C* on one breast. He had both his arms back as if he was giving the two of them a friendly hug and he was the only one in the whole three rows who was grinning. The gap in his teeth was there as clear as day and, as I looked back and forth between my printout of Roger's Photoshopped corpse-shot and the little face in the back row, all my doubts fell away.

I set to studying the names under the photo, aware that my pulse was racing. I was going to ID a murder victim.

But his name wasn't there. There were nine girls as well as Tam on the back row and the names underneath were Patti, Linda, Maggie, Vera, Wanda, Mickie, Sallie, Gudrun, and Clarice. He wasn't listed.

I turned a page, casting my eyes over the fun-loving scamps in the Latin Club—beaming smiles all round—and then the Future Nurses of America—faces like skelped arses and Tam in the back row again, arms around his neighbours to either side, face split with a grin like a pumpkin lantern and no name in the legend. Future Business Leaders and the Acapella Band were two bunches of girls and boys who had been caught mid-orgy if their pictures were to be believed, and there was no sign of Tam anywhere. But I caught one last glimpse of him among the girls who were destined to be librarians, mouths so pursed they could have been practising a collective "Ssssshhhhh!"

So. I sat back and gazed into the middle distance, wondering. Tam was a member of the class of 1968 and a Future Homemaker, Nurse, or possibly Librarian of America. How weird was that? For 1968? And what about Tam being in the class but having his picture missed out? How weird was *that*?

A nasty wriggling feeling was beginning to steal over me, starting at the back of my neck. Were Fur Collar and Big C and the rest of them in the Homemakers' Club not smiling because Tam was there? Were they annoyed that they hadn't managed to freeze him out? Were they just a big back-combed bunch of 'phobes? It would explain their expressions.

Or was I being unfair to girls born in 1950?

So what if I was? What kind of people were running the school who had let this happen? I flicked forward to where the faculty photos were laid out. Dale Dwight Johnson, the headmaster, straight from *Mad Men,* was flanked by a Dean of Girls and a Dean of Boys. I stuck my tongue out at both of them and turned to the so-called counsellors who, in my view, sucked at their jobs. And the school nurse had obviously just climbed out of the cuckoo's nest for the photo op. Business, fine arts and foreign language, maths and music. They all gazed out at me so pleased with themselves, with such unwarranted smugness and pride, while a kid in their pastoral care was ostracised. Physical education ... I stopped.

All the female teachers had been Mrs. Something up till now: Mrs. Salter, Mrs. Moon, Mrs. Grady. But here were the gym teachers: Miss Brand, Miss Jensen, Miss McNamara, and Miss Reinhardt (not pictured). I gazed at them. Did they know, this phalanx of strapping lesbians, that a poor lonely gay kid was kept out and cold-shouldered, when all he wanted to do was fit in and be accepted? I was glad Miss Reinhardt was too ashamed to be seen.

Although, as I flicked through the sciences and got to the librarians, bus drivers, and cafeteria staff, the number of unpictured individuals rose. There were only a few custodians in the group shot and half a dozen jannies lost forever, like they weren't worth the effort. Like this was just a popularity contest and not an official record after all.

Then another thought occurred to me. Because this *was* an official record, wasn't it? Oh not the Future Homemakers and the touchdown action shots. But a bit of this was a *facebook*. The origin story of actual Facebook was right here between these covers.

I flicked back to the end of the senior portraits again. And there it was. There was the name of the only student who did not have his picture included but had to have his name recorded officially just this once. *Not Pictured* it said in tiny writing. *Thomas Oscar Shatner.*

Bastards.

I clicked a few photos with my phone, slammed the book shut, and pedaled home.

Jen

I love the Last Ditch on a quiet Friday night when Roger's not on call and Kathi's all caught up with the service washes. I loved them when we used to gather in Todd's room, or in the office, and I love them even more now that we gather in Creek House.

Would I like to be in charge of issuing invitations? Would I prefer that to coming round the side of the motel past the oleanders, seeing the belch of smoke from my chimney, and realising that Todd had lit the stove already?

Well. You can't have everything.

"Bombshell! You'll never believe it," I said, entering the living room. The four of them were gathered there. Todd and Roger on the couch, Kathi on one end of the other couch, Noleen in the armchair. They're always very careful not to couch it up in two pairs, not to make me feel like the spare leg, which makes me feel like a spare leg with athlete's foot and a bunion.

"I see your bombshell and raise you a meteor strike," Roger said. If Todd had said it, I'd be looking round for a pinch of salt, but Roger isn't given to hyperbole.

"Is the case solved?" I said. Of course, I hoped it was. Anything else would be heartless and tacky.

"Not even close," said Roger.

"Yay!" I said, without meaning to. I sat down on the other end of the couch from Kathi and accepted the glass she put in my hand.

"And I was right," Todd said. "I am vindicated. I am a genius. I could probably be a certified private detective once I put in a few hours to get my license."

"Five hundred hours," said Noleen. "Stick to cocktails." She drained her glass and reached over to the shaker for more.

"Well, we'll see," Todd said. "Now then, Lexy, remember I said I thought a whole lot of the poem had been neglected on Halloween?"

"All the drinking," I said. "Yes. But, Todd, honestly, I really do have news."

"You'll get your turn," Todd said. "I'm bursting with this. And Roger was wrong by the way."

"Bursting with news but takes the time to get that in," Noleen said.

"Roger thought Tam was in his seventies," said Todd. "Well, he wasn't. He was sixty-eight."

"A whole two years off," Roger said. "And not even that if he repeated a year."

"And yet no one ID'd him," Todd said. "No one in the senior center knew him. Because although he graduated from Beteo County High, he hasn't lived in Cuento since."

"Which means what?" I said. "He was killed and brought back here to be dumped?" I was wondering how this nugget slotted in amongst all the stuff I'd learned and theories I'd formed.

"But no!" said Todd. "Think about it, Lexy. He graduated in 1968!"

"So he's not quite seventy," I said. "What am I missing?"

"It's 2018," said Todd.

"Right."

"It's fifty years later."

"And?"

"What happens fifty years after you graduate high school?" said Todd.

"I dunno. Nothing in Dundee. Why, what happens here?"

"A high school reunion!"

"Ohhhhhhh!" I said. "That is a definite possibility. He was back in town for his fiftieth high school reunion? When is it?"

"It's come and gone," Todd said. "It was pretty huge too. A lot of hard partying. And it was held ... wait for it ... at the farmers' market!"

"Okay," I said. The farmers' market was Cuento's wild side. There's kale, to be sure, but there's also bands and food trucks, and when the kale's all sold and the picnic blankets are rolled up, there's dancing and drinking. "So they held their reunion at the farmers' market. So what? I've seen wedding receptions there." Then my brain caught up with my ears. "Wai—wai—wait! They all got together and got plastered *at a market*?"

"Back to our tale," said Todd. "'One market night, Tam got hammered pretty tight, and by a chimney blazing finely, of foaming ale they drank divinely.'"

"Wait a minute though," I said. "If the reunion was at Halloween, Tam was four days dead by then, wasn't he?"

"Who has a reunion on a Wednesday?" said Todd. "Pay attention, Lexy. The reunion was at the farmers' market. Which is ...?"

"Saturday," I said.

"Which is ...?"

I gave a long, low, gobsmacked whistle. "Four days before we found him." It fitted perfectly with everything I'd learned. He had come to his high school reunion and they'd killed him.

"Now all we need to do," said Todd, "is find someone from the class of sixty-eight who still lives here in town, show the picture, and get his name."

"No need," I said. "That's my bombshell. I've got his name. And I think I know why he was killed too. Look." I handed my phone to Kathi, who was nearest. I had the picture zoomed in on Tam, Vera, and Wanda in the back row of the Homemakers.

"That's definitely him," she said. "He needs to fire his honeys. Or teach them to smile anyway."

"Don't say *honeys*," said Roger, leaning over and taking the phone. "Yeesh."

"His name," I said, "believe it or not, really is Tam. Thomas anyway. Thomas Oscar Shatner."

"Tom O. Shatner?" said Noleen. "Poor schmuck. His parents should be taken out and—" She cleared her throat. "Bad choice of words. But they should be."

Roger was swiping with Todd looking on. "Where's his picture?" he said. "You don't have a shot of his actual—Oh." He had seen the pic I'd taken of the little note saying Tam wasn't there. "They missed him? That's a cardinal sin for a yearbook squad."

"I think it was deliberate," I said. "I think they missed him out on purpose. And I think I know why someone killed him too, all these years later."

Roger looked up at me, with a look on his face that could turn the milk. "Are you saying what I'm thinking?" he said. "He's only in the Homemakers, Nurses, and Librarians clubs? That's … "

"Weird?" I said.

"*One way to play it*, I was going to say. I went the other way."

"What are you talking about?" said Kathi.

"I hit the gym, got some ink, and ran with a gang," said Roger. "And Todd did the same."

"Except for the ink," Todd said. "Being perfect already. But I thought about it. I could have gone the way Thomas went. Easily."

"What are you talking about?" said Noleen.

"I think Tam," I began, "or should we call him Tom? Did they staple the hat to him after he was dead as an insult, or just because that was his name?"

"*They*?" said Noleen. "They who? Someone at the reunion? Why would they insult him?"

"I think he was gay-bashed," I said. "I think the Jimmy wig and the horse's tail and the cutty sark were all misdirection. This was a hate crime."

∞

The next question was whether to go straight to the cops this instant and tell all to the duty officer or wait until morning and tell Mike. On the one hand, she was the detective in charge of the case. On the other hand, she despised us. On one hand, she was herself a gay woman, which had to count for something. But on the other hand, she had the worst case of internalised heteronormativism I had ever encountered. On one hand, this was a police matter and our duty as citizens, or visa-holders in my case, was to hand over the information to the police immediately. On the other hand, if Mike had listened to me about the ring in the first place, they would have known who Tam was days ago. On a third hand, mind you, I still couldn't explain where the ring had disappeared to. But on a very unlikely fourth hand, if they had paid attention to all the other signs and asked about *Tam*

O'Shanter around Cuento—put it in the paper and on the local radio—someone would have remembered Thomas Shatner, surely.

But Shiva aside, the man was dead and we had a lead. To the Cuento cop shop, en masse, we had no choice but to go.

And all our soul searching about Mike or no Mike turned out to be academic, because she was still there as we marched in lock step through the foyer. The dispatcher looked up from behind her plexiglass with nothing worse than an expression of inquiry on her face. But Mike, standing beside her looking over some paperwork on a clipboard, gave a prize-winning scowl.

"You're working late," I said.

"I've got a murder to solve," Mike said.

"And we've got information for you," I said.

"More jewelry?" Mike said. "More poetry?"

"Have you put a name to the vic yet?" said Todd.

"Don't say *vic*," said Mike, Roger, Noleen, and me in chorus. Three of us smiled at the snap. One of us scowled even more.

"Because we've ID'd him," said Todd.

"If you've been interfering in police matters, I'm going to take a pretty dim view," Mike said.

"I consulted public records in a public place," I said. "I don't think I even contravened copyright; four pages out of two hundred."

"His name," said Kathi. Kathi was usually pretty low-key. She didn't say much, never threw her weight about, didn't even laugh out loud that often. Of the four of them it had taken me longest to warm to Kathi, or rather to decode her. Now I loved her with as fierce a devotion as the rest of them. As the rest of them loved her, I mean. And as I loved the rest of them too. Be that as it may, every so often Kathi surprised us all. And this was one of those moments. "His name," she said again, "if you actually want to know his name."

"Are you messing with me, Mrs. Muntz?" said Mike.

"I wouldn't dare, Detective Rankinson," Kathi said. "I'd hate to have a dim view taken."

"You're spending too much time with this one," Mike said, jerking her thumb towards me. "Her with the mouth."

"You get *Mrs. Muntz*," I said. "And I get *her with the mouth*."

"Look," said Roger, "do you want to know who the dead guy in the slough is or don't you? If you know already, we'll go, but if you don't know yet, how can it not be killing you?"

Mike gave an elaborate sigh and buzzed out from behind the divider. She planted herself in front of us and opened her notebook.

"His name is Thomas Shatner," Todd said. "Thomas Oscar Shatner."

"Tam O. Shanter?" Mike said. "You're telling me you think that corpse is named Tam O. Shanter?"

"Shat-ner," said Todd. "It's not a joke. That's his name. He was sixty-eight years old and he graduated from Beteo County High."

"Right," Mike said.

"We don't know where he lived, but we think he was back in town for the reunion."

"At the farmers' market?" Mike said. "Someone saw him there?"

"We have no information on that," said Todd. "But it was the fiftieth reunion of his year. And he died with his class ring on."

"How many times must I say it?" Mike said. "There was no ring!"

"Okay," I said. "There was no ring. I imagined it. I saw ripples of water that looked like BCSHS six eight and so I went to the library and looked in the yearbook and found him there. Total coincidence." I had been pecking at my phone and now I handed it to her.

"This is him?" she said, looking at the Homemakers photo. "He was identified in the caption?"

"Well, no," I said. "They missed his name out of the caption."

"But do you have his senior picture?" She put an index finger down on my phone and looked at me. "Do I have permission to swipe?"

"Of course," I said.

Todd squeaked. I assumed he was thinking of Tinder and ignored him.

"He didn't have a … is that what you call it? … a senior picture?" I said. "But if you keep swiping"—Todd squeaked again and again I ignored him—"you'll see that he was missed out of the collection. There's just a note of his name. Now, we think that's significant, don't we?" I looked at Roger for corroboration but he was frozen, staring aghast at Mike's fingers. "We think he was bullied at school. Ostracised. And we think—"

"So you don't have a photograph with a name?" said Mike. She was still swiping. Todd squeaked a third time and Noleen made a low moaning sound in her throat. "You have a photograph of a young man with a glancing physical similarity to the victim and you have a name with no photograph."

"Oh come on!" I said. "Come off it!"

"And you have nothing more than that?"

Swipe.

Squeak.

Moan.

"Lexy Campbell," Mike said suddenly. "I am arresting you on suspicion of involvement in the murder of John Doe."

"What?" I said.

"You have the right to remain silent. Anything you say can and will be used against—"

"What are you talking about?" I said. "I didn't kill him!"

"—you in a court of law. You have the right to an attorney."

"I didn't see him until I pulled him out of the slough four days after he died."

"Four days," said Mike. "Good guess."

"*You* told me that!"

"If you cannot afford one, one will be appointed to you by the court."

"We can afford an attorney," Roger said. "Lexy, stop talking."

"Okay," I said. "Mike, I did not kill Thomas Shatner. I didn't *know* Thomas Shatner."

"With these rights in mind, are you willing to talk with me about the charges against you?"

"No," said Todd and Roger.

"Snap, jinx, I own you both," I said. "Mike, I saw a ring, I went to the library, I found out his name. I took photos of the yearbook. That is all."

"So how do you explain this?" Mike said. She turned my phone back to face me. I did not know, did not have the smallest clue, what I was going to see there. I still didn't understand why Todd had squeaked and Noleen had moaned. "If you didn't know John Doe, where did this come from?"

It was Roger's photo. It was Tam, Photoshopped back to life, cut off the deck of Creek House, and pasted onto a pleasant scene in a beer garden. He didn't look dead. He didn't even look drunk.

"Umm," I said.

"I'm calling my attorney," said Roger. "Stop talking, Lexy."

"Okay," I said again. "Mike, is it illegal to photograph a corpse?"

Mike stared down at that picture again. Her eyes flared. "It's illegal to converge on a crime scene to spectate or record and thereby impede emergency personnel in the performance of their duties," she said.

"How did we impede you if you didn't even know we had recorded anything until now?" I said. "And we didn't converge. We were there already."

"Sightseeing at the scene of an emergency," Mike said. "California penal code 402(a) PC."

"What emergency?" I said. "He was bloated up like a lifeboat."

"402(a) PC?" said Noleen, stabbing at her phone.

"And you'll never get that spliced Miranda past an attorney," Kathi said. "You should have said it straight through and not let Lexy distract you."

"Your word against mine," Mike said.

But Kathi held up her phone and shook her head. "Wrong again. I got it all. Smile for the camera."

Mike breathed in hard and long, swelling up until I thought her buttons would pop. Then she let it all go again. "Smart phones have ruined this world," she said. "Get outta here."

"I'm unarrested?" I said.

Mike pointed wordlessly towards the door.

"Thank you," I said. "I look terrible in orange. And listen, check it out, eh? Once you've cooled off and stopped being annoyed. Thomas Oscar Shatner. Seriously."

But Todd was dragging me by my elbow and Noleen was pushing me with both hands in the small of my back. Kathi was still recording. Roger was talking to an attorney. And Mike looked like she might easily change her mind. It was time to go.

Eleven

Blessed, miraculous, luxurious, heavenly Saturday morning. It must suck to love your job and not feel any different when you wake up at the weekend. I yawned so hard I did a spit squirt, then put my hands above my head and pushed against the panelling boxing in my bed at the top. Last, I straightened my legs and pushed my feet against the panelling boxing it in at the bottom. Six months of power yoga and I'd be able to split this little boat in two. As it was, I made it give one small creak then relaxed.

"It's wasted on you," said Todd's voice.

I pulled off my sleep mask and stretched out a hand for the coffee cup I knew would be there. I don't even flinch when Todd's at my bedside these days.

"What is?" I said after the first sip.

"This bed with the solid wood bracing at the top and bottom," Todd said. "So much resistance and all you do is stretch in it."

"Todd, I told you before," I said. "I am ready and waiting for a kind, funny, honest, intelligent, solvent, woke, genitally intact—"

"Racist!"

"American isn't a race. Male, between thirty and fifty with no drama, no resident kids, no strong feelings against having any more kids, and no guns. Find him for me and I'll happily break my bed. Until then, why don't you and Roger come for a sleepover one night?"

"Girl, please," Todd said, which I took to mean Roger and Todd could sink Creek House without trying. "Anyway ... Kathi's got some sewing for you to do, easier than a zipper this time. And Roger has some very interesting news about Tam. And I need a wingman. Interrogations begin today, Lexy. I've got three lined up and they're bound to lead to more."

"What the hell time do you get up in the morning?" I said. "Not just you. All of you! What interrogations?"

"Of sixty-eight-year-old Cuento-ites who might have been at the reunion."

"How did you get their names?" I said, swinging my legs out of bed.

"And get a pedicure!"

"It's winter!"

"What if I find him today? Captain Foreskin?"

"Then I'll get a pedicure."

I stumbled along the corridor to the bathroom, leaving Todd to choose an outfit for me. Is it disgusting to take your coffee into the loo? If Todd ever did find me a guy, or if I did it myself, would I have to stop? How long could I be single before moving back into intimacy with someone would be more effort than I could face?

"You should hold your pee a coupla times," Todd shouted. "Good for the pelvic floor."

Or maybe I wasn't as rusty as all that at intimacy anyway.

∞

The sewing job Kathi had on her docket this morning was to reverse the crotch rot in a pair of linen floods. She pulled them out of a packet and spread them on the folding table to show me.

"They're pretty new," she said. "But they've worn out in the inner thighs already. Eighty dollars' worth of pants. Twenty dollars per wear."

Dollars-per-wear was a big thing with Kathi. She priced out her jeans and polo shirts at fractions of a penny and had plenty to say about my wardrobe. Almost as much as Todd did, in her way.

"I said I could fix it," she said, poking her hands through the holes. "Can you fix it?"

"It's one of the great ironies," I said turning them inside out and taking them off Kathi's wrists. "They look like the ultimate fat pants. But if you've got the slightest little whisper of thigh rub, you'll turn them into assless chaps in six months. I don't suppose you asked if she's willing to sacrifice the pockets, did you?"

Kathi shrugged.

"Have you got a phone number for her?"

"I do," Kathi said, "but I was really hoping for slick, quick service. Rather than a lot of dithering. You know?"

"Maybe she'd think a phone call was extra-attentive," I said. "If she's the sort to buy them in the first place and pay to have them mended ..." I was checking the pockets as I spoke and both of them were in tatters anyway. "Hm," I said. "Pockets not functional. But on the other hand, pockets definitely well-used. I really need to check what she wants, Kathi. Give me the number."

"What the hell shreds both pockets in four wears?" said Kathi. "Keys? Pocket knife? This chick needs a tool belt."

"They're elasticated," I said. "A belt would pull them down." I squinted at the phone number on Kathi's order screen and dialled it.

"Speak!" said a voice.

It sounded familiar.

"Oh!" I said. "You're not a cat groomer, are you?"

"What?" said the voice. "Who is this?"

Kathi was miming a lot of strong foul language at me and slicing her finger across her throat. I hung up.

"What the ...?" she said.

"Sorry," I said. "I'll call back from your line. She won't know it's the same person."

"Right. She'll think it's some completely different extra from *Outlander*. Jeez, Lexy."

"Oh, yeah." I felt so at home here now, I kind of forgot that I stuck out when I opened my mouth. "Sorry. Right, you phone. And ask her if it's okay to stitch up the pockets and use the fabric to effect the repair."

"*Effect the repair*," Kathi repeated, dialling. "That's good."

"Tell her it'll give a better silhouette," I said. "Pocketless."

Kathi nodded and then started speaking. She listened to the answer, gave me a thumbs-up, and then kept listening. Her eyes widened. Her mouth formed an O shape as if to start asking "What the ..." again but she remained silent. Eventually she cleared her throat, said, "It'll be ready on Monday. Thank you for using Sew Speedy," and hung up.

"What?" I said.

"The pockets are shredded from her key chain," she said.

"Right," I said. "Like you thought."

"Because her keychain is made out of her cat's jawbone," Kathi said. "It's dead."

"I'll bet it is. Is that a thing? In California."

"It's not even a thing in the Inca Empire! It's gross."

I couldn't argue, but then the things that I thought were gross around here was a long list. I was dreading my first funeral, because an open coffin with a rosy-cheeked corpse in it struck me as beyond barbaric. I was no fan of the open salad bar either, if I'm honest. And as for mud baths! I was *in* one the first time it occurred to me that the mud wasn't changed between customers, and that this sucking, sticking cloying vat of organic goo, just the perfect temperature for bacteria to replicate in, had been sucking and sticking and cloying to that old guy who'd come waddling out of the changing room as I was going in. I felt the pustules begin to heave under my epidermis as I sat there. I felt funguses blooming and viruses spreading. When the attendant had the nerve to say *detox* I couldn't even laugh.

"So I can use the pockets?" I said. "I only need one. Or one half of two. Tell you what, Kathi. Keep the other two bits on file under her name and tell her when this lot wears through again—and it will unless she goes on a major diet—you'll repair them again for free."

"*You'll* repair them again for free?" Kathi said.

I hadn't been willing to discuss the fee breakdown for Trinity Solutions, because I didn't want to give it oxygen, so I didn't know if I was being kind or being had. I nodded and bent my head to start sewing.

∞

Todd was waiting for me when I left the Skweeky Kleen (featuring Sew Speedy) half an hour later. He was perched on top of the bonnet of his sparkling black Jeep. A stranger would assume he was posing there, getting a bit of height so that his golden perfection could be seen by more of the lesser mortals around him. I knew he was keeping his feet off the ground where the insects live. My heart ached a bit and then melted a bit as he gave me a brave smile. So when Della and

Noleen both ambushed me in a sweet pincer move, they each got me a good one.

Della opened her door with a kitten under each arm. "His skin is broken," she said, brandishing Flynn at me. He meeped forlornly.

"Today," I said. "I promise, Della. Today."

"He is crying."

"I can hear that. Look, hold him up."

I had put a pair of scissors in my back pocket while I was sewing and forgotten to remove them. As Della held Flynn out, belly forward, I made a few snips into the wads of congested fluff in his armpits. They split like loaves of garlic bread, still holding at the hinge side nearest his skin, but now with a bit of play in them. Flynn stopped meeping and let out a rusty little purr instead.

"There," I said. "That'll hold him."

Della put him down and watched him walk away, the clods of matted fur now dangling like windchimes. "Ugly," she said.

"Is Florian okay?" I said.

She turned him round and lifted his tail, getting him closer to me than I would have wanted before I managed to step back. "What the hell are you feeding him?" I said, even though I knew what she was feeding him because I was buying it. Like I bought the fish food and the live shrimp for the seahorse and the bedding and day-old veg for the rabbit. I left it outside their room so Della didn't have to say thank you, but she was still angry about being beholden. Hence the war of the groomer currently being waged.

"He climbed up on the counter and ate a bowl of refried beans," Della said.

I swallowed hard.

"They took thirty-five minutes to go through him," she added.

"Della, you've got to bathe him!" I said. "You can't leave him like that until I find a groomer. You can't let Diego play with him when he's covered in bean-shite!"

"Diego is at the Mathnasium," Della said. "Of course I'll wash him. I just wanted you to see."

"Well, thanks," I said, quietly taking back everything I had ever said about baby pictures being the worst thing ever. I backed away and turned to find Noleen's face an inch from mine.

"Jee! Zuz!" I said.

Noleen's face in close-up was a wonder. From a distance she was a plain woman, with strong features and no ornamentation, but from the four-inch distance I stumbled back to, she was beautiful. Her eyes were clear and flecked in seven different colours and her eyelashes and brows were a strong natural black. Her grey hair sat in little curls like Julius Caesar's without the leaves, and her skin was perfect. She was lined, but she was poreless and she had less of a 'stache and chin strap than I did although she had twenty years on me.

"Good morning, Nolly," I said. "You're looking lovely this morning."

"Sarcasm rolls off me like split mayo," she said. "Listen up."

"I meant it!" I said. "You look very well and very prett—pared for anything." I had bottled it. Noleen's t-shirt this morning said *I will cut you*. Even for her it was a bold choice. "I mean, I'm listening."

"You need to get with Trinity," Noleen said. Her voice was low and from the chin jerk that went with her words, I gathered Todd wasn't to hear. "Get over yourself and get with it. 'kay?"

"Any reason you can share?" I said.

"If Kathi loses the Skweek, this whole place'll go down," she said. "And the new owners'll slap an eviction on you quicker'n you can dial the international code to tell them at home you're coming back."

"But business is good, isn't it?" I said. "You were full all summer, nearly. And most weekends since."

"Yeah, that's right," said Noleen. "Business is fine. I'm just asking you for favors on account of how much I love asking for favors." She moved even closer. I could see how smooth her lips were and how well-flossed her teeth were. "It makes me feel all warm inside to discuss my private business and beg for help."

"What do you use on your skin?" I asked her. Truly, she was poreless. Even the creases at the sides of her nose looked like marble. Mine looked like peppered jerky.

"The tears of wiseasses," Noleen said.

"Aren't the tears of asses … piss?" I said. "And I wasn't being a smart arse, by the way. I meant it."

"Kick me while I'm down, why don't you!" Noleen said. "So that's a hard no, is it?"

"You are a lot of work, you know," I said. "No, it's not a hard no. It's not even a soft no. It's not a no."

"So that's a yes."

"No," I said. "Look, Noleen, I don't even know if Trinity Solutions is legal. Is it a company? Is it registered? What's the liability? What if someone takes the hump at something Todd says or does—"

"Don't say *hump*."

"—and sues us. Doctors can't use their insurance for lawsuits that aren't medical, can they? And a solicitor's fees would shut you down quicker than a rival dry cleaners, wouldn't it? And I can't get sued, because if I lose, I'll get deported."

"Only if it's a crime of moral turpitude," Todd put in. He had sneaked up behind me. "Not if it's a civil dispute over a contract to deliver services. What are we talking about? Who's suing you?"

Noleen gave me a look that said *over to you, sweet cheeks,* but before I was forced to dredge up an answer, my phone started ringing. To be precise, it started singing "Car Wash." I looked at the screen, saw a picture of my mum and, unable to put one and one together and get two, answered.

"Lexy?"

"Mum?"

"There you are!" she said. I looked round wildly at the car park, chain link, drained pool, and walkways of the Last Ditch. If my parents ever visited me in California, I was in no doubt that it would be a surprise.

"What? Where?" I said. "Where are you?"

"Where do you think I am?" my mum said. "I'm at home."

"Me too," I said.

"Bare-faced lie," my mum said. "Either that or you're not answering your phone. I just called you at home and left a message then I tried you on your mobile. Where are you?"

"I am fifty feet from my front door," I said. "Mum, how are you phoning a mobile?"

"Oh! Oh! *How did I get this number?* you're asking! That's cold even for you, Lexy."

"Because the only reason I'm shovelling out cash for a landline every month is so that you and Dad can call me. If you've wrapped your head round calling me on a mobile number, I can yank it."

"And what am I worth to you every month, Lexy?" my mum said. "What's the outlandish sum that you can barely thole to keep your own mother close to you across the miles?"

"Ninety dollars," I said, beaten.

"Ninety! That's... That's..."

"Sixty pounds."

"That's daylight robbery. See, this is why you're always short at the end of the month, Lexy. You fritter it all away on things you don't need. You've always been the same."

"I bought a Nissan Micra for cash on my seventeenth birthday!" I said. I had saved my pocket money and Saturday job wages for two years to get that little car and it broke my heart ten years later when the head gasket went and it wasn't worth repairing.

"Who needs a car at seventeen?" my mum said. "My point exactly."

"Didn't stop you taking lifts in it."

"And how do you think that made me feel?" said my mum. "You dropping me off at Keep Fit in that old rust bucket instead of a natty little hatchback."

"Wha—?" I said.

"Showing me up."

"Wow," I said.

"What's happening?" said Todd.

"Is that Todd?" said my mum. "Now, Lexy, you know I don't like to interfere, but he seems like a very nice young man. Family-minded. Very polite and helpful." That was one mystery solved then. *Todd* had given my mum my mobile number and tutored her on international dialling to a cell phone. "The only thing I didn't manage to find out was what he does for a living."

I paused. If I told my mother that the nice young man was a doctor, she'd be on the next plane over with a big folder full of sample menus, a list of free dates, and her own veil wrapped in tissue paper. If I told her we were in business together, ditto. And none of the other jobs I could think of—bus driver, bingo caller, milkman—seemed like real things that people still did. The truth—that he was off on long-term sick-leave with a psychological disorder—would slow her down, but Todd was standing right there and I didn't want to hurt him.

"He's married," I went for.

"Now, Lexy, we both know that's not true," my mum said." I asked him what his wife would think of him spending so much time with you"—oh, she was good—"and he said he didn't have one." Oh, he was great. "Why would you say otherwise?"

"Mum, is there anything I can help you with? Because Todd's waiting for me. We're going out for the day." Oh, I was best. She couldn't get off the phone quick enough, horrified to think that her daughter and a nice, family-minded, polite, helpful young man were being delayed going on a picnic together. "Take photos and tag me," she said.

"I will," I lied. I wouldn't. If Mum saw Todd, she'd pay an extra plane fare for the priest and bring him with her.

"Why is my mum's ringtone 'Car Wash'?" I said when I had hung up.

"You said you hated when people chose ringtones to match people. So I went random," Todd said. "Duh."

"Silly me," I said. "Okay, then. Let's go."

Twelve

So how did you find them?" I said to Todd once we were on our
way. "These potential witnesses."

"I looked on the *Voyager* website for stories the day after the reunion, got some names, found one who lives in Cuento and still has
an entry in the phone book, and that's where we're going."

"One?"

"I'm sure the first one will be able to give us addresses for some
more, even if just to get rid of us. Don't you think?"

"So you're not planning a charm offensive then?" I said. "Bad cop,
worse cop, is it?"

"Might be a struggle if Mike got there before us," said Todd. "And
I bet she did. I bet she went straight from sneering at our lead in front
of us to scampering off to chase it behind our backs."

But, when we got to the house where the Beteo County alumnus
of 1968 lived and knocked on the door, it was clear that the visit was a
bolt from the blue.

We were up in the mountain streets, not as fancy-schmancy as The
Oaks but still pretty well-to-do. California status symbols took me a

while to decode. None of the houses are old and none of the gardens are big, so the Georgian-rectory-with-a-paddock-ometer I'd always used to peg poshness was no use to me now. And at first one two-tone wooden house looked much like the next one. They both looked like sheds. I knew better now. If the street ran in a straight line between one stop sign and the next, you were still climbing the ladder. If the street had pointless bends in it or—best of all—was a loop, you'd arrived. If there was a half-moon window high above the front door so it looked like you'd got an upstairs, but really it was just a dusting nightmare and made the whole place feel weird, you'd really arrived. And then there was one that incensed me. If your drive was made of tarmac, you'd only recently arrived on Loopy Avenue. But if your drive was made of red bricks laid out in a pattern, you'd had time to get your feet under you. That was the thing I couldn't get over. There were bricks everywhere. Acres of bricks. Miles of bricks. But they were all lying on the ground, and the houses—in this state beset by wood-chewing pests of unimagined variety and appetite—were still wooden. Millions of dollars' worth of caulk-guzzling, paint-inhaling wood was available for termites on any given day.

As we wound our way around the loops of Lassen Avenue, pulled up at the foot of a long drive with the bricks laid out in a giant-fish-scale design and looked at a house with a half-moon window above the front door and an extra arched window even higher than that, I was already imagining the people who would open the door to a sea of beige, offer us a bottle of water from a fridge bigger than my once-beloved Nissan Micra, and lead us to the farthest away spot in the ground floor where bums could be parked so we would see how huge and tidy their house was.

I've seldom been more wrong. For a start, the front porch was still decorated for Halloween, four days after the fact, and not because the decorations were so impressive they were worth saving. There was a cornucopial pile of gourds stacked around the front door and some cornstalks lashed to the deck supports, and all over these were plastic spiders and fake cobwebs of the dollar-store type. Luminous skeletons, dull now in the morning light, swung above the porch rail with their shrouds billowing and their plastic shin bones clacking. There must have been a seated skeleton too, because its cobwebbed armchair was still there.

Todd clucked his disapproval. "Honestly, all she needs to do is vacuum off those gross webs—*Brrrrr!*—and she would be good through Thanksgiving."

"I know," I said. "I'm new here, but I know." I had removed the black cats and orange glittery BOO! sign first thing Thursday, cut up the carved pumpkin for compost, and let the rest of the squash stay on, with the addition of some brown ribbons and a few feathers. They weren't turkey feathers but they did the job. "Sshh," I added, hearing movement in the house.

The door yawned open on a woman I couldn't believe for a minute was sixty-eight. She had chestnut curls down her back and fake lashes sweeping her cheeks as she blinked at us.

"Mrs. Heedles?" Todd said.

"Ms.," said the woman, which explained a bit. She was divorced and not averse to trying again.

"We'd like to talk to you about Thomas Shatner," I said.

She turned to face me. "Thomas … Shatner?" She seemed bemused; not actually able to frown much, but puzzled.

"From high school," said Todd. She turned to face him now. She was swiveling from the hips instead of moving her eyes or her neck. The eyes I could understand. Those lashes looked heavy and the glue holding them on couldn't be a picnic, but was her neck fused? Can you lift your neck so much you can't turn it?

"Ah yes," she said. "From high school. You better come in."

The house, beyond the porch, was ready for a photo shoot. We did indeed parade through a succession of rooms, past floral arrangements and thick rugs still showing hoover marks, to get to a little den, snug, family room, and/or parlor at the back of the house near the glittering granite kitchen.

"Can I get you anything?" Ms. Heedles said. "Coffee? Juice? Water?"

"We're good," said Todd. "So you went to high school with Thomas Shatner?"

"I did," she said.

"And did you keep in touch?" I chipped in.

"I did not," her voice had dropped an octave and her mouth turned down at the corners as far as it could go. Not far, what with the collagen hiking up her cheeks and the Joker twist to her lips, but I shivered.

"But he was at the reunion," said Todd. It wasn't a question.

"I couldn't say. There were a lot of people there I didn't recognise. Some people have let themselves go so completely."

I nodded. And some people had made themselves over so completely. I was willing to bet a lot of the class of '68 didn't recognise this Little Divorcée Annie.

"He had that very distinctive gap between his front teeth," I reminded her.

She winced. She physically winced. It was an extreme reaction to suboptimal orthodontistry, even for these parts. She was swallowing repeatedly and her face was turning pale.

"Are you okay?" I said. I glanced at Todd. Had we hit the jackpot with our first throw? Had we found Tam's murderer, who was now remembering the gap between his front teeth and the look on his face when she shot him in the belly?

"Fine," she said, unconvincingly. She swallowed again. Then she shot to her feet and bolted away along a corridor. We heard one unpleasantly liquid belch before a door slammed shut.

When she came back, her face was mottled and her eyes were swimming. "Forgive me," she said. "A little digestive upset."

"Oh?" said Todd. "We wondered where you went."

The thought that we hadn't heard her being so unladylike as to honk up in her powder room seemed to calm her.

"What did you want to ask about Thomas?" she said.

"Can I get you some tea?" I said.

"Or ginger ale?" Todd added.

She shook her head. "No thank you. I'm not the best person to ask if you're trying to get in touch with him," she said. "I'm the wrong Maureen. The wrong Mo. Mo Tafoya went to the same middle school and elementary as Tam, besides high school. *She* might be in touch still."

"In touch … with Tam?" I said.

"But can't you find him in a database or whatever you call it?" she said. "Don't you have records? He's not missing, is he? You said he was at the reunion."

"We're not—" I began.

Todd laid a hand on my arm. Well, like a vise lays itself, he did. I'd have finger marks in the morning. "Thomas Shatner is dead, Ms. Heedles," he said.

"Is he," she replied, her voice flat. "What did he die of." It wasn't a question. It sounded like a lament.

"You didn't know?" I said.

"No." Her voice was more animated now and, as she rolled the thought around, her face came alive again too. Maybe it was just that her stomach had stopped pitching. But I didn't think so.

"And what do you make of the news?" I said.

"What do I make of it?" she echoed. "What do I make of the thought of Thomas Shatner being dead and rotting and flies eating his eyes and rats feasting on his flesh?" she said. Pretty safe bet her stomach had calmed down. "I say *good*." She delivered it like a punch.

"That sounds personal," I said. "I know you said you fell out of touch, but were you *ever* close to Tam?" Woman scorned, I was thinking.

"Close?" she said. "Of course not. Thomas Shatner didn't have relationships with women." I felt Todd stir at my side. "Thomas Shatner wasn't the type to get 'close' to any woman. I'm surprised you don't know that if you're investigating his life. At long, long last."

"Ms. Heedles," Todd said, "we're very grateful to you for speaking so plainly. Because we do indeed think Tam's murder is a hate crime."

"Hate crime!" she said. Her stomach might be settled but there was enough bile in those two words to strip the enamel off her teeth and leave her hard wood floors in need of refinishing. "What 'hate crime'? What a lot of nonsense!"

"Whoa, whoa, whoa!" I said. "Gay bashing is a hate crime whether you like it or not."

She stared at me in frozen effrontery, blinking metronomically and opening her eyes very wide between blinks. After a moment, she shook her head and gave a mirthless laugh. "This country is going to the dogs! And if it's a crime to say so, then arrest me. If freedom of speech has been suspended completely, just get the cuffs out and take me downtown."

It was long overdue. I cleared my throat, put on my best innocent voice, and said, "We didn't mean to mislead you, Ms. Heedles, but we're not police."

∞

We were out of there before the cistern on her powder room loo had finished filling. It gave a final-sounding little hiss just as the door slammed shut behind us.

"Not a towering success," I said, standing on the porch, scraping a wisp of fake cobweb off my calf.

"What?" said Todd. "You're kidding. We've got confirmation of the hate crime hunch. We've got another witness's name—Maureen Tafoya. And we've definitely got a suspect."

"You think so too?" I said.

"She had a flashback when you mentioned his teeth," Todd said. "She saw him dead, for sure."

"Can I help you?" said a voice from behind us. I was still facing the door dealing with the fake cobweb, which was sticky stuff, but I saw Todd's eyes flash and his cheeks flush. I know the signs. I sucked my stomach in and put a smile on my face before I turned round. And right enough, there before us on the path was a young man of great beauty and enormous ego—going by the skinny fit of his outdoorsy gear, which had plenty of zips and straps but was otherwise painted on and not with a thick brush either. His face fell when he saw me.

"We're leaving," I said. "So no."

He was staring at me, with a look so frozen, so hostile, so outraged by my very existence that I could feel my hackles rise. I wanted to take a handful of tampons out of my bag and juggle with them or take my bra off down my sleeve and fling it at him.

"Right, right, right, good," he said. "I'm just visiting. My aunt Mo. Is she in? Is she a friend of yours?" He was talking to Todd, but he managed to force himself to turn to me. "Or yours?"

"The mildest of acquaintances," I said. "And, like he said, we were leaving anyway. Enjoy your visit."

We edged round him on the path despite the broad shoulders he had to go with his narrow hips, meaning we practically had to limbo past him. He was wearing walking boots that wouldn't have disgraced a terminator but he didn't seem keen to step onto the grass.

"Weirdo," said Todd as we got back in the Jeep. Pretty Boy had parked an inch from our front bumper, his *Keep Tahoe Blue* and *Get Down in Monterey* stickers close enough for us to tell he'd had them for years and wasn't some newbie, despite the head-to-toe Patagonia couture. I smiled at Todd. It was kind of him to pretend he didn't know why Mr. Beautiful had nearly swooned at the sight of him then nearly gagged at the sight of me.

"Letting the side down a bit, he was," I said.

"Huh?" said Todd.

"Random predation? Such a cliché."

"Pred...?" said Todd, once again being kind enough to pretend he had no clue what I meant. "I didn't get that vibe off him, but you're the expert."

I considered capitalising on that admission with a bit of a nag about Trinity Solutions, then bit my lip. We had enough going on today.

∞

It wasn't hard to find Mo Tafoya. She was right there in the phone book, just where Todd said she would be, right there on 14th Street in the older part of town. Her path was short and made of poured concrete, the block was straight from one stop sign to another, and the house was a ranch. But at some point someone had decided to throw up a high gable and add a pointless window above the door. The Tafoyas weren't hoboes.

They were no better at seasonal housekeeping than Ms. Heedles, though. The porch was another abandoned collection of black cat silhouettes and crêpe paper witches' hats. At least they'd removed whatever horror had been set up in the rocking chair in the corner. It was still wound round with dirty bandages but contained no Freddy, Caspar, or random zombie.

It was no stretch to believe the woman who answered this door to our knock was sixty-eight. She had the hair I was planning to have when I was seventy-five: long, grey, and wild. She wore the clothes I was planning to start wearing when I was eighty: a hemp kaftan with a serape on top, woollen socks underneath a pair of Birkenstocks. But she had a face I hoped I'd never see looking back at me from the bathroom mirror. Her eyes were pink and her cheeks were pale. Her mouth trembled, and when she spoke, her voice was faint and wavering.

"Yes?" she said.

"Mrs. Tafoya?" said Todd. "Maureen Tafoya?"

"Yes?" she said. She glanced at me.

"It's about Thomas Shatner," Todd said.

"He's dead," she blurted. "Did you know?"

"Yes," I said. "And we'd like to talk to you about him. If you've got a minute."

"*You?*" she said. Todd and I shared a glance. Neither of us knew what she was asking. "I mean," she went on, "are you the police?"

"Oh," I said. "No. My name is Lexy Campbell and this is Todd Kroger. It was me, well us, who found him. His body. Tam. Thomas."

"Tam," said Mo Tafoya. "You found him, you say? You better come in."

Inside, the house went with the hemp kaftan rather than the plastic witch hats. It smelled strongly of incense and curry and it was a realtor's nightmare. The walls were red, all the way up to the dizzy heights of the cathedral ceiling, and the ceiling itself was stencilled in cobalt blue and a shade of orange that would put a pumpkin to shame. There were rugs and cushions thrown around like there'd just been a search in a souk and in the middle of the painted coffee table, a brass hookah with at least six coiled pipes sat in pride of place.

"Nice…" Todd said, before words failed him.

I actually liked it, so I took over. "What a beautiful house," I said. "So colourful, Mrs. Tafoya. How long have you lived here?"

"Mo, please. Since it was built," she said. She threw herself down onto a pile of cushions that might have had a couch underneath it somewhere. "We moved in in 1970 as soon as we got married and we've been here ever since. They'll carry me out feet first."

"Lovely," I said. "I mean, not death. But you know … home."

I meant that too. People staying put seemed normal to me. People chasing all over with their stuff in a U-Haul seemed weird. I wasn't a good advert for it anymore, seeing as how I was here in *California*, but I still appreciated the commitment.

"Well, Cuento's not the place it was," said Mo. "It used to be a community, not a dorm."

It was tough to know how to answer that. Everyone thinks the world just about staggered on until they came along then fell to bits. It's only natural.

"So you knew Tam was dead?" I said, getting down to business. Mo Tafoya froze and stared. "Only, not everyone seems to."

"I read the article in the paper," she said.

"It didn't name him," Todd pointed out.

"Well, no, I mean, not the first report. No, it didn't. But he's been IDed now. Not at first but now. They've identified him now." Mo gulped when she finally managed to stop talking, but at least she didn't bolt for the bog. She just sat there with her lip trembling and her eyes swimming and stared back at us.

"They ID'd him from the high school yearbook," I said.

She closed her eyes and drew her brows up as if she was fighting some enormous internal agony. "Oh," she whispered.

I watched her for a while, noticing the way her eyes darted back and forth behind her closed lids and the way she had bunched up a fistful of bright serape in each hand, twisting them as if she was trying to milk a goat. I turned to Todd with my eyebrows raised. He shrugged.

"We think it was a hate crime," I said. "A gay bashing."

Mo Tafoya's head dropped forward so that her hanks of hair fell over her face like two long grey curtains. "That's right," she said. "That's what it was."

Her head was curled right down now. If she opened her eyes she'd be staring at her belly button. It must have taken decades of yoga to get a spine that bendy.

"Did you see him at the reunion?" I said. "You were *at* the reunion, weren't you? You with your love of community."

Mo lifted her head and opened her eyes. "I was," she said. "It was a wonderful night. We can show these kids a thing or two about having a party! They think they invented all-night dancing. We were the originals."

"And *did* you see Tam?" I said.

"Thomas was there," Mo said. "I stayed away from him."

"Oh?" said Todd. "Why was that?"

Mo shook her head and said nothing. Her eyes were shining with unshed tears.

"And what was the dress code?" I said. "For the reunion?" I added, when she didn't answer. Because the clobber we'd found Tam in—minus the hat—didn't say *party*. Californians are casual to a fault. You can go weeks without seeing a man in a tie or a woman in tights, as long as you stay out of banks, but the mom jeans and blue crew-neck weren't partywear. I'd have expected a sixty-eight-year-old man—gay or straight—to have at least a Hawaiian shirt on.

"Dress code?" Mo said. "Sm—smart casual? Business … optional?"

"Right," I said. "So you didn't speak to Tam. Who did you see him speaking to?" She shrugged. "Can you remember? Did you see him leave?" She shook her head. "Who did he leave with? What sort of time?" Shrug. "Do you know where he was staying while he was in town?" Shake. "Was there a block booking for the out-of-towners? Or might he have stayed with a friend?" Shrug. "Who was his best friend at high school?"

"John Worth," Mo said. "John was the senior class president. Captain of the football team."

"Did he date the head cheerleader?" I said. I knew this stuff from films. It still tickled me that it was true. It was like suddenly meeting Hogwarts alumni.

"Briefly," Mo said, reminding me these people were real.

"And does John still live in Cuento?" I said.

"His sister does. She lives in the old place. John's staying there while he's in town."

"Great," I said. "And where's that? Do you have a phone number?"

"For John *Worth*?" I didn't know if her squeak of disbelief was because I thought she'd hand his number over to a stranger or because even fifty years later she couldn't imagine having the phone number of the captain of the football team. "No, no, no. No phone number. Why would I need a phone number?"

"Okay," Todd said. "We'll find him. Is his sister's name Worth too? Did she ever marry?"

"Women don't have to change their names when they marry, young man," Mo said. "I've been happily married to my Herm since 1970 and I'm still proud to be Maureen Tafoya."

"Well, you go, girl," said Todd. "*Pride* is indeed a wonderful thing."

Mo's eyebrows drew up into hooks again, turning her eyes diamond-shaped. She gave Todd a beseeching look as we both stood, thanked her for her time, and said goodbye.

Thirteen

ow many different ways did that fail to add up?" Todd said once we were back in the Jeep and driving away.

"All the ways," I said. "Starting with her blunder about knowing the name of the body." I was on the *Voyager* app, scrolling through the adverts to get to the news. "Bugger," I said. "They *have* ID'd him. About forty minutes ago. She could have read it."

"She didn't *just* find it out. She would have said so," Todd decreed. "We've got ourselves another suspect, Lexy. Also-Mo definitely knows something."

"No way," I said. "Witness. Not suspect. Hippies don't do homophobia."

"Maybe John Worth will shed some light on it all," was all Todd said, which was quite restrained of him. Then his restraints burst. "John Worth! I can see him, can't you?"

"I can't see him as the best bud of the only gay in the village," I said. "Any more than I can buy Also-Mo being a bigot. She had a bong on the coffee table, Todd. She had prayer flags in her roof space. She thinks Cuento's gone suburban. You're right. Nothing about this adds up."

"But she told us at least one outright lie," said Todd. "Did you ever look at the press pics of the reunion at all?" I shook my head. "Look now. They're bookmarked."

I took his phone and clicked through. "Wow," I said. "It's *still* 1968 for these guys, isn't it? Also-Mo isn't the last hippie standing."

"She might be," said Todd. "They're not stuck in the summer of love. Those are costumes, Lexy."

I zoomed in on a couple of men standing posing for the camera and whistled. He was right. These weren't real hippies like Also-Mo. These were middle managers wearing Freak Brothers wigs and tie-dyed t-shirts. One of them had a pair of pink flares on, but the other hadn't gone that far and was still wearing his crisp chinos.

"Why would she lie about the reunion dress code?" I said. "It's so easy to check."

"No idea," said Todd. "Moving on. Call Noleen while you've got my phone, and ask her if she knows where the old Worth place is."

"Where are we going in the meantime?" I said.

"Historic downtown Cuento," said Todd. "As long as it's not a farm, any place with 'old' in its name is going to be downtown somewhere."

Historic downtown Cuento is an area three by two blocks with brick-fronted buildings that used to be family department stores and drugstores with soda fountains, and are now bicycle repair shops and yoga studios. It's zoned so's you never have to cross the road to get a cup of coffee, and you never have to cross two to get some Korean barbecue. It is, in other words, California. Oh how California historic downtown Cuento is! And I love it. There are dog bowls and shade trees and outdoor pianos. There are pocket parks with chess tables and Little Free Libraries. There's a book shop. There's an art cinema. There's a Jamaican barber just to stop it feeling too precious altogether.

And there's Mama Cuento. She's an eight-foot-tall statue on the corner of First and Main, where she stands with her hands on her hips and her head thrown back saying *hmp-hmp-hm* to everyone who passes by. Her bronze head is wrapped in a cloth and her bronze feet, just peeking out from the hem of her dress, are bare. Her collar is open as if she's been working in the heat of a long day and her face has seen it all. I assumed she was African American at first, because of the colour of the bronze (which was pretty stupid of me) and the headwrap, I suppose. Todd reckons she's Latina because of her name, but she's pretty goddamn tall for a Latina lady and she's got a long lean-muscled back that doesn't exactly scream Mexico. Most of Cuento thinks she's "regular American," and if you take that to mean Native they roll their eyes and mutter at you. Noleen told me once there was a move to change her name to Town Mother back in the fifties, but it went nowhere.

Anyway, we hooked round Mama Cuento and into the residential bit of the historic district, with me on the phone to Noleen to mine her city memories for directions. She didn't know the street address, but she told us it was the one with the wraparound porch and the two turrets "painted the color God regrets" and it didn't take long to track it down. It was purple, with a bit of orange and black in the trim, a house made for Halloween. And yet *this* was the place where the residents had got their act together to de-pumpkin-ise in good time. As we went up the walk, a large woman in grey sweats was cramming an armload of black crêpe paper into the wheeliebin.

"Let me help," Todd said, sweeping her aside and applying his considerable muscles to a bale of paper, straw, tattered ribbons, fake cobweb, and tangled lantern-lights, compacting it enough to close the bin lid.

"Thank you," the woman said. "Thank you so much." She seemed upset; fluttery and with a lot of looking over her shoulder as if someone might be watching.

"Is this bin bag going in too?" I said, holding one up. "Trash—can—bag—garbage—sack?"

"If there's room," the woman said. She was wringing her hands now like the heroine of a Victorian romance and her breath was coming quick and light. I'd never had to catch someone as they fainted and I didn't fancy my chances with this little fireplug.

"Are you Miss Worth?" Todd said, when the bin bag was squished in and the lid was down again. "John Worth's sister?"

"Becky," she said. "Yes. Why? Are you reporters?"

Which was an extremely peculiar conclusion to jump to. Todd sent a side glance at me, but I had no more clue than he did how to answer.

"No," I said after a long pause. "You can relax. We're not reporters and we're not police."

Becky's shoulders dropped. "Thank God," she said. "So ... who are you?"

"We found Tam's body," I said.

"What? When? Where?" Becky said. "Was it you that put it in the creek?"

Which was an extremely peculiar question to ask.

"No," I said. "I live in the houseboat at the back of the motel on Last Ditch slough and we hauled it up with our beer box at a Halloween party."

"Oh," said Becky. "You're that therapist!"

"I'm that therapist. And we feel involved now. So we want to find out what we can about Tam Shatner."

"Right," said Becky. "Right. Well, that was Johnny's year, not mine. I didn't ever get to know all the details, but you know … small towns … we heard rumors and rumbles. And now this!"

"Mm," said Todd. "You understand why we're so concerned, don't you? If this was a hate crime … "

Becky frowned. "A hate crime?" she said. "What d'you mean? Aren't hate crimes like the Klan?"

She would have said more but the screen door at the back of the deep porch opened and a man came thundering over the boards to lean on the porch rail and bellow at us.

Bellow at her, I realised once I started paying attention to what he was saying.

"What are you doing?" he said. "Who the hell are they? What have you said? Did you—" But he bit that off. "I told you to come back inside." Eventually he managed to make himself stop talking and stood there, gripping the rail with two meaty fists. I saw a class ring winking on one finger. He was breathing like a bull, and—added to his strong forehead, broken button nose, and underbite—it was a pretty comprehensive impersonation.

"John Worth?" I said. If I looked closely, I could just about trace the boy I'd seen in the yearbook. He had been burly with a fair complexion, a twinkling blond crew-cut, and dimples. This man had doubled in weight, lost his hair, and turned the deep brick red of a golf bum. He had pale blue tattoos on his forearms and ropes of gold chains tangled in his grey chest hair. He would definitely have worn a Hawaiian shirt to his high school reunion. He was wearing one now. And cargo shorts and flip flops.

"Who wants to know?" he said.

"Lexy Campbell," I told him. "And this is Todd Kroger. We want to talk to you about your friend, Tam Shatner."

"No friend of mine," Worth said.

"Oh now, Johnny," said his sister.

"I wouldn't have pissed on him if he was on fire," he added. "What do you want to know about him?"

"Who killed him, ideally," I said. "But we'd settle for who saw him at the reunion, who spoke to him last, when he left, and where he went."

"I spoke to him last." Worth was still gripping the porch rail to look down at us, and as he said these words he flexed his fingers and took a tighter hold. His class ring made a dull clunk against the painted wood. "I saw him arrive, I went straight over, and I threw him out of there. Told him he wasn't welcome and he should haul his sorry ass back to f—"

"Back to …?" I said.

"Excuse my language," Worth said. "I shouldn't cuss in front of a lady."

"And he left, did he?" I said. "He took off like a good boy?"

"He walked away on his own two feet," Worth said. "He ate nothing. He drank nothing. He spoke to no one. He arrived, I told him to fuck off, and he fucked off."

"Excused," I said. Worth blinked at me, uncomprehending.

"And how many people were there in total?" said Todd. His voice was worryingly calm.

"Hunnert fifty?" Worth said. "All of us and some spouses. Coupla dozen kids too."

"You really think Tam Shatner was the only one at that party?" Todd said. "Out of a hundred and fifty people? You're kidding yourself. Or did you send anyone else away, like you sent Tam?"

"Maybe Tam was the only one who was stubborn enough to attend," I said. "Maybe all the others in the class of sixty-eight wouldn't stoop to it."

"What?" said Becky.

John Worth said nothing. He just looked at Todd out of his little bullish eyes, all squinted up from the pads of fat on his cheeks. He munched his jaws a bit too. Perhaps he'd found a morsel between his molars and wasn't literally ruminating. But it didn't help him look any less bovine. "Only one what?" he said, eventually.

"Oh right!" scoffed Todd. "You didn't know what he was."

"What he *was*?" said Worth.

"So why'd you run him out?" I said.

Worth let go of the porch rail and his arms fell heavily at his sides. "I didn't," he said. "He wasn't there. I shouldn't have said that. I don't understand what's happening."

Join the club, I thought. What I said was, "So you didn't see him, didn't run him out of the reunion, didn't follow him?"

"Follow him?" said Worth, raising his massive head. His breathing sounded laboured.

"Well, he could hardly get shot in the middle of a party," said Todd. "Not without someone noticing. Even with a silencer."

"Shot?" Worth's voiced was ragged and his colour was changing.

"Yes," I said. "Shot. It was in the paper." But even as I said it, I wondered if my memory was betraying me. *Dead four days* and *foul play* had been in the paper. I would need to check.

"I thought he drowned," Worth was saying. His face wasn't even red now. It had darkened to a colour I'd be hard-pressed to name.

"He drowned?" said Becky.

"Aren't you supposed to be at work?" said her brother. Becky looked at her phone and started. She trotted over to a car parked on the driveway at the side of the house and hopped in, peeling out on two tyres into the quiet street. I watched her go and then blinked, focussing on the other car, presumably John Worth's car, still parked there. It was that same cat groomer's decal again, 02-15-11 COCO, but this time I knew it was on a different vehicle from the one that had been in front of me in the coffee queue and parked at the Thrift. This one was red and low-slung. A ... Cala ... Cama ... A red car.

"Is that yours?" I said, pointing. "With the phone number on the back?"

Worth stared at me. His face wasn't red now. It had gone white behind his tan, a truly awful shade to behold. Todd was looking down at his phone.

"Let's go, Lexy," he said.

"Yeah, get off my property," said John Worth. "And don't come back."

"Not even to piss if it catches fire," I agreed.

"Lexy!" Todd hissed. "Let's go."

Fourteen

"What is it?" I said, when the front door on the old Worth place had slammed and we were *off his property*, back on the street quick-marching to where the Jeep was parked.

"Roger."

"Is he okay?"

"He's got information."

"Well, just wait while I get a good hold of this stone and squeeze some blood out!" I said. "What information?"

"Tam wasn't shot," said Todd. He chirped the Jeep open and clambered in. "Why were you asking about John Worth's car?" he said, when I had clambered in too.

"Right," I said. "Let's change the subject. That seems like a great idea. What do you mean he wasn't shot?"

"Roger doesn't want to put it in an email or say it over the phone. So we either wait till he's home tonight or we go up to the hospital and grab him between rounds."

"Let's take him a burrito," I said. "Poor thing, having to work on a Saturday."

I'd only visited Roger at work once before, when I presented a workshop on "self-care in times of crisis" to a parents' support group. It wasn't successful. None of the parents believed my combination of pizza and bad telly would deliver the results I knew it would, and when I told them it had got me through a divorce and they asked what about the children and found out I didn't have any, they all folded their arms and gave me the stink-eye. Some of it was figurative, but some of it was literally elbows and eyelids. But even the workshop wasn't as bad as the complimentary lunch afterwards in the cafeteria. A salad of pink-edged iceberg lettuce and chewy croutons with shriveled grapes for fancy and one of those bog-awful flavoured waters.

Todd was pulling up at the taco wagon and my stomach was already rumbling.

Ten minutes later, with three giant Al Pastor burritos *ir* and three twenty-ounce watermelon juices, one with light ice because of the daylight robbery ice scam I was onto, we were on our way.

"*Ir!*" said Todd.

"It means 'to go' *en Espanol*," I pointed out.

"It means 'to go' like 'I go, you go, he she and it go.'"

"And he knew what I meant."

"He knew what you meant because he's had years of gringos who think they can speak Spanish saying it to him."

"Don't say *gringo*."

"Sorry. *Gabacho*."

"Don't say *gabacho*."

"You have no idea what *gabacho* means, do you?"

"I can guess."

"*Para llevar*."

"Don't say—"

"Oh for God's sake! *Para llevar* means food 'to go.'"

"Are you okay?" I said. It wasn't like him to be so testy.

"Worried about Roger," was all he would give me. Then we were on the freeway and he had to concentrate. It's not that big a city, Sacramento, but it wears its "worst drivers in America" badge with pride and Saturdays aren't any better just because the Capitol staffers have all piled up to Tahoe or down to San Francisco. The weaving, texting, and random speed changes took every bit of Todd's attention until we came off at the hospital exit. And the ambulances didn't help much.

"How do you feel, coming back?" I said as we made our way from the car to the paediatrics entrance.

"This isn't coming back," Todd said. "I didn't work here. I worked in ambulatory care, way across campus."

"Ambulatory care!" I said. I knew he meant outpatient and it still tickled me.

"What do you call median strips again, Lexy?" Todd said.

"Central reservations," I said. "What do you call GPs?"

"Primary care physicians," said Todd. "What do you call a plain-clothes cop who's not a sarge?"

"I'm not sure how the ranks map onto each other."

"What are the possibilities?"

"Either detective inspector, detective chief inspector, chief superintendent, or maybe just detective constable. Yeah, you win."

∞

Todd might never have worked at the kids' bit of this sprawling hospital, but he was known here. The nurses on the frontline greeted him like the messiah. There were hugs, tears, selfies, and even one cheek-pinch before Roger answered his page.

"Hey," he said. "You're just in time for lunch. It's seafood day at the mac-and-cheese window."

I held up the package of food and tray of drinks. "Burritos and watermelon juice."

"From Chipotle?" Roger said.

"Have we met?" said Todd. "From the wagon on E Street and they're getting cold."

I felt mean sitting in the café eating a shoebox-sized roll of goodness while everyone else choked down fishy pasta, but we were far enough away not to hear the moans of jealousy. Roger had insisted on this quiet corner and then he sat with his broad, scrub-clad back facing the room, daring anyone to come and disturb us. Todd gave a couple of finger waves to people he recognised but then shifted so no one could see him. I was in plain sight, but no one was likely to come belting over to bother me.

"So," said Todd, after a good bite, a luxurious chew, and a slug of juice, "he wasn't shot."

Roger swallowed, took a glug of his own drink, and shook his head. "He wasn't shot. And the police—well, Mike, I suppose—are kicking themselves for being fooled."

"I would think she is," I said. "How do you think you've seen a GS—gunshot wound if you haven't? Belly-button piercing gone wrong?"

"Oh no, it *was* a gunshot wound," said Roger.

"An old one?" Todd guessed.

"Okay, I'll stop toying with you," said Roger. He took a mammoth bite of his burrito. He was in the middle of it now, through to the good bit, and he chewed in a state of bliss with his eyes closed. Then he swallowed, huddled even closer, and spilled all.

"The on-call pathologist on Wednesday night was someone I happen to know," he said. "Todd, don't freak, okay?"

"Is this the Maurice guy?" Todd said.

"This is the Maurice guy," Roger said. "Lexy, I have no interest in this guy—he looks like Mr. Burns and dresses like Columbo—but he isn't getting the message. He's ... friendly bordering on stalker, you know? And he knew where the corpse was found and ... I wasn't happy to discover it, but ... he knows that's where I've been living."

"He does?" said Todd.

"Which, yes, is a worry," said Roger, "because I haven't changed my official address and all the mail goes to a PO box and so I'm not sure how he found out, but anyways. Here's the silver lining to a pretty black cloud. He told me what they found in the autopsy."

"He emailed you?" said Todd.

"No, he's not dumb enough to do that," said Roger.

"He called you?" said Todd. "He has your number?"

"Not that I know of," said Roger. "No, he came over this morning, oh-so casual, shooting the breeze."

"Over from where?" said Todd. "Where does he work?"

"Pathology," said Roger. "What with him being a pathologist and all."

"Todd, please," I said. "We can loop back. What came out in the autopsy?"

"He was wearing a Halloween costume," Roger said.

"Right," I said. "A Jimmy wig. Stapled on."

"No," said Roger. "Under his clothes. He was wearing a second-skin costume. It had chest hair and fake junk and a fake bullet wound. It was on under his sweatshirt and mom jeans. Made of some kind of nerf-style stuff. Neoprene maybe."

"It was a fake—" I started to say, much too loud. Then I bent over and whispered instead. "It was a fake bullet wound? And Mike fell for it? Oh my God, she's never going to live this down! She thought a fake bullet wound in a neoprene onesie was a real bullet wound in a guy's actual flesh? Wow!"

"Four days in the water can do strange things to a corpse," Todd said, perhaps trying to be fair.

"But he wasn't in the water four days," Roger said. "That's another thing Maurice told me. He spend three days happily decomposing at an ambient temperature, outside but not exposed, and only then did he hit the water."

"He spent three days lying out in a ditch somewhere without anyone finding him, dressed in a fake birthday suit, junk and all, with a hat on, and no one reported it?" I said.

"So what did he die of if it wasn't a bullet wound?" said Todd.

"Sitting," Roger said. "Not lying, Lexy. Sitting. From the pattern of hypostasis in his butt and lower legs. He was sitting. And he wasn't out in the wilds. There was no rodent damage. He was somewhere pretty sheltered."

"How?" I said. "How could he be sitting outside for four days? What, like at a bus stop? On a park bench? I know Mo Tafoya said Cuento's not the community it once was, but that's nuts."

"I think," Roger said. "This is only my theory, but I really do think it's … seasonal."

"Huh?" said Todd.

"As in, calendar specific," said Roger.

I was stumped, but light was dawning on Todd. "Oh. My. Godetia corsage," he said. "He was sitting propped up on someone's porch as part of a Halloween scene, wasn't he?"

"Looks like it," Roger said.

147

"But why would someone do that?" I said. "I mean, why would someone do that?"

"Buys time," Todd said. "Let's a murderer get away."

"You're assuming he was murdered," Roger said.

"He was at the high school reunion," I said. "And there's definitely something fishy about that. We've spoken to three people and they're all pretty jumpy, aren't they, Todd?"

"Was it natural causes?" Todd said. "Did he just party too hard?"

"Ohhhhh!" I said. "If he drank himself to death at the party maybe his dependents could sue the Alumni Association. Or the Farmers' Market. Is that it?"

"We'll make an American of you yet, Lexy," Roger said. "Straight to litigation! No, he didn't drink himself to death. Well, not in the way you mean. He was poisoned."

Roger was used to the idea, having had all the time since the Maurice guy blabbed it to him. He took another caveman bite of his dwindling burrito and waited to see what we made of the bombshell.

"Food poisoning?" I said. I looked into the open end of my own burrito. I love that taco wagon and I hate sissies, but you do hear things.

"Nope," Roger said. "Hydrogen peroxide."

Todd winced.

"What's that?" I said.

"Caustic soda," said Roger.

"What's that?" I said.

"Lye," said Roger.

"He drank *lye?*" said Todd.

"He drank lye."

"Who drinks *lye?*" I said.

"Which is what made Maurice so sure it was murder and not suicide," said Roger. "No one in their right mind could make themselves drink lye. It would be like trying to suffocate yourself by holding your breath. But that's what killed him. It burned out his throat, burned away his gut. It even dissolved the composite they used to fix the gap in his teeth. On its way down, you know."

"Wait, what?" I said. I clutched Todd's arm. "Mo! Original Mo! Mo H! Roger, we spoke to a woman this morning who went bolting off to her bathroom to puke when we mentioned the gap between Tam's front teeth!"

"That's pretty suspicious," Roger said.

"And we also spoke to another woman who's got an empty rocking chair on her Halloween porch," I said.

"And one seriously freaked-out dude I'd swear knew Tam wasn't shot," Todd added.

"Are you saying you tipped off a murderer?" said Roger, going still.

"She's going to kill us for interfering, but we need to tell Mike, don't we?" I said. My heart sank at the thought of it.

"I'll do it," Todd said. "She hasn't just tried to arrest me and had to back down. I'll do it with tact and decorum. We don't need to ruffle any feelings or upset anyone."

While those words were hanging in the air I became conscious of movement at the far side of the cafeteria. Something large and red was barrelling towards us, weaving between tables but knocking over the occasional chair. It was a nurse, I realised. Or it was a nurse if nurses wear red scrubs and, right enough, no one else in the cafeteria was decked out like a blood clot. She was moving at quite a pace.

"It *is* you," she screeched as she got within a few yards of us. She looked familiar but I couldn't place her.

"What the?" said Roger, craning over his shoulder.

"What did you say to him?" the woman bellowed. She tripped over some guy's foot as he stuck it out into her path and she stumbled for a few lurching steps. Then she righted herself and kept on rolling our way. "What did you do to him?" she shouted. "What have you done? What did he ever do to you?"

The guy who'd tried to trip her up was chasing after her now. *He* was dressed in grey scrubs, which rang a faint bell, and he'd surely had them tailored to his physique. They hugged him like spandex. The red scrubs of the running woman hugged her like spandex too, because her physique was scrub-shaped. She could certainly haul it around though. She was nearly upon us. I still couldn't place her. But at my side Todd gasped.

"Becky?"

Of course!

"Becky Worth?" I said. "What's wrong?"

She was in no mood for talking. She came right up to the table, took me by my lapels—well, the zip of my hoodie—and shook me. "What did you do? What did you do?"

"What are you talking about?" I said. "Stop shaking me!"

Todd was trying to prise her fingers off me. "Hey, hey, hey," he said. Roger was on his feet, reaching out.

The grey scrubs guy was here too now. He stepped between Roger and the woman in red. "I'll take care of this," he said. "Let me get rid of this for you."

"Maurice?" Roger said. He shot a look at Todd, who let go of Becky's hands. Becky took the chance to shake me even harder, sending eighteen ounces of watermelon juice and two thirds of a large burrito on a carnival ride round my insides.

"He's had a heart attack," she said. Sobbed, really. She was sobbing now.

"Mr. Burns?" said Todd, looking between the svelte guy in the grey scrubs and Roger's face, which was purple. "Columbo?"

"And it's all your fault," Becky was saying. She had lost some of her fire now. I managed to get out of her grip and pushed her into a chair. "What did you say to him? What did you want with him? He was fine and now he's dying. He's a good man."

"I'm sorry to hear he's ill," I said. "Although if he got to a hospital still alive after a heart attack, he's probably not dying, you know. But I'm going to have to disagree with you on one score, Becky. He is *not* a good man."

"Good men certainly are thin on the ground around here," Todd said.

Maurice flicked him a glance but had little attention to spare from Roger. "Are you okay?" he said. "Should I call security?"

"Why would you say that?" Becky was asking me. She blew a snot bubble out of one nostril and even if she had just assaulted me and even if her brother was a murderer, I hated to see a fellow woman so humiliated in front of these three gorgeous men. I passed her a tissue.

"Blow your nose," I said. "Because he's a homophobic bigot, Becky. That's why."

"Who is?" said Maurice. "Roger, is someone harassing you?"

"Yes," said Todd. "Someone is. Someone not a million miles away."

"And who are you?" Maurice said, looking at Todd as if he'd been tracked in on a shoe.

"He's not a homophobic bigot," Becky said. "Why would you say that? He works down in L.A. He's a sound engineer. He's got more gay friends than anyone I know."

"Maurice, this is my husband, Todd," Roger said. "Light of my life, fire of my soul. Like I told you."

151

"*Loins*," said Todd. "The quote is 'fire of my loins.' You friend zoning me now, Roger?"

"What is he talking about?" said Becky.

"I'm at work, Todd," Roger said. "*Loins* is not appropriate language."

"Saying he wouldn't piss on a burning gay is homophobic enough for me," I said. "And he knew Tam wasn't shot."

"What's she talking about?" said Maurice. "Roger, I told you what I told you in confidence."

"When someone's married," said Roger, "confidence extends to the spouse."

"My brother didn't kill Tam Shatner," said Becky. "What did you say to him after I'd gone?"

"I'm not saying he did," I said. "If me asking questions about Tam has given John a heart attack, I think that's on him. Not on me."

"But he's really, really not a bigot," Becky said.

"No one ever admits to being a bigot," said Todd.

"No, but—" Becky said. Then she glanced at her watch. "I need to get back to him," she said. "I promised I'd only be away five minutes while they moved him out of the ER into the ICU. I've got to go."

"Do you have someone coming to support you?" I said. "Do you want me to come with you?"

Becky snorted as if she'd rather have Dick Cheney wax her legs than put up with me as a shoulder to cry on. Then her face crumpled. "If you would stay till our sister gets here from Reno," she said. "Thank you."

"You go on," I told her, "and I'll be right behind you." I turned to Todd. "Put the rest of my burrito in my fridge for later," I said. "And swing round by the Worth place. See what she was cramming into the wheeliebin in such a hurry this morning. And look in my diary for a time you and Roger can come to see me."

"What?" Roger said.

"I mean it. Mr. Burns indeed! That was a rookie mistake, Roger. Maurice, would you like to go out for a drink sometime?"

"With you?" Maurice said.

"With me."

"Uhhhhh, no," he replied.

"Exactly," I said. "Now listen: you've got as much chance with Roger as I've got with you, so do yourself a favour and move on. Okay?"

"Why do I need to come?" Todd said as Maurice swished off with as much dignity as scrubs ever allow. "This is a clear case of Lexy Campbell says one-side-sucks."

"Okay," I said. "I'll see Roger alone."

"No way," said Todd, as I knew he would. "I want to hear what you both say about me."

I kissed them both on the cheek and together we left the cafeteria. Todd, though, stopped dead in his tracks as we passed the drinks dispenser.

"Oh God," he said. "That's not even funny."

He pointed towards a hospital health poster pinned on the wall behind the fountain. *Drink less soda for health!* it said, on top of a shot of Coke fizzing over ice cubes.

"Hard to argue," Roger said. "How could anyone—even a murderer—kill someone by making him drink *lye*?"

"Here in the land of the well-ordered militia," I said, "what's the point of all that mess and bother instead of a nice clean bullet?" Todd and Roger were both staring at me. "*I'm* not asking!" I said. "I'm trying to put myself in the murderer's shoes. Like Roger said: why lye?"

Fifteen

I've had a life. I mean, I'm married and divorced, I've travelled, I've solved a murder, I've been the target of a mafia vendetta. I've lived. But that Saturday afternoon was the first time I'd sat at the bedside of a probable murderer, patting his sister's hand and pretending I wasn't pumping her for information.

"Was John overworking?" I said. "Between his sound engineering and his part-time business?"

Becky shook her head, barely listening. She was studying her brother, as if she could will him back into consciousness by the sheer intensity of her gaze. She was mistaken. He was deeply out of it. His breath fogged the plastic mask over his nose and mouth and then cleared it. Fogged it and cleared it. And his eyes were still, glinting in a slit in his eyelids. His feet flopped outwards under the thin blanket and his hands were resting on their backs on top of it, his fingers curled, not a twitch anywhere, even when the little clothes peg pinched him every half minute to measure his blood oxygen.

"Or was it the reunion?" I said. "Did he overdo it?"

"He was a little pink around the eyes on Sunday morning," said Becky, "but it was his fiftieth reunion." She reached forward and brushed the shock of sweaty sandy hair back from his brow. "I think his color's starting to look a little better, don't you?"

"Perhaps," I said. In truth between the overhead lights, the greying cotton gown slipping below the tidemark of his golfer's tan, and the tubes and wires snaking all over him, John Worth couldn't have looked worse unless someone had given him a black eye.

"It was a different time," Becky said. "Fifty years ago. We didn't know any better." I held my breath. Was she changing her story? About to acknowledge her brother's shortcomings after all? "Cheerleaders baked cookies for the team, decorated their lockers. We even laundered their uniforms in Domestic Science. Can you believe that?"

"It's all pretty outlandish to me," I said. "Or maybe *glamorous* is a better word. Homecomings and proms and reunions. It's like something from the movies."

"Really?" Becky said. "Nothing glamorous about it, if you ask me. Bunch of seniors drinking too much and sleeping in the wrong beds."

"And when you say *seniors* ... " I said. "Do you mean the high school seniors at the graduation or senior citizens at the reunion?"

She did a little nose laugh. "You're right," she said. "*Nothing's* changed. They were just the same this year as fifty years ago. Booze, tears, and drama." She sighed. "It was sweet, in a weird way. All of them together again."

"All of them?" I said.

"Most of them. There's one they never get to come back and celebrate. Joan Something. They always hope, but she's missed forty-nine parties since graduation." She reached out and took hold of John's hand, squeezing it. "Crazy not to see people while everyone's still here. We'll all be gone soon enough."

"There's always one, though, isn't there?" I said. "It's a shame, when the committee goes to so much trouble. And … is it just the one night or is it like a festival?"

"Our exotic, glamorous high school reunions?" Becky said. "It's just one night."

"Well, that's nice then, isn't it?" I said. "That your brother's still here days later. It must be you he wants to spend time with, mustn't it? I mean, there's no other reason for him to stay on in Cuento?"

I wondered if I was treading too close to the heart of the matter. But I'd been staring at the bark of the trees and missed the wasp's nest dangling from the wood.

"Nice?" said Becky. "You think *this* might be nice?"

"Not this exactly," I said. "But before … "

"… the massive heart attack."

"Yeah, before the massive heart attack. He spent some time with you instead of working. I do always think you Americans work soooo hard. Two jobs isn't even unusual, is it? It's very admirable."

But I'd lost her and there was no getting her back, even with flattery. Even with true flattery, like this right now. Because I meant every word: they did work hard, with their four-day vacations crammed into a long weekend and one day off for Christmas. Right now Becky Worth was working hard at piecing together everything I'd said to her.

"What side business?" she said. "His job at the studio, you said. And a *side* business?"

"The pet grooming," I said.

"What?"

"Cat grooming service?" I said.

"I'm the one who works in the veterinarian's office over in Cuento," Becky said. "Not Johnny."

"Have you swapped cars?" I said.

"We did, last weekend," she said. "But only for a day. Why? Why are you so interested in the reunion? You're not cops, you're not reporters. He already said that dead guy left the party alive. Or wasn't there at all." She was still gazing at John, but she was frowning. Any second now, she'd turn and look at me and I wasn't sure I'd be able to get my expression innocent if she did.

"It's for these two kittens," I said. "I saw the advert on the Cala ... ?"

"The sacred El Camino!" Becky said, actually rolling her eyes. "I couldn't believe he let me drive it! But, what 'advert'?"

I opened my mouth to answer but before I could utter a word there was a massive movement from the bed. John had lifted a hand and was plucking at his mouth. "Maaaaarrrh," he said; a bone-chilling sound, coming from deep in his barrel chest and amplified by the dome of the mask.

"Johnny!" Becky said and stood to bend over him.

He reached up with the other hand and grabbed her by the neck. "Maaaarrrhhh," he said.

"Johnny?"

"Hey!" I said.

He swivelled his head as far as the mask would let him and let his gaze settle on me. "Nooooo!" he said, which was pretty clear.

"Let go of my neck, Johnny honey," his sister said. "You're confused."

"I'll get someone," I said, sliding out of my seat as he took a swipe in my direction. I edged out of the room and headed back to the nurses' station. But one of his machines must have alerted them already because two of them were bearing towards me at the fastest clip possible without a walk turning into a run.

"He's awake," I said. "A bit distressed, but definitely awake!"

The nurses brushed past me and on into John Worth's little side room. I shifted from foot to foot, swithering on which way to go. Back to see what was bothering John or home to the Last Ditch to find out what Todd had grubbed out of his bin?

Then a red light went on above the door to his room and one of the nurses came flying out, tugging an alarm hanging from a cord around her neck. I pressed myself back against the wall to let her pass and then scurried away.

∞

Todd was sitting in my living room when I finally, finally, finally got back, after the Uber ride from the seventh circle of hell. I sneaked in round the back of the Skweek, battling an extra twenty feet of oleanders so I didn't have to pass Della's room, to find him sitting in my armchair staring at a black plastic bin bag resting on a white plastic sheet in the middle of the floor. He had an aerosol container in each hand, caps off, trigger fingers on nozzles, ready to go.

"Where have you *been*?" he said. "I thought the sister was only coming from Reno."

"Uberland," I told him. "I'd have been better on the bus. Have you just been sitting here the whole time?

"Sorry. Kathi wouldn't let me take it into one of the rooms and I didn't want to do it in the parking lot."

"That's not what I meant," I told him. "I'm just amazed you've managed not to open it."

"Open a garbage sack?" said Todd. "Are you crazy? I have no idea what's in there. You open it, you skanky ho, and I'll zap the critters before they escape."

"What critters?" I said. "Did you feel it moving when you brought it over?" Todd shuddered and I saw a rash of goose pimples pop up on his forearms. He had pushed his sleeves back in case they interfered with his quick-draw aerosol action. I took a closer look at the cans. "Todd, is that the stuff from Costa Rica? You can't spray that in here. Or at least let me open the window."

I opened the window then, pulling on a pair of latex gloves—there were always latex gloves lying around anywhere Kathi spent time—I undid the orange ties on the sack and folded it back.

"Well!" I said.

Todd was pressed back in his chair with both arms held straight out in front of him. "What is it?" he said, sounding strained.

"There's nothing in here for you to worry about," I said. "Lay down your weapons and have a look-see."

Todd narrowed his eyes at me, but he knows I would never ambush him with fruit flies or maggots. He set the canisters down, rose warily up onto his tiptoes, and peeked over the rim of the bag. Then he whistled, stood back down on his heels, and came closer.

"That is very interesting," he said, whipping out his camera. "You take it out and I'll photograph it."

"Or," I said, "we call Mike to come and take it away."

"Right, right," Todd said. "You unpack, I'll snap, then we put it back and call Mike."

"Deal," I said. "Okay." I snapped the blue gloves to make sure they were snug on my wrists and plunged my hands in. "Item one," I said, pulling them out again. "Jimmy wig." I turned it inside out. "No visible staples."

"Check," said Todd.

"Item two: kilt. Not a real one. Cheap costume quality."

"Kilt," said Todd. "Check."

"Item three: leather-effect waistcoat. Aka vest. Not a real one. Cheap costume quality."

"Village People biker vest," said Todd. "Check."

"Draught excluder," I said, pulling out a long sausage of fabric stuffed with straw. "Home-made. And another draught excluder. And a huge draught excluder. And a—why are you not saying check?"

"Because I'm speechless at how dumb you are," Todd said, watching me pull another one out of the sack. *"Draught excluders?"*

I was rootling in the bottom of the bag for the last item. "And a severed head," I concluded. "Oh! They're not draught excluders, are they? They're arms and legs."

"And a torso," Todd. "To put the kilt on."

"Ew," I said, pulling a tiny little draught excluder with two round supports out of the bin bag's last corner.

"So...that's true?" Todd said. "Scottish men don't wear anything underneath?"

"It's true," I said.

"But they do those dances with all the swinging around."

"They do," I said. "But on a real kilt—not this thing, but on a *real* one—the pleats are stitched down to hip height and the sporran chain adds a bit of battening too. And remember it weighs nine pounds."

"What does?" said Todd, round-eyed.

"The kilt, you pig!" I said. "It's really hard to get it to fly up from Scottish dancing. Now, a Scottish-Jewish wedding, on the other hand? When they lift the groom up on a chair?"

Todd was quiet for a minute, imagining. And I was quiet for a minute revisiting some happy memories. Then we shook ourselves back to attention.

"So this fake Mel Gibson dude was dressed up and sitting on John Worth's porch over Halloween?" Todd said. "And then all of a sudden, when the *Voyager* publishes Tam's identity, Worth dismantles the display, like it's some big emergency."

"With his sister's help. But even with his sister's help it's so stressful he has a heart attack. Oh, he came round by the way. He heard me talking to his sister about the reunion and he pretty much willed himself awake. It was like Moby Dick breaking through the waves, Todd. You should have seen it!"

"But how does draft-stopper-fake-guy relate to real dead Tam?" Todd said.

"A decoy? Only, that just raises the question … ?"

"Where *was* Tam?" said Todd. "The non-fake dude, in the fake-nude suit."

"Presumably with a kilt of his own on top," I agreed. "Isn't there a big spread in the *Voyager* the day after Halloween? Porch-decorating finalists?"

"There is," said Todd. "And I bet the photographer has five thousands shots of porches all over town that didn't make the grade."

"Do you know him?" I said. "Any chance you could bat your eyelids?"

"Her," said Todd. "And no. I tried to get her to delete a pic of me in a fun run one year where I looked as fat as a blimp and she got really weird about it. Photographers, you know."

"We should hand this over to Mike," I said.

"Not yet," said Todd. "Not before we put this back in John Worth's garbage can for Mike to find."

"You're right about that," I said. "But I didn't just mean the stuff, I mean the lead. Mike could get a search warrant for the photos. We really need to hand over what we know."

"We do," Todd agreed. Technically. But his voice was as dead as a dude who'd been ripped up into five draught excluders. "Or, even if we can't get the photographer to cough up, we can check out all the photos that made it onto the website."

161

"There's something I'd like to do too," I said. "After dark, I'd like to go through the Moes' wheeliebins."

"*Wheeliebin!*" said Todd.

"Garbage carts, whatever," I said. "See if they've just shoved everything in there for the dustmen on Monday."

"*Dustmen!*" Todd said.

"Sanitation engineers, whatever."

"But why?" said Todd.

"Because I think John Worth killed Tam and stashed him on someone's porch and that someone found him and chucked him in the slough. But if they didn't unstaple his hat, they might have skimped on all the other clean-up too."

"But unless it's one of the Moes," Tam said, "it could be anyone. It wouldn't even need to be someone from the class of sixty-eight, would it?"

"No," I admitted. "But we could *try* cross-referencing porches with the yearbook. We *might* get lucky. Mind you, the library shuts in twenty minutes so we're going to have to hustle up there and speed read."

"Or," said Todd, "wear that coat with the kangaroo pouch. Twenty minutes isn't enough."

"Téodor Mendez Kroger, MD," I said. "Are you suggesting I steal a library book?"

"For a good cause? For the weekend? Absolutely."

Sixteen

This time, I knew where the yearbook was to be found and didn't need to alert a librarian to our presence. I strode to the shelf, slipped the book under my arm, went round the corner, jammed it into my pouch pocket, and sashayed back to Todd in New Mystery. I had to sashay instead of striding because of the way the four pounds of book made my poncho swing. If it swung on its own while I marched along behind, it would raise suspicions. This way, it looked as if my Marilyn Monroe wiggle was the source of it all and the only question to pop into an onlooker's head would be why someone channelling Jessica Rabbit when it came to gait was wearing a poncho.

"What are you doing?" said Todd as I sidled up. "You might as well carry a sign saying *I'm filching a book*."

"It's wanging about. What am I supposed to do?"

"Don't say *wang*. Give it to me and I'll stick it down the back of my jeans."

"You'll never be able to walk with something this heavy in your jeans," I said.

Maybe it was all down to his marvellous posture, and maybe I should go with him to one of these yoga classes he was always nagging me about, but with that solid slab of yearbook tucked in the back of his waistband he strolled out of the library like a Cold War spy crossing Checkpoint Charlie. He might have tensed a bit going through the security gate but evidently a fifty-year-old high school yearbook wasn't worth a magnetic strip and no alarm went off as Todd passed the sensors.

"Where to?" I said, when we were back in the Jeep. "Home?"

"Way to fail to hustle like a dying European monarchy, Lexy," Todd said. "No way. We need to get on this. I'm going to drive back to the Moes' houses to check their garbage cans while you cross-check porch tableau finalists on the *Voyager* website with graduates of the class of sixty-eight. And if you find any matches, we'll check their garbage cans too. We'll be done in time to take the evidence to Mike if she's working as late as yesterday. Can you read in a moving vehicle without barfing?"

"In an automatic doing twenty-five in a forest of stop signs?" I said. "I think I'll be okay."

By the time we stopped at Mo Heedles's house—or rather, around the nearest looping corner on Lassen Avenue, so she didn't see us—I had confirmed that there was at least one more Jimmy-bewigged porch zombie and he was slumped at the front door of one Lampeter family.

"Look for Lampeter in the yearbook," Todd said. He was turning a blue latex glove inside out leaving the fingers on the inside.

"What are you doing?"

Todd leaned over me into the glove box and took out a Mars Bar. He unwrapped it, broke half off, and dropped it into the glove.

"Does that look like dogshit?" he said.

"Totally. How many times has it melted, and can I eat the other half?

He tied the glove shut. "Does it look like a poop bag?"

"Yip. Can I eat the other half?"

Todd took his belt off and attached his titanium pitcher's necklace to the buckle end.

"Does that look like a dog's lead?"

"Not bad. Can I—"

"Didn't you know Roger keeps candy in the glove compartment?" Todd said. "In case of diabetic hitchhikers."

I was speechless. I had been in a car with a melted Mars Bar all these times and never knew.

"Look for Lampeters," Todd said again and let himself out of the driver's door. His disguise was perfect. He was, to a T, a dog walker with a turd to get rid of. And this being Cuento's second-poshest neighbourhood, the wheeliebins were at the kerb nice and early for Monday's pick-up. I didn't understand it—back home, wheeliebins lolling kerbside was the mark of the ghetto—but I'd seen it often enough not to question it anymore.

I was bent over the yearbook, Lampeter-hunting, when Todd threw himself back in to the driver's seat, started the engine, and peeled away, still with the makeshift poo bag dangling from one hand and the makeshift dog lead dangling from the other.

"Shit, did she see you?" I said.

"No," said Todd, taking a corner on two wheels. "I'm just enjoying myself. Did you find anyone? Want me to take a turn?"

"Not yet," I said. "I take it you didn't find anything in the bin?"

"Nothing Halloween-related," Todd said. "More used Q-tips than I ever wanted to see, but no plaid and no 'draught excluders.'" I ignored his air quotes. "Are you nearly finished?"

"I keep getting distracted," I said. "It's all so mysterious. Junior Varsity, Sophomore Metro League."

"I can't imagine school life in Dundee," Todd said. "Is it just rows of little barefoot kids scratching on slates with pointed sticks?"

"Invitational Track Meet. What does it all *mean*?"

"Quit goofing off, Lexy. You'll only find half the student body back there in 1968, years before Title IX."

"Eh?"

"Flip to the senior class and do it methodically."

I flipped. I actually flipped too far. And then I flipped out.

"Oh. My. God," I said.

"Join them up," Todd told me. "You sound insane."

"Pull over," I said, clicking the overhead light and holding the book up. "Here she is. Joan Lampeter. Here they all are! John Worth gets a whole page spread of his own and there they are, facing page. Maureen 'Mo' Tafoya, Maureen 'Mo' Heedles, some kid called Patricia 'Patti' Ortiz, and Joan Lampeter! Like a backing group."

Todd whistled. "President, Secretary, Treasurer, Class Councilor, and Class Councilor," he said.

"And I'll tell you something else too," I said. "Becky Worth told me today that someone called Joan is missing. The only one who stays away from the reunions."

Todd whistled again.

"Is there any way this is a coincidence?" I said. "There they all are, as cosy as cosy can be. All but one of the names that came up as soon as we scratched the surface of this inquiry."

"It's a stretch," said Todd. He was driving again. Gagging to get into Mo Tafoya's bins, I reckoned. "Who's the vice pres?" he asked, as we turned into 14th Street. It was even darker than Lassen Avenue, Cuento-ites loathing light pollution so much they might have been vampires. I held the book up closer to the light. There was some writing in the centre of the page in the bit of space between the girls' pictures.

"Oh. My. God!" I said again. "And don't tell me to join them up because ... Oh."

"My?" he supplied.

"God. Vice President, not pictured. Guess who?"

Todd didn't so much park as just stop in the middle of the road. "No way," he said.

"Thomas Oscar 'Tam' Shatner," I said.

"Oh," Todd agreed.

"My," I added.

"God. Well, well, well. Looks like what Becky said might be true."

"John Worth was no knuckle-dragger if he made the only gay in the village his deputy?" I said. "Or is it voted on?"

"Nope," Todd said. "President is voted on, but the deputy is the president's pick. This keeps on getting weirder." He opened the door. "Get online, Lexy, and see if this Patti ... "

"Ortiz," I said.

"Yeah, see if Patti Ortiz still lives in Cuento. Or at least see how many Ortizes live in Cuento and then we can try them all and see if they've got an Aunt Patti somewhere."

"Are you going to go up the path to where the bin's stashed?" I said.

"Can't think how else to rake through the garbage, can you?"

"What if someone sees you? They won't buy the dogwalker act if the bin's not kerbside, will they?"

"Nope," said Todd. He tossed the glove with the half Mars Bar into my lap. "Help yourself."

But there are limits. I flicked it onto the floor. "So ... what are you going to do?"

"I'm going to do my Drunk with a Full Bladder," Todd said. "Even if one of the neighbors sees me and challenges me, they'll wait till I'm done."

"Ew," I said, but as I watched him I thought he was probably right. He weaved along the street then made a wide tacking turn into the shrubbery separating Mo Tafoya's garden from the house next door. He was fumbling at his zip as he disappeared into the shadows. I wouldn't have followed him.

Minutes later, he came lurching back out again. Empty-handed. Just in case anyone was watching, I clambered over the drinks holders into the driving seat. Cuento-ites might not be uptight enough to call the cops because a drunk took a leak, but they would surely dial it in if he drove off afterwards.

"Well?" I said, as Todd got in the passenger side.

"Nada. Wherever Also-Mo put her zombie, it wasn't in her garbage. Did you find Ortizes?"

"You find them," I said, starting the engine and moving off slowly. "I can't phone them anyway, with my memorable accent. Oh!" A sudden thought had struck me. "Remember Also-Mo saying *You?* that weird way when we rocked up on her doorstep? Do you think it was me? My voice? Maybe? Because she didn't know either of us, did she? So what was she reacting to?"

"No clue," said Todd. "Hey-hey! I found some Ortizes in Cuento. Oh boy, that's just the first page. I found a ton of Ortizes in Cuento."

"Any Patricias?" I said. "Try Facebook?"

"Or I could just start dialling," Todd said. "Where are we going by the way?"

"I thought we'd go back to the Worths' to re-stash the bin bag for Mike," I said.

"Ight," said Todd. Then he sat up a little straighter in his seat. "Mr. Ortiz?" His voice had turned way more Mexican than usual. "Hi, is Patti there? Oh yeah? *Ay, perdone. Tengo el número equivocado.*" He hung up. "One down. Fifty-seven to go."

He had made it through nine *ay perdones* and one heart-stopping wrong Patti, who came to the phone and turned out to be twenty, by the time we pulled up at the old Worth place. It was in darkness. Becky and the sister from Reno must still be by John's bedside.

"Who was still calling their baby Patti twenty years ago anyway?" Todd said. Then he was off again. "Mrs. Ortiz? Is Patti there?" There was a silence. "What?" he said. He clicked the phone to speaker and held it out.

The voice of an elderly woman came out of the phone, shaking with emotion. "You leave us alone, you sick son of a bitch! You think it's so long ago it doesn't hurt every day anymore? You think it's okay to have that bastard back in this town? You think you helping? *Métetelo por el culo!*"

"Insert ... Like *insert*?" I said when the call was dead.

"Yeah," said Todd. "Your Spanish is improving. And that was pretty peppery language for a woman who sounded as old as my granny."

"Old enough to be Patti Ortiz's mother?" I said.

"Maybe," said Todd. "But it's a leap."

"Not really," I insisted. "'So long ago' could be fifty years, couldn't it? And a 'bastard who's back in this town' might do for Tam Shatner."

"But what could a poor lonely gay like Tam Shatner have done to Patti Ortiz that would make her mother be that angry fifty years later?" Todd said. "What is it? What are you thinking?"

169

He was right; I *was* thinking something. I was grasping at the loose waving ends of about five different wisps of thought and I was scared if I tried to say them out loud, I would end up blowing them away.

"Promise you'll listen quietly and hear me out," I said. Todd nodded, wide-eyed. "Okay," I went on. "Now why would Mrs. Ortiz there assume that you were a sick son of a bitch phoning up and messing with her just because you asked for Patti? Why wouldn't she just think you were someone asking for Patti?"

"Oh my God, you're right!" Todd said, very much not listening quietly and hearing me out. I could feel the wisps of idea being swept away on the tide of his excitement. "The only reason she'd know I wasn't really calling for Patti is if Patti is missing! Patti is gone! Patti has been gone 'all these years.' And oh! Oh! Oh! Becky Worth said it, didn't she? She said they keep hoping a missing girl comes back but she's missed forty-nine reunions!"

"But that was Joan," I said.

"But Becky wasn't in the same year. She probably only knows them as a group—Mo, Mo, Patti, and Joan. And she knows one went missing. But she doesn't remember which one. She made a mistake. What's Joan's full name?"

I flicked through the yearbook. "Joan Frances Lampeter."

"Great," said Todd. "How many Joan Frances Lampeters you reckon are on Facebook? Why look at that, I do believe it's just one. And here she is … yep, looks about sixty-eight to me … and lives in Cuento, CA!"

"But no one said she was *missing*," I reminded of him. "We're just building castles here, Todd. Becky Worth just said she didn't come to reunions. Why are you grinning?"

"Because Joan Lampeter is sixty-eight years old and, not to be ageist or anything, but her privacy settings are a hot mess. She might set her posts to friends only but her pictures are a free-for-all."

"And?" I said. "Show me before I untie your glove and smear your hair with Mars Bar."

Todd held out his phone. I peered and felt the skin on the back of my neck prickle. There was a woman in a linen dress with a cocktail in one hand and the other arm slung around Mo Tafoya. Behind them were the pillars holding up the roof of the Cuento Farmers' Market. "She was at the reunion," I said.

"Unlike Patti Ortiz," said Todd. Then, as a fist pounded on the window of the Jeep, he shot up high enough to bang his head and flub his phone. I heard the screen crack as it came down. Outside the window, looking like a Halloween pumpkin on account of how she was holding her torch under her chin and shining it upwards, was Mike.

Todd wound down the window. "Evening, Detective," he said. "Can we help you?"

"What are you doing here?" Mike said.

"Here?" said Todd, craning to look up and down the street. "Cuento? I live here."

"Here at John Worth's place," Mike said.

"Who?" said Todd.

"Wait," I said. "Are we interfering with emergency responders in the execution of their duties again?"

"What are *you* doing here?" Todd said.

"Following a lead in the Shatner case," said Mike. "And you know what I hate doing when I'm following up a lead in a case? Repeating myself. What are you doing here?"

"We're probably doing the same thing you're doing," I said. "Following a lead. But we're only doing it because we didn't think you were doing it. And since you're doing it, we'll stop."

"It's cold anyway," Mike said. "We're too late."

"What?" I said. "Because they've cleared the porches?"

Mike gave me a look she had never given me before in the months I'd known her. Well, it was the same look of exasperation and annoyance I was used to, but it was mixed with something new. It was mixed with something that looked a lot like respect.

"You got an in at the *Voyager*?" she said. "Because if that punk of a photographer told you after I told her to keep it to herself, I will hurt her."

"Uh, the First Amendment might get in the way of that," said Todd, whatever the hell that meant.

"No," I said. "We came at it from the other end. From the yearbook." Then I shut my mouth so firmly it made a slapping sound. Because the yearbook—purloined from the public library—was right there on my lap and Mike would love nothing more than to stick us with a theft charge.

"The yearbook?" was all she said.

"The 1968 high school yearbook," I said.

"How did that tell you anything about the porches?" she said.

"We guessed," I said. "From the stapled-on Jimmy wig. And the fact that he died at Halloween and didn't turn up for four days. He was hidden in plain sight, wasn't he?"

"I'm not here to answer your questions," Mike said, snapping back into full-cop mode. Pretty late, if anyone was asking me. "But how did the yearbook bring you to *this* porch? This one in particular?"

"We were starting at the top," Todd said. "With the senior class president. Why? Is ... what was his name, Lexy?"

"John Worth."

"Is John Worth a person of interest?"

"Like I said, I ask the questions. And if I hear that you've been cruising round town snooping at porches, I will make sure you pay."

"That's not a question," Todd said.

"You should consider yourself lucky I caught you here, on porch one," Mike said. "Go home and stay out of this."

"That's not a question either," I said. "But you're welcome and we will."

"Welcome?" said Mike.

"For the tip about the ID of the dead guy," I said. "The class ring."

"Just for the love of God, f—" said Mike, but she caught herself in time. "Fly away home before I arrest your asses for curb crawling," she said. Then she walked off.

"Florida," I said as we watched her get into her car and leave.

"Huh?"

"Remember John Worth said Tam Shatner should haul his bum back to F— And then he pretended he was going to say 'fuck' and he didn't want to swear in front of a lady, but then he swore anyway?"

"Oh right," said Todd. "That *was* weird."

"He was going to say *Florida*," I said. "Mike said an *F* that was going to turn into a *U* there. Then she said an *F* that was going to turn in an *L*. It looks really different. One gives you duck face and one gives you chipmunk face. Try it in the mirror. Tam Shatner lived in Florida."

"So?"

"I dunno. Might be useful. It's a long way to come to a reunion, isn't it? Why are we still parked here, by the way?"

"Because if Becky Worth gets home and finds her garbage missing, she's gonna call the cops and tell Mike we were here earlier and you gave John Worth a heart attack. A man we've just pretended not to know."

"Oh, yeah," I said. "Well, trot on then. Ditch the bin bag and then let's go home and see if Kathi and Noleen can make any sense out of all this, eh?"

For the third time, Todd climbed down from the Jeep and made his way to someone else's wheeliebin to break all sorts of laws. He wasn't a dog walker or a desperate drunk this time. There was no point, when the bag he carried could be used to clean up after an elephant and when the Worths' collection of bins sat out in the glare of their security light, far from any peeing shadows.

Minutes later, I saw him coming back to the Jeep at a run. Well, not really a proper run, more as if he was trying to move as fast as his legs would carry him without looking as suspicious as running at night makes you look. Like he was on castors and one was wobbly.

He still had the bin bag too. He threw himself into the passenger seat and hissed, "Go, Lexy! Get out of here. Back up to the stop sign and get gone."

"I'm not reversing up a street when cops are hanging around," I said, doing a U-ey with a bit of a wiggle on the end and then driving away sedately at twenty-five like a good girl. "Whyn't you ditch the bag?"

"I did!" said Todd. He was bunched up on the seat beside me hugging the bag like a teddy bear. He didn't have his seatbelt on. "This isn't it!" he said. "This is another one! It was sitting on the doormat. Must have been put there since Becky took John to the hospital."

"But it could be anything," I said. "It might be jumble, or—"

"Jumble?"

"Uhhhhh, donations for a yard sale," I said. "Or it might be—Ew! Don't open it! It might just be rubbish. Pizza boxes and more Q-tips."

But it wasn't. I saw the flash of tartan and the tuft of fake ginger hair at the same moment Todd did. He folded the top back over and shoved the bag down by his feet. Then he put his seatbelt on and sat up while we drove past the cop shop on the way home.

Seventeen

We scooped up Kathi and Noleen on the way past the office. They were folding service-wash laundry on the signing-in desk, waiting until ten when Noleen would finally give up on the hoped-for walk-ins and switch the night bell on.

"What's that?" said Kathi, pointing to the bin bag swinging from Todd's hand.

"Another porch zombie," Todd said. "Not garbage. Can we tip it out here if I put newspaper down?"

"And I'll tell the Skweeky Kleen clientele that their undershorts were folded and packed in the same room as someone else's trash?" said Kathi. "Should I get stickers made?"

"You and your stickers," I said.

"Who and whose stickers?" Noleen chipped in.

"You lot," I said. "All of you. With the bumper stickers. But I take it back. Sorry."

"Ain't no stickers on my ride," said Noleen. "And I wanna say two things to you, Lexy. One, there's no better way to get outta jury duty than a bumper sticker. It's public, see? So they get to ask you about them in discovery."

Todd was laughing. "What was it you had again, Nolly?"

"*Keep Gitmo Open*," Noleen said. "Worked like a dream when the defense got to me. My feet didn't hit the ground. Course, I also had a *Close Gitmo Now*, in case the prosecution asked first. Guess which one peeled a chunka paint offa my bumper when I got outta the courtroom?"

Kathi and Todd both just laughed. I couldn't have guessed to save my life and get a free margarita, so I said nothing beyond, "What's the other thing?"

"What?" Noleen said. "Oh. Yeah, well it's not *us lot* that's got that horny caveman painted on the side of a hill fifty feet high, is it? Speaking of signs."

"How do you even know about ...?" I said.

"PBS documentary," said Noleen. "The Cerne Abbas Giant, right?" I shrugged.

"Anyway," I said. "What about Mount Rushmore? And Crazy Horse?"

"Could we table this for now?" said Kathi. "While you get that nasty garbage bag out of here, please?"

"We'll take it to Lexy's and go through it right now," Todd said. "It'll be long gone by the time you get there."

"No," Kathi said. "I don't want to miss the opening. I just want to be able to walk out and grab a shower if it's gross."

"Deal," said Todd. "We'll go and make ... sidecars, I'm in the mood for ... and grill some shrimp? When you close at ten, we'll be waiting. I need to process some of this stuff before we find out any more. Don't know about you."

"And Roger?" Kathi said. "Should we wait for him?"

"Roger needs some time alone to reflect on his choices," said Todd primly. Kathi and Noleen shared a troubled look.

"Roger very kindly gave us some tip-top info earlier today," I said. "But he's got a semi-stalker at work that he said was ugly and isn't."

"Baw-bag," said Noleen.

"Twunt," Kathi agreed.

"You can't cheer me up with British swearing," said Todd. "I am very angry."

"How about if I call him a douche nozzle?" I said. "An asshat? A mother—"

But a chorus of *whoa*s told me I'd better not finish that one. Our cultural exchange still had a ways to go.

∞

"So what do we know?" Noleen said, as she kicked off her crocs and put her socks up on the hearth just after ten.

"Thomas Oscar Shatner," I began, "graduate of the class of sixty-eight, out gay back when it was brave—er" I added hastily, as Todd started to bridle, "left Cuento for—we think, Florida, but that's based on how much of Henry Higgins's identical twin I am, so best call it soft data—and came back to town to attend the fiftieth reunion on Saturday, where—or after which, anyway—he was poisoned with—"

"*What?*" said Kathi.

"Roger busted the autopsy results," I said. "The bullet wound was fake. He drank lye."

"He drank *lye?*" said Noleen.

"Who drinks *lye?*" said Kathi.

"And then was left sitting on someone's porch dressed up as a Scotsman—we think, based on the hat—until Wednesday, when he was redressed as a regular joe and dumped in the slough. Now here's where it gets interesting."

"Because that was such an everyday tale?" said Noleen.

"Earlier today we saw three porches, didn't we Todd, where figures had been removed. One of them was at the house of the class president of the class of sixty-eight, one John Worth—"

"I know John Worth," said Noleen. "And Becky. Veterinary nurse. Nice kid."

"Right," I said, wondering—and not for the first time—how old Noleen was and what she used on her skin. "Thank you for directing us to their place. We got there just in time to find Becky trying to get rid of a dummy, a kilt, a Jimmy wig, and sundry other bits and bobs."

"But … if there was a dummy," said Kathi, "that means Tam wasn't there. If 'dummy' still means mannequin. Right?"

"Right," I agreed, "but there was an empty armchair on the porch of Mo Heedles, and an empty rocking chair on the porch of Mo Tafoya."

"Who?" said Kathi. "I think we need to catch up."

"Hence the current catch-up session," Todd said, still sounding grumpy for him. "We found Maureen Heedles because she was at the reunion and still lives in Cuento. Nothing more than that. But we lucked out. She turned us on to Maureen Tafoya,"

"Her, I know," said Noleen. "Woodstock never ended?"

"That's the one," I said. "And then we discovered that both Moes, along with Joan and someone called Patti, were John Worth's … bevy of lovelies." I had been flipping through the yearbook and I held it up to show them all the full-page picture of John Worth, back when he was burly, rather than bloated, and the four quarter-page shots of Mo Heedles, looking older than she did now under her helmet of back-combed hair with her thin brows and her pale lips; Mo Tafoya, showing the first signs of her prayer-flagged future with a broochless, scratchy-looking polo-neck and a centre parting in her hair; Patti Ortiz looking up from under her fabulous brows with a gaze poised on a knife-edge between innocence and sizzle; and Joan Lampeter, fresh-faced and freckle-dusted with her hair back-combed on top to be sure but flicked up in feathers behind as if it knew the end of school and setting lotion was on its way.

"Bevy of lovelies!" Kathi said. "The student council, you mean?"

"She looks familiar," Todd said, putting down his napkin and bending forward to peer at the open pages of the yearbook. "Joanie. Doesn't she?"

"We saw her photo at the reunion," I reminded him.

"Oh please," said Todd. "Fifty years later? No, it's not that. I'm sure I've seen that girl in a different context. And recently."

"There's no way the pictures could have got switched round is there?" I asked. "Because there might have been a news story about one of these girls. But not that one. And Becky Worth got them mixed up too, didn't she? She said Joan had dropped out of view. But it was Patti."

"Patti Ortiz?" said Noleen. She took her feet down off the hearth and sat up straight. "It's not Patti Ortiz you're talking about, is it, Lexy?"

"It is," I said. "What do you know about it?"

"Patti Ortiz was older than me," Noleen said, "but her name was still the name our parents were using when we got to high school and went driving and dancing. And parking."

"You *did*?" said Kathi.

"Yeah, I did," Noleen said. "Whenever some 'phobe tells me I don't know what I'm missing, I can straighten them out, no pun intended, in extreme detail."

"Never mind all that," I said. "What do you know about Patti Ortiz? Because Todd spoke to someone we think was her mum tonight and she was not okay with the idea of chatting."

"I don't *know* anything," said Noleen. "That's the point. *No one* knows anything. Patti Ortiz just disappeared off the face of the earth. Right after graduation. I mean, the night of graduation. She went to the party and she never went home. She was never seen again."

"Fifty years ago," I said. "Her poor mother."

"Mother, father, and a brother," Noleen said. "The brother never came home from 'Nam. The dad died a while back too. Heart attack, stroke, something. But the mom, old Mrs. Ortiz, is still in Cuento. Still waiting. With the porch light on every night. Fifty years, Lexy, like you said."

We were all silent for a moment after that. Todd slid his phone out of his back pocket, I guessed to text Roger. It was Kathi who spoke first. "Speaking of porches ... "

I had forgotten about the bin bag. But there it was.

Todd spread a few double sheets of *Voyager* on my nice hardwood floorboards and unfolded the neck of the bag. Kathi pulled her feet up, in case of scampering rats or sloshing bin juice, I supposed, and Todd got going.

"*Draught excluder*," he said, pulling out another of the fake limbs we'd seen in the earlier stash. "Private joke," he told Kathi and Noleen. "Fake kilt. Jimmy wig. Fake junk. Fake Braveheart vest with bootlace ties."

"Fake junk?" said Noleen. "The wiener and meatballs?"

"To have an authentic Scotsman sitting up on a porch at eye level with passersby," said Todd.

"Ewwww," said Kathi. "I thought that was a myth." Then she held up a hand. "There's someone on deck," she said. "Jesus, if it's Mike, we're all in trouble."

But I was ahead of her. I knew there was someone on deck and I knew it was Della. She wasn't keen on water and so, when she lifted her back foot off dry land, she always gripped the PG&E pole hard enough to make the boat sway, just once.

"Come in," I said. Della edged round the door. She was still wearing her uniform from work although she had taken off her hairnet and changed her clogs for a pair of slippers. She was holding a baby monitor under her chin—Diego must be asleep in their room—and a kitten in each hand. "Oh God!" I said. "Della, I'm sorry."

"No sorries needed," she said, bending down to let Flynn and Florian go. And go they did. Unimpeded by armpit nests, they streaked once round the living room at floor level, once more at tabletop, mantelpiece, and shrimp bowl level, then shot up the curtains to balance, eyes rolling and tails lashing, on the pelmet. "They are groomed, Lexy. You are free."

"They look fantastic," I said. "Where'd you take them? What do I owe you?"

"Nothing," said Della. "It was free. Free cat grooming for anyone named Deifilia today."

"Son of a—Good for you," I said. "Seriously? Deifilia?"

"It's a beautiful name," Della said. "It means 'daughter of God.' What isn't serious?"

"So where was this?" I said. "One of the mobiles?"

"Aristocats up in Madding," Della said. "Main Street. Very fancy."

"Probably the best idea," I said. "Those folk that work out of the back of their cars are a funny bunch. Rude, for a start. But that reminds me. Todd, remember Becky Worth didn't know what I meant about John Worth's little part-time cat-grooming business?"

"She wasn't the only one," said Todd. "There's no way that guy is a cat groomer, Lexy. What are you on?"

"Hey," said Noleen. "Newsflash. We don't need to be talking about freaking cat groomers anymore. The cats are groomed. I'm thrilled the cats are groomed, since they both just ran through the shrimp. But let's change the record, huh?"

"You're still going to eat the shrimp?" said Kathi. "You're sleeping on the cot tonight."

"And who cares if John Worth is a cat groomer or a horse dentist or a poodle manicurist?" Todd said. Then he stopped.

"What?" I said.

"Dunno. Something. But it's gone." Todd shook his head. "The question is how come a big honking homophobe like him asks the only gay in the class to be his vice president. And how come a woman like Mo Tafoya—who's pretty much NPR in human form, right Lex?—hasn't woken up in the last fifty years, even if Mo Heedles is still putting on fake family values."

"Fake?" I said.

"Divorced," said Todd.

"What about her nephew?" I said. "That guy we met today?"

"What *about* her nephew?" said Todd.

"Wait, wait, wait," Della said, holding up both her hands like a cop at a traffic stop. "Rewind. Fill me in."

I refreshed the sidecars and caught her up. She nodded and sipped, nodded and sipped, and she didn't, unlike everyone else, ask who drinks lye. She asked a much cleverer and more useful question altogether.

"Who has access to lye?" And she followed that up with, "No one at Party City or Halloween Central will remember anyone buying a Scottish costume, but they might remember someone who bought four, right? For the porches of John Worth, two Moes, and Joan. Could we get pictures and show them to the clerks?"

I clicked my fingers at Todd to start writing some of this down while she was on a roll. But the roll was finished.

"What does a girl who ran away after graduation have to do with a gay man being poisoned fifty years later?" she said.

"Nothing, right?" I said. "Nothing. Poor Patti Ortiz isn't part of this, is she?"

"Maybe none of them are part of it," Todd said. "I mean, the murder. Maybe Tam Shatner didn't so much 'come to his fiftieth reunion' as he 'left Florida.' Maybe the trouble followed him here and all John Worth or one of his honeys did was try to get rid of the body."

"On a four-day time delay," I said. "That's a puzzle, but otherwise … maybe."

That's how Roger found us. Five of us with empty glasses and emptier expressions, all staring into the middle distance trying to … Well, trying to do a number of different things.

I was still stuck on the cat groomer aspect of John Worth's peculiar life.

Todd was tracing a finger over the photograph of Joan Lampeter, still trying to work out where he knew her from.

Della was Googling "lye" and gagging.

Noleen was trying to dredge up more memories of the story of Patti Ortiz.

Kathi was gazing at the crumpled bin bag, doing some deep breathing as she tried to stop minding it being there.

Flynn and Florian were snoring on the curtain poles.

Eighteen

The trouble with investigating pop-up fancy-dress shops the week after Halloween, though, is that they've all popped down again. Party City was shuttered with nothing but a flapping banner to show that it had ever been, and Halloween Central was in the throes of becoming Holiday Central, in time for Christmas. I banged on the door and asked one of the polo-shirted ... elves, I suppose; lately goblins but elves now for the duration ... how I could find out if a purchase of Halloween costumes had snagged anyone's attention.

The elf took a long flatulent suck on the dregs of his twenty-ounce soda and shook his head. "You wanna know if we noticed someone buying a costume before Halloween?" he said.

"Not *a* costume," Noleen said. Noleen had announced, somewhat surprisingly, that she was coming with me today. "Four costumes all the same. Memorable, huh?"

"Four?" said the kid. His scorn was palpable. "Try sixteen for a soccer squad. Or twenty for a baseball team." He took another drag on the straw. It whistled this time and that convinced him he was finished. He dropped the cup into the pile of receipts, garment tags, and dead leaves he was sweeping up and twirled his Swiffer back into go-mode.

"So you wouldn't remember selling four of these?" Noleen said. Todd had photographed the kilt outfit before he'd sneaked the bin bag back onto John Worth's porch later last night.

"I would remember selling four of those," the elf said flatly. "Since we didn't stock them. That's a Welsh man-skirt, right? Yeah, we didn't have any of them."

"No Welsh man-skirts?" I said. "Really?"

"You'd have to go up to Evangeline's for that," he said.

"Evangeline's!" I said. "Nolly!"

She nodded at me. Evangeline's was where the cutty sark came from.

"While we're here," I asked the broom elf, as he walked away. "Did you sell fake naked suits?"

"Huh?" he said. The lid came off the discarded soda cup and ice cubes rattled out and across the floor.

"Neoprene birthday suits with integral genitals," Noleen said. But I guessed there were three words in that that he didn't know and an expression he didn't understand and he merely shrugged, then swerved to Swiff up the ice cubes.

"What *is* Evangeline's?" I said when we were back in Noleen's car. It was her oasis in a germ-free life and, as a result, truly filthy. I had to kick my feet around like a scuba diver to make space for them amongst the chicken buckets and Pringles tubes.

"You ever been up to Old Sacramento?" she said, in reply.

"Old?" I said.

"Eighteen forty-nine," Noleen confirmed, but not in the way she thought she was. I considered telling her the New Town in Edinburgh was started in 1767, but no one likes a smart arse and Noleen's sweat-shirt today had a picture of a pink pony cantering away across a rainbow and the slogan *There Goes My Last Fuck*. When I'd seen her, I'd started a sentence asking her if it was the best choice to go intervie—

But I hadn't finished it.

∞

"Cool shirt," said the girl behind the bar at Evangeline's. And bar it was, even though this was a shop and not a saloon. It was polished mahogany, ten feet tall, twenty feet long, and only one of the arresting sights in here. The iron-cage lift to get up to the first floor had made me feel like Sam Spade. The flocked wallpaper, pannelling, arched doorways, and finials were straight out of a shoot 'em up Western. And the costumes stretched as far as the eye could see. Ghostbusters jostled can-can dancers, Disney princesses shared rails with Stormtroopers, gangsters and their molls were everywhere. One of the flapper dresses looked good enough to wear for real to a cocktail party. I checked the price tag. I couldn't afford it. So I drifted over to where Noleen was chatting up a serious Goth, packing Dracula masks into a cardboard box on the glossy bartop.

"I'm surprised you're still open," I said.

"Year-round," said the girl. She had so many rings on she was having a spot of bother with the Sellotape dispenser. I took it from her and screeched out a good long tongue of it, using it to reinforce the box. "This week's quiet, but once the holiday invitations go out we'll pick up again." Then she ran her tongue bolt along her lip rings making a noise like wind chimes. I grimaced an apology. She was right. I *had* been staring.

"Well, since it is your quiet week," I said, "we were wondering if you could help us."

"We're interested in some kilts and Tam O'Shanters that were bought here," Noleen said. "And leather vests and ... I don't know what you call them, but they're like fake naked suits? Men's?"

"Right, right," said Goth Girl. She was stapling shut the packaging on the Dracula masks, but her fingernail extensions made the stapler a bit of a challenge. Noleen took it away from her and cracked out a row of staples like a pro. "Yeah, the three kilts and the streaker suit," the girl said. "I remember."

I felt my heart leap. That's not just an expression, it turns out. I truly did feel my heart lift up in my chest and leave me with a bit of indigestion as it subsided again.

"Four," Noleen said, "wasn't it?"

"Four *hats*," said Goth Girl. "The plaid hats with the pom-poms and the red hair poking out?"

"Right," I said.

"But only three kilts," she said. "I remember because I asked the guy if he had miscounted and he basically told me to butt out."

"What a cheek!" I said. The box was full and I plied the Sellotape again while Noleen started on the next one. Goth Girl was leaning against the counter with her arms folded. "Big guy, right?" I thought about how best to describe John Worth. "Beefy, fair hair, fifties."

She shook her head, many bits of metal jangling. "Thirties at most," she said. "But beefcake, sure. Asshole. He looked at me like I was deranged when I asked if he wanted another kilt."

"He was lucky you had a brain cell free to notice what *anyone* was buying last week!" Noleen said. She turned to me. "It's pandemonium in Evangeline's right before Halloween."

189

"Oh well," the girl said. She shoved a load of unsold Frankenstein masks towards Noleen and me so we could keep at it. "It wasn't Halloween. This was a while back. September. Maybe even August. I told him there was time to order another kilt and vest to go with the fourth hat, but he told me he was just the errand boy."

"Just the errand boy," I echoed. Definitely not John Worth then.

"You've got a good memory," Noleen said.

"Is that why you're here?" said Goth Girl. "Double-checking?"

I had no idea what she meant and so I said nothing. Noleen looked at me, but I only shrugged.

"Because I already told the first cop all this," the girl went on.

"You think we'r—You made us as cops?" said Noleen.

"Undercover, right?" she said, looking again at the pony on the rainbow. "Where *did* you get that shirt? It's nice quality for an offensive one. Most of the really offensive ones are cheap crap. But that's decent." She was rubbing a bit of Noleen's cuff between her thumb and forefinger when a phone started playing "Despacito."

"You gonna get that?" Goth Girl said. And she was right. It was mine. Bloody Todd!

"Hello?" I said.

"Nolly's not picking up," came Kathi's voice on the line. "I've got something to tell you."

"Good or bad?" I said. Her voice was unreadable.

"Wrong question," Kathi said. "Significant or insignificant, and the answer is I don't know. It's something someone brought into the Skweek."

"An alteration?" I said. I'd been neglecting the sewing machine for the last couple of days.

"A kilt," said Kathi. "A real kilt. Wool. Weighs a ton."

"Nine pounds," I said.

"But it's just one and we're looking for four. So like I said, who knows if it means anything."

Noleen had extricated herself from Goth Girl's interest in the unusual quality of her shirt and from the much more worrying possible interest in whether we were undercover cops, as well as from the prospect of doing all the work for the rest of the shift to save the kid's nails and knuckles. She was over by the head of the staircase.

"Sorry," I said to Goth Girl over my shoulder, as I hurried to join Noleen. "Gotta dash. Got a lead."

"Nine pounds?" said Goth Girl. "Decapitation?"

$$\infty$$

"So obviously, Mike is on the case," I said as we barrelled back across the causeway over the Sacramento River towards Cuento. "She was at John Worth's last night and she's been to Evangeline's asking about the costumes. So we just need to take the kilt from the Skweek and hand it over to her." I waited. "Right?"

"Wrong," said Noleen. "Did you hear me saying our business was hanging by a thread, Lexy? We can't hand over a customer's belongings to the cops. We'll be shut down in a hot minute."

"Which is … fast?" I said. I wasn't being arsey. I honestly don't know. It depends whether it's melted or fried, to my mind. "Don't look at me like that. We don't like gay bashers, do we? We want them caught and punished, don't we? Well, then."

"How about this," she said again, as we were passing the farm stand at the turn-off to the motel. "Hey look, persimmons are in."

"*What* are in?" I said. "I thought persimmon was a colour."

"How about this," Noleen said. "We'll ask Mike how the case is going and if—IF—she mentions anything about kilts or plaids or Village

People vests or anything like that, we'll tell her about this kilt. I'll get Kathi to hold off on cleaning it until then."

"Why?"

"DNA, doofus," Noleen said.

"There won't be any DNA!" I said. "Doofus yourself. Listen. The streaker suit wasn't so the kilt looked authentic from below. It was so none of Tam's DNA got on the outfit."

"Why not burn it?"

"Because it's real," I said. "It's probably a family heirloom."

"Why not use a costume one from Evangeline's?" said Noleen. "Instead of risking a family heirloom."

"Because … the decoys were a late addition to the plan?" I said. "But that Goth reckoned the guy—What guy, by the way?—came in over a month ago to stock up."

"Let's see if the dry cleaning tells us anything," Noleen said, pulling up in the proprietors' parking space at the Last Ditch and leaping out. I took a bit longer, needing to shake a polystyrene box off my foot and wipe away some noodles from my instep. But I caught up as she climbed the stairs and we entered the Skweek together.

The kilt was laid out in all its glory—it's a woolly skirt, but it's part of my heritage—on the folding table but Kathi and Todd were not, as I had expected they might be, hanging over it like a pair of pathologists at an autopsy. They were both, rather, bent over Kathi's desk, staring at a screen.

"So you reckon this is the missing costume?" Noleen said. "What you looking at over there?"

"Della found Tam in Florida," Todd said. "He's been there since 1968. He must have hopped the rails right after graduation."

"Interesting," I said. "But what are you looking at over there?"

"What are we *not* looking at!" Todd said. "Privacy settings like Swiss cheese again and he was a party animal. Lots of photographic evidence of his life down there."

"And?" I said.

"And we've got this seriously wrong," Todd said. He lifted his head for the first time as Roger came in behind us. "Fire up the 'dar, baby-cakes," he said, "and tell me what you make of this here."

Roger took the seat and Noleen and I clustered in behind him, like adoring magi. The picture on the screen was Tam at some kind of party on a pier or the deck of a ship—ropes and riggings anyway, all hung with fairy lights. He had a cigar in his mouth and was grinning around it. His Hawaiian shirt was open to the waist and he had a chain round his neck and an arm round a small woman in Polynesian costume.

"Pray Away?" I said.

"See?" said Todd to Kathi. "Even Lexy can tell."

Roger clicked the right arrow. The next picture was the same night, the same party, the same cigar, shorter and horribly wet-looking at the business end. Tam was sitting at a poker table with three more red-faced grinning men. The short woman was gone but there was a blonde hanging over one of the other men, nibbling on his earlobe and mugging for the camera.

"Maybe he was closeted," Roger said. "Overcompensating? Over-friendly? Over-refreshed even. Uh-oh." He had swiped past a picture of Tam on a golf course, then one of him on a zip line, one of him posing with a roller-skate waitress at a Sonic, one of him in a Hooter's for God's sake, tucking a tip in a waitress's waistband, and now we were looking at a shot of him at some kind of auto expo.

"Wait a minute!" I said. "You two love your cars. That Jeep gets looked after like a sphynx kitten."

"It's not the car that's bothering me," said Roger. "It's the model."

Right enough the picture of Tam showed him, once again, with his arm around a girl, this one in high heels and swimsuit with a sash on.

"So?" I said. "Overcompensating, like you said. Of course he's going to pose with a Lara Croft in her bathing costume if he can. Closeted, like you said."

"Look at her face," said Roger.

"That's what I said," Kathi chipped in.

I looked at her face. She was smiling but it was pasted on her mouth like a police aware sticker on an abandoned car. And her shoulders were round her ears. She couldn't get away from Tam because one of his hands was clamped hard on her bare midriff and he was grinding her other hip against his groin. I looked past her false lashes, and smoky make-up right into her eyes. Where had I seen that look before? That look like she was trying to pretend Tam Shatner wasn't even there.

"He's not gay," said Roger. "Wasn't, I mean. He wasn't even just straight. He was a pig. A predatory, handsy, entitled, straight, white, male chauvinist pig. We've got this all wrong, people. How did we get this so wrong?"

"Aha!" I said. "Where's the yearbook?" I had realised where I had seen that miserable face before, that frozen grin and those hunched shoulders. Kathi produced the stolen volume and I flipped through the glossy pages until I found those Future Homemakers of America, and Nurses, and Librarians too. "Look," I said. "He's been that way his whole life. Look at him, the scumbag. He's not in any of the group shots with other boys. He just photobombed these ones where the girls couldn't stop him. Look at their faces! They hated him. They're completely blanking him. We were right about that. But we couldn't have been more wrong about why."

"Tell you something else for nothing," Kathi said, much more solemn. "Now it makes more sense that a guy like this is mixed up with a girl running away from her high school graduation and not being seen for fifty years, doesn't it?"

"Aw man," I said. "It certainly does."

"It muddies everything else, though," Noleen said. "I wanted the killer of poor lonely gay Tam caught. But if John Worth lured him here and bumped him off in the name of womankind..."

"But John Worth made Tam his vice president," I said. "All those years ago. John Worth was either just the same or at least turned a blind eye."

"He could have woke since," said Roger.

"But wait, wait, wait," said Todd. "We can't do this. We can't play judge and jury. We need to get that kilt over to Mike in case there's evidence on it. I'll do it if no one else wants to. It doesn't matter what the guy did or didn't do in his life. Killing people is wrong. Killing people with lye is way wrong."

"Now, wait a minute," said Noleen. "This isn't your call, Todd. This is Kathi's and mine."

"What about me?" I said.

"Because we own the business," Noleen said. "Not because of what's in our underpants."

But before the argument could go another round we heard feet pounding on the stairs and the door of the launderette blatted open.

"Stop!" It was a man I'd never seen before, breathing in big ragged gulps. "Stop. I made a mistake. I wasn't supposed to be here!" He looked wild-eyed around the Skweeky Kleen until his gaze fell upon the kilt still spread out on the folding table, its side straps unbuckled and its pleats in disarray.

Nineteen

The intruder wasn't the only one who could have been sprayed silver to make a day's wage on a boardwalk somewhere. The five of us were transfixed too. Whoever this was, he'd comprehensively blown his cool. It was hard to imagine a more definite sign that the kilt was dodgy.

"Is there a problem?" Kathi said. "I was just preparing the garment for processing."

"So … you haven't done anything yet?" the man said. He was really only a boy, I thought, now I'd had a proper look at him. "Is there a charge if I take it back?"

"No," Kathi said, "but you won't get a better deal in Cuento today, you know."

"It's just that, to be honest with you, my … boss … wanted me to have an alteration done as well so that's why I was supposed to go to Wash-n-Dry cleaners."

"Oh, we can do alterations here," Kathi said. "What was it you wanted to have done?"

"Hang on there a minute though, Kathi," I said. "I can hem a pair of jeans but I'm not sure I could tackle a kilt."

The man turned his wild eyes on me and I could have sworn each of his pupils was moving independently of the other as he darted glances all over. "Y—you?" he said. "Aren't you the Blame Game therapist? Or is there two of you?"

"Two of me?" I echoed.

"Sew Speedy has a team of experienced tailors ready for any project," Kathi said.

The man dragged his gaze away from me and back to her. "Yeah, but the thing is, you see, to tell the truth," he said, "my … boss … has an account at the Wash-n-Dry and they've done this kind of alteration before."

"Right," Kathi said. "Well, if you're sure then."

"I do honestly think it's best," the man said. He waited.

"Go for it," said Kathi, gesturing to the kilt.

"Uhhhhh, can I have a bag?" the man said. "Just to get it out to the car without … "

"Without … ?" said Todd.

"Um. I ran out without my duffel. To be frank, when my boss told me I'd … "

"You'd … ?" said Roger.

"Never mind," the man blurted. Then he rolled the kilt up like a tarp, opened his rain jacket, zipped it closed again over the wad of wool, and waddled off.

"What the fuck?" said Noleen once the echo of his footsteps on the metal stairs had died away.

"How many lies did he just tell?" said Todd.

"Well, to be honest, and tell you the truth, and be frank," I said, counting off on my fingers, "his boss hasn't got an account at a rival dry cleaners and he isn't getting a kilt altered and he's never had a kilt altered before."

"And his 'boss' isn't his boss either," said Roger. "It's Sunday. So like Noleen said, what the fuck?"

"If I had to guess," Noleen said, "the kilt is a family heirloom and the owner—the fake boss—couldn't stand it being covered in corpse juice, so he sent Boy Wonder to get it cleaned but for some reason the kid came here—twenty feet from where the body was found—instead of where he was supposed to go."

"You're a genius," Kathi said. "I bet that's it. You've cracked it, Nolls."

Roger and Todd both smiled. It's so easy for the happily married to enjoy others' happiness. Noleen just about managed to smile too, even though public protestations of affection weren't her favourite thing. I smiled like I had a coat hanger in my mouth. I've done far too much psychological training to get caught being sour about someone fizzing over with admiration for the love of her life.

"If only we knew his name," Todd said when all the hearts were warmed. "Then we could take this straight to Mike. This is a bona fide lead."

"We know his first name," said Kathi. "Because that's why he ended up here. I put the sign out this morning: fifty percent discount for all Andys."

"And I suppose someone took a photo of the kilt, right?" I said. Todd nodded but still looked puzzled. "So we're in with a good chance of getting a last name." No lightbulbs were on yet. "If we reverse engineer the tartan," I said, "we'll find a clan name. My money's on Worth."

"Is Worth a clan?" said Kathi. "Is Worth even Scotch?"

"No idea," I said. "But it's a better bet than Ortiz and Tafoya."

Todd was scrolling already. "Jesus Christ," he said. "These'd give you a migraine quick enough. No such thing as a Worth plaid, Lexy. Or Lampeter. Or Shatner. Or … O'Shanter, even."

"Try McShanter," I said.

"Nope."

"McLeod?"

"Why? Holy Jesus, that's one ugly-ass plaid."

"No reason. I just wanted you to see it. It's quite something, eh? Well, Téo, it looks like you just need to look up green tartans and work your way through."

"And what are you going to do?" Todd said. He looked a little bit bug-eyed already as he raised his eyes from his screen and blinked them hard.

"I'm going to Mike," I said. "She owes me. She didn't believe me about that bloody ring but it got us Tam's ID in the end. Who's coming with me?"

There was silence. Roger broke it. "Who's coming with you to tell Mike she owes you and remind her of when you were right and she was wrong?"

"Anyway, what makes you think she's working Sundays now?" said Noleen.

"It's a murder inquiry," I said. "She's probably working day and night."

"You watch too much TV," Noleen said. "City of Cuento doesn't have the money to pay Sunday overtime just because some scumbag's dumb enough to drink lye."

It was a good point well-put.

"So here's what we'll do," Noleen went on. "We'll take today to work out what to say to Mike tomorrow to fulfill our civic duty and keep the motel and laundromat out of it. Okay?"

"Sounds fair enough to me," I said. "The motel and the laundromat *are* out of it, apart from anything else. Tam got tangled in the beer-chilling rope of a houseboat moored in the slough downstream from where his body was dumped after he was killed God knows where, God knows why. This is nothing to do with the Last Ditch at all."

Roger was staring at me, chewing his lip.

"What?" I said.

"That's strange, isn't it?" he said. "The cutty sark on the 'burial ground' speaks to local knowledge, doesn't it? And lying in wait for Kimberly's horse to cross the footbridge speaks to real detailed local knowledge. But dumping a corpse upstream in a slough with a big old houseboat parked in it? That's sloppy. Raises questions."

"Raises one or two of the eleventy billion questions," I said. I looked over at Todd. He was hunched over his phone still sniffing out tartans. "I'll do a coffee run and then let's really put our heads down, eh? I want to speak to Mrs. Ortiz as well, if we can find her. Coffee first though." I waited for Todd to offer to go with me—or even for me, since I know he doesn't rate my coffee-ordering abilities—and right enough, my words did slowly permeate the fog of checkered wool forming behind his eyes.

"I'll drive you," he said. "Roger can you take this over? Blue squares with a green windowpane check and a white line through the green. I got up to Kerr. It's a pretty one. I could totally pull off a Kerr plaid."

"Oh you got up to Kerr, did you?" said Roger. "Just the Ms to go then."

Todd blew him a kiss and hustled me out the door.

∞

It was chucking-out time at the various churches of Cuento and the drive-thru at Swiss Sisters was backed up all the way to the railway underpass. We joined the end of the queue.

"So ... did Patti Ortiz run away to Florida with Tam Shatner?" I said.

"They both disappeared after graduation," Todd said. "It's a possibility. Now we know that Tam was a ladies' man, it's a definite possibility."

I reached over onto the backseat for the yearbook and flipped to the first photograph of Tam, there in the back row with the Future Homemakers. "And there *is* Patti," I said. "At the end of the row. Isn't she lovely?"

"Cute," Todd agreed. "Doesn't seem too much of a stretch for her."

Way up ahead of us someone got their coffee and left. Down here we edged into the dimness of the railway underpass.

I laughed and put the overhead light on so I could keep looking. "Right?" I said. "Future Homemakers of America! It's like they're saying 'I firmly believe some guy is going to marry me' and some of them deserve a medal for self-confidence. Jeez, look at this one! What's her ... Oh God, the poor thing. Gudrun Andersen. *Gudrun!*"

"It sounds even worse in your accent," Todd said. "Like you've swallowed a hair and you're trying to get it back up."

I lifted one side of my mouth to acknowledge the joke, but truth be told, I felt like I'd had enough attention on account of my accent for a while. "Sometimes things get better," I said, flipping another page.

"Like?" said Todd.

"Like these games mistresses could be married now," I said.

"Games mistresses!" Todd said. "Gimme a look." I handed the book over. "They do look happier than Mrs. Handmaid and Mrs. Surrender, don't they?" he said. He handed the book back and it fell open at the double page where the Moes, Patti, Joan, John Worth, and the tiny letters spelling out Tam Shatner's name were to be found.

"Does your gaydar work on women then?" I said.

"My gaydar doesn't work at all," said Todd. "It used to, before David Beckham and the grooming revolution. These days, unless it's as obvious as Tam at the motorshow, I'm sunk."

We inched forward another car length. "Jay-sis," I said. "There should be two windows. One for coffee and one for metroccinos." Todd had heard this complaint too many times to bother answering it. "Parp your horn."

"Don't say *parp*," Todd said, but he parped his horn, which helped. That is, it didn't do any good but it was pretty goddam loud here under the tunnel and it made me feel better.

"Anyway, you're too modest," I said. "What about Tahoe Guy yesterday?"

"Who?"

"Mo Heedles's nephew," I said. "Yesterday."

"He's not gay," Todd said. "He was checking out your ass until he saw me seeing him do it."

"Nah," I said. "He was throwing you off the scent. He clocked you, decided to mess with you, and leered at my bum. He practically puked when I turned round."

"Huh?" said Todd. "What are you talking about?"

"He looked at me like I was a cockroach in his cream puff."

"Don't say *cream puff*."

"P-syllid in his profiterole."

"The *P* is silent," Todd said. "And can you stop talking about critters while we're sitting in this dungeon of a railroad underpass?"

"Sorry!" I said. "Turd in his taco."

"Thank you. I saw that look. I thought he was overcorrecting the ass-ogle."

"Todd," I said. "That guy yesterday would have jumped your bones right there in his auntie's front garden if I hadn't been there spoiling it all. The ogle was yours."

"Wrong," said Todd.

"Shame we'll never get a chance to find out."

"I found out yesterday," Todd said. "That was a straight man. Outdoorsy, probably a gym bore."

"Lake bore," I said. "Blue Tahoe, remember?"

"Right, right," said Todd. "A surfer. Did you see his shoes?"

"What?"

"He had the straightest shoes I've ever seen in my life. If those games mistresses' yearbook photos were full body shots and we could see their shoes, they'd look like the dancing slippers of Liberace and Beyoncé's secret love child in comparison."

"Poor Beyoncé."

"Conceived in vitro and carried by a surrogate," Todd continued. "Funded by the Secret Federation of Gays."

"Them!" I said. "I thought they were concentrating on bringing floods and tornadoes."

"The elected ones are," said Todd. "I'm talking deep state."

"I do love you," I said. "You talk more crap straight and sober than most people do on mushrooms."

"I'm married in case you forgot," said Todd. "You should listen to your mother sometimes, Lexy. Before you wither on the vine."

A low blow, that. I absorbed it quietly.

∞

When we got back to the Skweek with a tray of outlandish coffee drinks and a bag of pastries that could close down a gym and open a heart hospital, we discovered that no one else had been wasting their time wittering on about Liberace. Roger, Noleen, and Kathi had all struck pay dirt.

"Lah-MAHNT," Roger said as soon as we were through the door. "Lah-MAHNT plaid."

"What?" said Todd. "Jeez, I got to Kerr then you swept in for the glory?"

"LAH-mnt," I corrected. "But yes, you're right." The picture of the kilt on Todd's phone and the picture on Kathi's laptop of the Lamont clan tartan were an exact match.

"And Mama Ortiz lives on K Street," said Noleen. "1200 block."

"And," Kathi said, "I found out a whole hell of a lot about Tam Shatner. Including why he came back to Cuento after all these years."

"Really?" I said, splitting a cinnamon roll with napkins over my fingers and handing her the big half. "Was it more than just the fiftieth reunion then?"

"Yup," said Kathi, looking pretty pleased with herself. "It wasn't the reunion at all. That was a coincidence. He came back to buy up a piece of real estate."

"He was moving back here?" I said.

"Nope," said Kathi. "There's no house on the property and the zoning is agricultural."

"Is he a farmer?" I said. "Is that what he did in Florida? Because they do say the citrus industry is shifting west, don't they?"

"They do?" Kathi said. "The stuff you know."

The truth was one of my clients was an orange grower with a brutal anxiety disorder and I'd learned more than I ever dreamed I'd need to know in order to help him navigate the vagaries of pests, prices, weather, and water.

"No," Kathi went on, "he was not a farmer. He was a waste management contractor."

"A what?" I said.

"A dustman," said Todd.

I flicked him the vees. "I know what it means," I said. "I was just emoting. Because that's like code for dodgy, isn't it? Waste management?"

"Not necessarily," said Kathi. "But it's not unheard of either. He was one of Central Florida's biggest *specialized* waste management contractors."

"Specialised how?" I said. "And how did you find this out?"

"I looked him up on White Pages and called the number," Kathi said. "Got a very talkative young woman by the name of Courtney who hates working on Sunday just because her boss is dead and the whole operation is headed—and I quote—'straight to Shitty City.' She confirmed everything we saw in the auto expo photo too, by the way. Thomas Shatner had an eye, two hands, and a long tongue for da ladieees."

"'Uck sake," said Noleen through a mouthful of muffin. "Tryina choke down some breakfast here."

"Never married," Kathi went on. "Not for lack of some Melania-grade gold-diggers giving it the old college try over the years. Never even lived with any of them. Just kept the rolodex turning. A real prince. So do you want an answer to your question?" I frowned. "About the specialism?" I nodded. "Roadkill disposal."

"Ewwwwww," said Todd. "Go back to talking about his tongue while we're eating, huh?"

"That is truly disgusting," I said. "But it must be lucrative if he was investing in farmland in California."

Kathi gave me a huge grin. "He wasn't," she said. "He was buying a very small parcel of land. It's surrounded by fields but it's not a field. And it can't be turned into a field because of ground contamination from former use as a homestead with a septic and propane tank and all that. But its residential zoning has lapsed."

"It doesn't sound like the start of an empire," I said. "Why would anyone buy it?"

"I do not know," said Kathi, "but the ever-helpful Courtney down there in Tampa provided the information that he had a watch on this property in case it ever came on the market and, when it did, she booked him a plane seat the same day."

"That is very, very interesting," I said.

"You're an easy mark," said Kathi. "Because I haven't even got to the interesting part yet."

"Parts," said Noleen.

"Both fascinating," added Roger.

"Go on then," I said.

"The little acre and a half parcel of land that's for sale that Tam Shatner has been waiting to buy for years on end is … the old Armour homestead."

My jaw dropped open. "Where the cutty sark was found?"

"The same. Guess what the other interesting fact is."

I chewed the last of my cinnamon roll and pondered. What were the options? A real estate deal had a buyer, a seller, and a plot of land. We knew two, so the last piece of the puzzle must be … "Who owns it?" I said.

"Don't know," said Kathi. "We can check that out tomorrow when the land registry office is open. But that's not it. The question is who's selling it."

"Isn't that what I said?" I said.

"I mean the realtor," said Kathi. "I mean which graduate of the class of sixty-eight is a real estate agent and currently has the old Armour homestead on the books."

I ran over them. "Mo Heedles," I said, thinking of her pristine house and its neutral tones. Her perfect hair and face and clothes.

"Close but no fluffy unicorn," Kathi said.

"Close to Original Mo?" I said. "You mean Also-Mo? Mo Tafoya with the prayer flags and the bong is a realtor?"

"That's California for ya," said Noleen. "Gotta love it, huh?"

Twenty

"You know that thing where you know you're missing something and you don't know what it is?" I said.

"Mm," said Todd. We were in his room now while he selected an outfit for our afternoon's mission.

"I've got a big stinking pile of that going on. It's like ... you know when you've got a bit of popcorn shell stuck on one of your teeth and you can't tell which one?"

"No. What?" said Todd. "For god's sake, Lexy, get your gums checked. *What*?"

"Okay! Jeez. Well, you know when you've got a hair on your face and you can't find it but you can't ignore it?"

"How many times have I offered to take you to my waxing lady?" Todd said. He was dressed now in a pair of grey-blue twill slacks of Roger's, a pair of black brogues, a white shirt, and a cashmere vee neck. And he had removed all his diamonds. He'd put plain silver hoops in his ears instead.

"I don't mean growing out of my face, Todd," I said. "God, you're annoying. I mean like an eyelash or something. Never mind. Why have you downgraded your earrings and then worn cashmere, by the way?"

"I haven't downgraded anything," Todd said. "I'm trying to look more Mexican. And there's no point taking earrings out if you've got pierced ears. It just makes you look like you're hiding something."

Of course we were planning to hide a great many things on this afternoon's expedition. It was pretty much a massive con, but I chose not to dwell on that. "Look more Mexican?" I said. "She'll know you're Mexican, Todd, from your perfect idiomatic Mexican Spanish."

"Okay, you caught me," Todd said. "I'm trying to look 'respectable Mexican,' like maybe I just went to church. Instead of 'me Mexican.'"

"Church?" I said. "Should I change too?" I was wearing my California winter uniform of yoga pants, Fuggs, and a hoodie.

"No point," said Todd. "You'll never pull it off. You better go with recent immigrant, clueless but harmless."

That, I could do. That, I could hardly avoid doing, even after nine months here. Whether I was wondering what day of the week Thanksgiving was this year, mixing up Labor and Memorial Day, or asking for a knife to eat a salad, I was basically the resident fool. A stick with a bell on the end wouldn't have been out of the question.

"What makes you think she'll talk to us?" I said. "She was fairly forthright on the phone."

"She didn't know who we were on the phone," Todd said.

"And who are we?"

He rubbed his hands with aftershave and slapped himself in the cheeks before answering. "I think we could go with 'people who found Tam's body,'" he said. "It's less to remember than a cover story."

∞

Mrs. Ortiz lived in a neat yellow house in old east Cuento. As we walked up the path, I saw a lace curtain flutter in the big living room window and by the time we were on the porch the door was open and she was facing up to us. She was tiny, truly miniscule, a little dot of a person, with white hair cut in a style so brutal it made Noleen's look like a salon do. She glared up at us out of miniature black eyes tucked into nests of wrinkles.

"I'm not buying," she said. "Don't care if it's God or brooms."

"We're not selling," said Todd. I was thinking Todd's church-going uniform was obviously a good one and wondering what about me looked like a broom-seller. "We want to talk to you about Patti." The door started to close.

"And Thomas Shatner," I added.

The door stopped moving and then slowly opened again.

"Did you phone?" she said. "Was it you who called and asked to speak to my daughter?"

"I'm very sorry about that, " Todd told her. "I was trying to find you and I didn't think about what would happen when I did find you. *Lo siento.*"

"*Lo sentimos,*" I said. "I was there too."

She sniffed deeply and then stood back to let us in. "You are forgiven," she told us. "Sit. I'll make coffee."

Her living room was as neat as the yellow siding. Her chair, to one side of the fire, had panniers on both arms, with remotes, knitting, a phone, and rolled magazines all ready for a quick draw. The bigger chair, on the other side of the fireplace, was dented from long use but its cushion was plumped up now and balanced on one corner. The table beside it was empty except for an amaryllis bulb just beginning to burgeon. Todd and I sat on the couch, facing the fireplace wall, from where a photograph of Patti, blown up to poster-size, looked back at us.

Mrs. Ortiz came back in minutes with a loaded tray. I recognised the beloved beverage of my youth—instant coffee—but not the plate of bright pink sponge cakes in paper cases that sat beside them. "Eat, drink," said Mrs. Ortiz, sitting down in her armchair. "Then speak."

The coffee, even with a dash of nostalgia, was truly disgusting, but the pink sponge cakes were so sweet—could they really be spicy?—that I couldn't taste it.

"So," said Todd after a sip of coffee that made him visibly shudder, "we understand that Patti left home years ago?"

"My Patti," said Mrs. Ortiz. "She went out to a party the night of her graduation and we never saw her again. She has never seen her nieces and nephews and her great-nephew now. I don't even know if she knows that her father is dead." She nodded at the empty chair on the other side of the fireplace. "I don't even know if *she* is dead. Sometimes I hope she is dead because that means she is not cruel. Sometimes I hope she is a cruel girl who left us and doesn't care because at least that means she is alive. Somewhere. With children and grandchildren of her own. But if she loves them, how can she not love us? Me?"

I couldn't think of one damn thing to say. And a glance at Todd showed him with tears in his eyes. It was Mrs. Ortiz who broke the silence.

"So what is it you came to ask me? All dressed up like a good boy." She smiled at Todd, who blushed as he smiled back.

"*No puedes engañar a una abuela,*" he said.

"I've lived too long to be fooled," said Mrs. Ortiz, but she said it a proud way, not a sad way.

"Tell us about Thomas Shatner," I said. "What you know of him from back then."

"He was a *bad* boy," said Mrs. Ortiz. "Not a boy with a leather jacket and a bottle of Scotch in his pocket. Not a bad boy to make a *mamá* afraid for her good girl. He was a *bad* bad boy. Mean. Cruel. I don't know what makes a person go wrong, but whatever it is, it had happened to Thomas before he got to high school and met my Patti. He was a bad, bad boy. No one liked him."

"And yet he was the vice president senior year," Todd said. "Someone liked him."

"John Worth," said Mrs. Ortiz. "But he didn't like Thomas. I think Thomas had something, you know what I'm trying to say?"

"Had something *on* John Worth?" I said. "Like something to blackmail him over?"

"*Blackmail* is a big word," said Mrs. Ortiz. "But there is no other way to make it sensible." She sighed. "Do you think I'm a foolish woman to be saying all these things about children's lives from fifty years ago?"

"Not at all," I said. "We think the students' lives, as you say—their problems and squabbles, from fifty years ago—are absolutely at the heart of what happened to Thomas Shatner last week."

"It's just, you see, that I spoke to them all, back then. Looking for clues. Looking for Patti. And then I've thought it over and over so many times all these years. It's all in my head and it won't go away."

"So what did they tell you, *abuela*?" said Todd. "Mrs. Ortiz, I mean."

"*Abuela* is good," she said. She gave me a flick of a look. "You can call me ma'am." But she was kidding.

"Well, ma'am," I said, winking at her, "I'd like you to start further back than what the other students told you after the graduation. I want

212

you to start—if it's not too painful to talk about her—with Patti and Thomas at school together."

"I love to talk about her," Mrs. Ortiz said. "She was my baby. My son came early in my marriage and then nothing for ten long years. Then my miracle. My Patti."

I did a quick calculation and upped her age from the eighties, where I had put her, into the nineties. Old enough to have been married, say, eleven years in 1950.

"And she *was* a good girl," her mother said. "She wasn't a genius or an angel and she wasn't going to be a movie star, but she was my good, good girl. And I loved her."

It was kind of wonderful to hear a mother being so clear-sighted and so unsickening about her only daughter and a long lost daughter at that.

"And everyone else loved her too," Mrs. Ortiz said. "It was different back then. For us. For … people like us." She gave Todd a questioning look, which I intercepted.

"You can talk," I told her. "I'm an immigrant but I know—"

"*Querida!*" said Mrs. Ortiz. "You are not an 'immigrant.'"

"That's what I was just going to say!" I said.

"There were names they called us," Mrs. Ortiz said. "Me and my good man who worked so hard. Sometimes it felt like the harder we worked, the more bad names. Like working hard made them hate us. So when Patti joined the junior class council and helped to make the decorations for the junior prom and she went to the junior prom with a nice boy who picked her up in a nice car and came to the door and said hello to her father and me? We were more happy than I can tell you."

"So … not Thomas Shatner?" I said. "The nice boy?"

213

"No one went to the junior prom with him," she said. "A boy like that. Then senior year came and she was on the senior class council too, and her grades were good. Not great, but good. And her friends were here every day after school, playing records and giggling. Nice friends, from good homes. Good girls."

"Mo and Mo?" I said. "And Joan?"

"The four of them," said Mrs. Ortiz. "See? I said to my husband. See? She is not lonely. She doesn't need us to move to a house near your cousins. She is happy here. He was worried about her. About where she would find a husband. About whether she would marry one of those … "

"*Gabachos*," I said, and she rewarded me with a small smile.

"That night," she said. "That graduation night, we argued."

"You and Patti?" said Todd.

"Me and Joe," said Mrs. Ortiz. "Her father. We argued about her going to the dance. The senior dance. Because she wasn't going with a nice boy who picked her up in a nice car. She was going with those girls. I told him it was sweet—all four of them going together in a rented car—but it wasn't the usual way. He found it strange and we argued."

"The girls all went to the graduation dance together?" I said. I turned to Todd. "*Is* that strange?"

Todd shrugged. "Not these days. Back then? Why did they do it, Mrs. Ortiz?"

"So that John Worth didn't have to choose," she said. "Or maybe better to say so that John Worth didn't *get* to choose."

"So they all went to the dance together," I said again. "But Patti didn't come home?"

Mrs. Ortiz screwed her face up. "That doesn't sound right," she said. "Patti was the one who wanted to come home. After the dance, all the kids were going to park somewhere on the edge of town. But Patti had promised me and her father she wouldn't do that. So she came home. She left to come home."

"Wait," I said. "You're telling me the other three girls just let her walk home on her own in the dark while they took the car off to park somewhere and keep the party going?"

"Not on her own," Mrs. Ortiz said. "Someone offered to escort her."

"Thomas Shatner," said Todd.

She shook her head. "John Worth," she said. "He swore on his Bible that he walked her to the stop sign at the end of that street." She pointed with a jabbing motion. "And watched her walk up the path and onto the porch. He swore."

"And Tam?" I said. "Was he with the others? Parked up somewhere, partying?"

"They said no," Mrs. Ortiz told us. "They said he left the dance at nine o'clock. He was drunk and the teachers threw him out. No one saw him later."

I considered this while I finished off the last of the pink cake and grey coffee. Todd looked at me as if I was eating worms. My theory that Patti and Tam ran away to Florida together had taken a bit of a hit from this news of him disappearing early on and Patti making it to her front porch with John Worth watching. Still, since we were here, I was going to check.

"And in the time since, Mrs. Ortiz," I began, "have you ever had any sense of where Patti might be? Has anyone ever thought they'd seen her? Anywhere? Have you ever had anyone else look for her?"

"Have I ever had anyone look for her?" The woman was glaring at me, but I honestly did not know what she was reacting to. Was it stupid to doubt that she'd turned the earth upside down looking for her little girl, or was I being Marie Antoinette to think this woman in her modest little house could afford to employ private detectives? "I spent every penny I earned on posters and radio ads," she said. "I hired people. I wrote to every cousin and cousin of cousin in the country, sent pictures ... then later the internet. Such sadness. You would not believe the sadness of the *mamás* and *papis* looking for their *niños*."

"And did you ever hear anything?" I said. Todd was dumbstruck. But then he's an anaesthetist, not used to asking tough questions of people.

"A few photographs of pretty girls," said Mrs. Ortiz. "None of them my Patti."

"And how about Florida?" I said. "Do you have cousins there?"

"I have cousins who moved there," she said. "But it's a big place. Why?"

"That's where Tam Shatner went after he left Cuento," I told her. "That's where he's been all these years until he came back here last week for the high school reunion. Well, not for the reunion exactly. But while it was on."

Todd took a sharp breath in then, making both of us look at him.

"This place," he said, "where all the kids went to park after the dance. You said it was on the edge of town. Do you know exactly where?"

Mrs. Ortiz nodded and pointed. "Out that way," she said, pointing. "There's nothing there now. Back then the old house was still standing. But it wasn't the house they cared about. They liked ... oh, now what was it? I'm getting old. I'm not so sharp. There was a story."

"An Indian—" Todd began.

"—burial ground!" she finished for him. "That's it. An Indian burial ground at an old farm out there. I don't see why a cemetery is a good place to go with a sweetheart, do you? When we were young,

Joe and me, we used to sit on the edge of a cliff looking out at the sea, breathing in flowers and listening to birds. Not looking at graves and hearing ghost stories."

"You were the wise ones," I said. "When did he die?"

"Only last year," she said. "He couldn't wait any longer. I can't wait forever. If you can tell me what happened to my Patti, maybe I will just lie down on my soft bed and go home."

"Or," I said, "if we find her, you can stay right here and catch up with all her news."

Mrs. Ortiz shook her head. "My Patti wasn't a cruel girl," she said. "She would never do this to me. When I go home, soon, I will join her like I will join Joe."

∞

"Do you think she believes it?" I said to Todd out on the doorstep. "That she'll be seeing Patti again on the other side?"

"No doubt."

"Hmph," I said.

"You don't?" said Todd.

I shrugged. "You're the expert. Speaking of which, what's the explanation for those fairycakes?"

"Don't say *fairy*cakes!"

"Cupcakes, rock cakes, scones, cookies."

"*Tres leches*," Todd said. "Delicious." I snorted. "Okay, better than the coffee at least," he said instead.

"She loved having someone to feed," I said. "Fifty years, Todd."

We drove off in silence. But he didn't take me home. Instead we went back to the old Armour homestead and got out of the Jeep and stood there on the mound and stared at where the cutty sark had lain and thought of Patti.

After five minutes, Todd punched me lightly on the arm. "Let's go," he said. "Tomorrow we take this to Mike. Agreed?"

"Deffo."

Twenty-One

Damn my Presbyterian work ethic! Or maybe, more honestly, damn my lack of belief that I could make a living as one of the therapists in such a therapist-stuffed town as Cuento! When a woman had phoned in sobs asking if I could do an eight o'clock appointment on Monday morning, I should have told her I kept banker's hours and could squeeze her in at ten for a consideration. I shouldn't even have had to call them banker's hours. They were just civilised hours, in my opinion. Eight o'clock was breakfast time. But here, where everyone hit the gym before five, eight o'clock on a Monday morning saw the week already curling up round the edges.

Here she was, wringing a hanky in her hands on my back porch. I was on the phone to Todd, so I lowered my voice.

"You can go without me," I said. "I can't stop you. On the other hand, if you take me, I'll soak up some of Mike's…"

"Bile?" said Todd. "Why are you whispering?"

"There's a client outside waiting."

"And what's that clacking noise?"

"I'm peeking through the blinds at her. She's crying."

219

"So? You're used to that, aren't you?"

"I was," I said. "I've forgotten, these last few months, what it's like to talk to people in acute distress. But this is some acutely acute distress. She's not just weeping. She's blowing snot bubbles and honking like a goose. I better go."

"Tell her she should have started therapy back when you'd have laughed at her and she might have avoided this," Todd said. "I'll see you at lunchtime."

"What are you going to do this morning if you're saving Mike to share with me?"

"I'm going up to the hospital."

"Great!" I said, loud enough to let the snottery woman on my porch know I was there. I waved in case she could see me.

"Not to work," said Todd coldly. "Not even to take a meeting about work. To see John Worth, in case he's conscious again and feeling chatty."

"Good idea," I said. "You could always stop by, though."

Todd hung up without saying more. I was on his side about the whole work thing, much as he never seemed to see it that way. He was an anaesthetist with cleptoparasitosis, a big scary word, but one that rendered him equal to a clown who was scared of needles or a teacher who didn't like airports. In other words, absolutely fine. Operating theatres were famously insect-free. And Todd wasn't so far gone that he didn't know that. The trouble was, cleptoparasitosis was a psychiatric diagnosis, and when the hospital's lawyers had heard those two big scary words, Todd was out on his bum sooner than they could say *mad bug dude who'll ruin us all*. Words of one syllable each, but terrifying.

I switched my phone to silent and went out the back door where my eight o'clock—this country!—was waiting.

"Hiya," I said, with a big smile on my face. "Dorian?"

220

"Lexy, right?" she said. "Thank you for seeing me."

"Of course," I said. "Come in. Make yourself comfortable. We've got some stuff I need to do, I'm afraid, but it won't take long."

It took longer than a therapeutic hour (aka fifty minutes) had to spare, mind you. I got her signature on a sheaf of papers, told her all about how I wasn't affiliated with any HMOs or insurance companies but she should check her own policy for possible reimbursements, and finished up with the required spiel about why and when I'd suspend confidentiality and call the cops on her. That bit's usually no more than awkward but this woman paled, swallowed, stopped crying, which was a bright side, and said in a wavery voice, "What do you mean by *harm?*"

I blinked. No one had asked me what *past incidents of harm to a child, elder, or vulnerable adult or threat of future harm to self or others* meant. I assumed they all knew better than me.

I glanced at my phone all the way over there on the windowsill out of the way and wished it was closer.

"But what counts as a child?" she said. "Or a vulnerable adult? Is it eighteen? Twenty-one? Vulnerable how?"

I stared at her, trying not to make it seem like I was staring at her. Which was it? Had she hurt a child? Or was she planning to shove someone off a bridge? Or, much more likely, was she simply very anxious and trying to parse my words for no pressing reason.

"Why don't you tell me what's wrong?" I said. "And then we can take it from there."

She folded her mangled hanky into a tiny little square, then pressed it into her palm and made a fist around it. "But if I tell you what's wrong and you decide it's harm and it's a child, you'll report me."

"Have you assaulted a minor?" I said.

"No."

"Or a senior? Have you withheld food, drink, warmth, or shelter from a frail relative?"

"No!"

"Well, that's that sorted out then at least. Are you planning to kill yourself?"

"No."

"Or someone else?"

"Probably not," she said. "But I see what you mean. Thank you. Okay. Thank you. I can talk now?"

"You can talk now."

She took a huge heave-ho of a breath. "I think my daughter's turning tricks."

"That is not where I thought we were going," I said. "That must be terribly upsetting. But it's not something that triggers the suspension of confidentiality. You can rest assured on that score. Tell me about it, if you'd like to."

"You see, I thought when you said *child* that she is my child, and when you said *harm* well I think that is harm. Serious harm. I can hardly believe it and I can't tell my husband. It would kill him. That's what I meant about not being sure if I was going to kill someone, you know? Because if I told him, this would surely kill him. She's his little girl. His baby girl. He adores her. And now she's ... selling herself like some low-life."

I nodded and kept my thoughts to myself. Thoughts like: all that daddy's girl crap didn't strike me as adorable or even that much at odds with the kid's plunge into poor choices. Thoughts like: *low-life* was subjective.

"So what makes you suspicious?" I said.

"She's hiding something," Dorian told me. "And she has all this *money*."

"But she might not be a tom—tart—pros—sex worker," I said. "It could be … all sorts of things." Drugs, I was thinking. Or a bank heist.

"I suppose she might have knocked over a bank," said Dorian. "She's a bold girl. But she's not tech-savvy. She couldn't run an online scam to save her life."

I was going to have to say it. "Drugs?"

"No way. She's outdoorsy. Ever since she was a little girl. That's why she came back to Cuento for college. Because of the mountains. And the lakes. And all the facilities. She's a bit of a health nut, if I'm honest. If my husband and I have a bottle of wine on a Friday night she's on the phone to Al-Anon. Practically."

"Well, but if she *is* such a health nut," I said. I was warming to Dorian. That was my kind of talk. Most people round here would have said *honours herself through her choices*. "I mean, sex work isn't the healthiest way to live, by and large."

But saying it right out like that had tipped Dorian over the edge again. She shook out the wadded up hanky—which I could tell had no absorbency left from the way it flapped like a damp flannel—and buried her face in it.

"How long has it been going on?" I said. "Does she live with you? Or how did your suspicions first get raised?"

"No, she doesn't," Dorian said. "I come from Cuento, but I moved to Colorado when I married. I still have family here. When my daughter came back here, I was happy! I thought she'd have relatives to look out for her! But then I saw this big deposit in her account and when I asked her about it, she wouldn't tell me where it had come from."

"Hang on," I said. "You saw a transaction in her account? How did you manage that? Are you a guarantor?"

"She's my daughter!" Dorian said. "We have no secrets."

"Right," I said. "Okay. So you have the passwords to each other's accounts. Okay. That's nice."

She was squirming. "She can't get into my account," she said. "Why would she need to?"

"Right," I said again. "But in a way it's good that she dumped the cash in her account, isn't it? I mean, if she had anything to hide, she would have hidden it."

"Well," Dorian said. She was squirming even harder now. She got up and went to put her hanky in the bin. Then she went all the way over to the other side of the room to get a fresh one, even though there are boxes of the things everywhere. "She didn't know I could see in there. She found out when I called her to ask where the five hundred dollars came from."

"Five hundred?" I said, briefly thinking I was in the wrong business.

"Twice," her mother said. "And she wouldn't tell me where it came from. All she said was that I would regret knowing and she didn't want to see the way I would look at her if she told me. So I got on a plane and came right out here. As anyone would. But face-to-face it was even worse. She was crying and begging me to stop asking. She said she was ashamed and she didn't know what had gotten into her. But she won't tell me!"

"Right," I said. "Okay. Well now, Dorian, I'm going to say something now you might not like. But it's absolutely what I believe and I think it will help you."

Telling her to calm down, back off, apologise to her daughter for invasion of privacy, and learn some relaxation techniques went down about as well as a shot of lye in a latte. I had never before tried to ground a helicopter parent and confiscate her licence to fly. It was interesting, but by the time I was finished, I was nearly looking forward to Mike in comparison.

"When are you going back to Colorado?" I said.

"When this is straightened out!" she told me. "I bought an open ticket and rented a car on a renewable daily deal."

Where did these people get all their money? Not from working, presumably, or else where did they get all their time? Cutting to the chase, I agreed to see her again, with her daughter in tow, in the middle of the week.

∞

"You are all crazy," I said to Todd, as we headed down the street to the cop shop. We were on foot. You have to make the most of the days that aren't too hot to bear in Cuento. Today was a pleasant sort of a light jumper and cleverly wound scarf kind of a day, maybe shading into a cute wooly cap and mittens later when the sun went down. Needless to say, Todd had a quilted coat on that reached from his neck to his knees and had put down the earflaps on his skiing hat. But he agreed that a stealthy approach was best.

"Who all?" he said.

"Who do you think? Americans."

"Ah, the honeymoon's over," said Todd. "I remember when you loved us."

"Win me back," I said. "Apply some of that can-do spirit and entrepreneurial vim and win me back again."

"Meh, maybe later," said Todd. He knew I didn't mean it. And to be fair, offering counselling and therapy isn't the classic way to meet the balanced portion of any population. I cast my mind over the people I knew best. Noleen was Mrs. Average apart from the aggression. Roger was as normal as they come. Della and Diego could have starred in adverts for breakfast cereal. Mike was … Nah, Mike was nuts. And here we were asking the dispatcher if she was available for us to talk to. Who knew where this would end?

Mike came out to the front reception area and stood chewing her lip and treating first me, then Todd, then me again to long speculative looks.

"Come on back," she said at last, buzzing us through to where the interview rooms lay. "Get you anything from the machine?"

I snorted. I had exhausted the menu of drinks from the Cuento cop shop long ago and they all tasted like they'd been swallowed once already. The chicken soup, twice.

"No really," Mike said. "We've got a matcha and a chai in there now. Not bad as far as vending machines go."

We chose one each, for research purposes. Mike edged back in with two cups and handed them over. I took a sip.

The closest I can get to describing it is to say if someone boiled spinach, then used the water to wash out those bootees dogs wear in icy weather, let it cool to tepid, then poured it into a cup with some cheese, they'd end up with a treat compared to the Cuento City Police instant matcha.

"It's something else, isn't it?" Mike said. "It's the eighth wonder of the world. So what can I do for you?"

"It's about Tam," I said. "Thomas Shatner."

"Oh yeah?" said Mike. "Well, that case is juuuust about closed. A few Ts to cross and Is to dot. But pretty much closed."

"Good," I said. "Is there a suspect in custody?"

"No," said Mike. "Why don't I ask the questions?"

"Good plan," said Todd. "Is that because you think it was John Worth and he's still in ICU?"

"How do you know John Worth is in the ICU?" said Mike.

"Have you been back to his house?" I said. "If Becky's staying by his bedside, she might not have found the bin bag on the porch. There's a bin bag on the porch with a Halloween costume in it, including a hat the same as the one that was on Tam's head when you pulled him out of the slough."

Mike nodded. I had no idea if she knew all this already; cops are spectacular at looking unsurprised no matter what you tell them. "Like I said, how about if I ask the questions?"

"Agreed," I said. "Do you know about the real estate deal?"

"What real estate deal is this?" she said.

"Tam was back in Cuento to buy a plot of land," said Todd. "The plot of land where we found the cutty sark that your colleague didn't seem all that interested in."

"Which is also the place where the class of sixty-eight gathered after their high school graduation, on the last night that Tam Shatner and Patti Ortiz were ever seen in Cuento."

Unless I was very much mistaken, cop rules or no cop rules, Mike's eyelids did give a tiny feather of a lift at some bit of that.

"The Armour homestead?" Mike said. "Someone's yanking your chain. It's not for sale."

"Really?" I said. "Or … someone was yanking Tam's chain to lure him back here. It's listed by Mo Tafoya, by the way. Worth checking out."

"Checked," said Mike. She spat the word through her teeth. "You don't need to worry that we've missed something, Ms. Campbell. We didn't miss anything."

"You missed the class ring," I said.

And again Mike's face registered some tiny outward sign of inner thoughts. This time it was a squinching down rather than a flaring up, but it was there.

227

"So who have you pegged?" Todd said. "If not John Worth or Mo Tafoya, how about Mo Heedles? Or Joan Lampeter?"

"How the hell did you get those names?" Mike said. "Is there a leak in my stationhouse?"

"You mean we're right?" I said.

"No," she said. "You're wrong."

We waited.

"Well?" said Todd at last. "Are you going to tell us or do we need to wait for the *Voyager* app to update?"

Mike took a long time considering whether to say any more. "I guess I owe you for the drinks," she concluded at last, pointing to the brimming cups of wrongness on the metal table. "We took a long hard look at all of those gals. And there's nothing. We got their phone records—nada. Their financials—nada."

"No transactions at Evangeline's Costume Mansion?" I said.

"No! Jesus," said Mike. "None."

"So who was it then?" said Todd.

"It was suicide."

"Suicide," Todd repeated. "Thomas Shatner stapled a hat to his head and killed himself?"

"Yes," said Mike. "It's unusual to staple a hat to your own head, but he was full of drugs. He probably never felt a thing."

"You're serious?" I said. "You're seriously serious? Suicide? Why?"

"Because he hated them all and wanted to spoil the reunion," Mike said. "He was one twisted individual."

"But dedicated," said Todd. "Taking his life to wreck a party."

"No," Mike said. "He was suicidal anyway. But he chose to come back here and do it at the reunion to wreck everyone's happiness. A real prince."

I nodded, thinking. What she was saying was arse gravy of the first order, but her take on Tam overall sounded sincere.

"And why the hat?" I said.

Mike nodded, also thinking. Thinking what she could serve up that I would swallow, I reckoned. "That's what clinched it," she went for in the end. "He knew what the theme was. For the porches. Of the alumni."

I chewed that over for a bit. Could I swallow it without choking?

"Look," Mike said, leaning to one side and easing her phone out of her hip pocket.

I leaned forward and Todd leaned in and we both looked. There was Mo Heedles's porch with the rocking chair occupied. There was Mo Tafoya's porch in the next shot, just the bobble on top of the hat on top of the Jimmy wig showing. Then came the extravagant wrap-around porch of the Worths' house and another be-tartaned zombie, followed by a house I didn't recognise at all, except for the outfit on the dummy propped on the deckchair beside the front door.

"Just the four?" I said.

"Yeahhh," said Mike. "Not much of a success rate for the alumnus committee."

"Well, it's thankless, isn't it?" I said. "Committee work."

"Even without suicidal weirdos wrecking everything," Mike agreed.

"So he shot himself in the belly, standing on the banks of the slough, dressed in a Jimmy wig, hoping he'd get some of his class-mates in trouble?" I said.

Todd said nothing. His eyes were closed as if this was a séance and he was Madam Zelda, communing.

"Yes," said Mike. Well, she had to, I supposed. I wasn't supposed to know the bullet wound was fake, since I wasn't supposed to have found out the autopsy results via Roger and his pathologist stalker. Ditto the hypostasis and other evidence of how he'd spent his first four dead days.

"And—just one last thing," I said. "What happened to his class ring?"

"Oh that," said Mike. "We found it."

Todd opened his eyes. I opened mine as wide as they would go.

"We do take notice of what witnesses tell us, Ms. Campbell," she said. "We sent a diver back down to search more thoroughly and he found it."

"When was this?" I said. "I didn't see anyone."

"No," said Mike. "You were out. We were glad we didn't disturb you."

Twenty-Two

"That was a load of complete, dried, pelleted, bagged, and tagged bullshit, wasn't it?" I said to Todd as soon as we were out of the cop shop and scurrying homeward. It was raining. It doesn't rain much in Cuento. It doesn't rain enough in Cuento, in fact, given the gallons it takes to grow an almond and the raging wild fires every summer.

"Ssshhhh," Todd said. "I'm concentrating." He whipped out his phone and began talking into it very fast. "NSA 042. Phew. I'm crap at remembering numbers. 1960s ranch, U-shaped drive, pepper tree in the front yard, north-facing street. Mint-green paint with black trim and white accents. Grey composite shingle roof. Pool."

"Good thinking, brain box," I said. "This is the fourth house with the porch zombie, is it?"

"Which I'm guessing is Joan Lampeter's, don't you think?"

"So what do we do? Ring up your pal on the force and get them to run a plate?"

"Mike's the closest thing I've got to a pal on the force," Todd said. "The license plate is just for confirmation if we find it."

"How *do* we find it?"

"We go for an online stroll."

"A mid-century ranch with a composite roof, a pepper tree out front, and a pool in the back?" I said. "In Cuento? You'll have to carb up. How did you know there was a pool, by the way?"

"Crystal Clear Pool Service sticker on the gate to the side yard," Todd said.

"Side yard!" I said. I loved that there was a word for that sliver of dirt between one outsize house on its midget plot and the next. Only people determined to look on the bright side and be delighted with life could have come up with it. It was like giving a French name to a scoop of vanilla ice cream that melted and turned your pie crust soggy, or the way they called everything a holiday even when you didn't get a day off work. Valentine's Day! Halloween! 420! Life was a constant party.

"You could let some of these go by, you know," Todd said. "You don't have to pick up on every tiny little thing."

"I was marvelling!" I said. "I was being nice. God almighty, Todd, if *you* ever went to Dundee *you'd* never stop whinging. The weather, the food, the drinks, the drunks, the buses, the drunks on the buses…"

"The no mosquitos, the no black widows, the no brown recluses…"

"The midges," I said.

"What are they?" Todd's shoulders came up round his ears.

"Nothing," I told him. "Sorry. Forget it. They're mythological. Like haggis."

"Haggis isn't mythological," Todd said. "They sell it in cans in that deli in Sacramento."

"Yeah, but hairy wild haggises running round the hills, always in the same direction because they've got one leg shorter than the other, aren't real. And neither are midges. Trust me."

"What choice do I have?" said Todd. I reached over and squeezed his arm. "So," he said, "while you go and tell a load more clients to stop whinging and pull their necks up—"

"Socks."

"—I'll start scouring the map of Cuento for Joan Lampeter's house."

"And when I knock off for the night, if you're still looking, I'll call Crystal Clear and find it out that way," I said.

"They won't tell you," Todd said.

"Let's see."

"Let's you, me, and fifty bucks see," Todd said, by which time we were back at the Last Ditch and going our separate ways.

∞

My two o'clock was the overanxious empty-nester to be. I talked her down from the wire and then up out of the doldrums and sent her on her way. My three o'clock was a thrice-divorced guy who had only just realised that if he didn't stay married to one of them one of these times, he was going to die alone. His current woe was that the "gals" who were swiping him right these days were only ten years younger than him and he didn't want them. "Shoulda had a kid or two," he said. "Like they were always bitching to make me." I sent up selfless thanks that he hadn't. Selfless because his kids would be clients by now, and thanks because I had enough daddy issues to deal with on my roster and wasn't looking for more. My four o'clock was a woman I wish I could have introduced to my three o'clock, but not in a swiping sense. She had multiple sclerosis and she had never met the right guy to bitch at about having children. "Who'll look after me?" she said. "When it gets bad, I mean."

I took a long look at her. She had a BMW key ring, so presumably she had the car to match it parked out front. Noleen would love that. A Beemer in the car park would give the Last Ditch a certain cachet. And she was wearing shoes with red soles, I noticed as she recrossed her ankles. I couldn't remember what brand they were, but I knew it wasn't Target.

"Are you rich?" I said.

"I'm comfortable," she answered, bridling. No one ever says they're rich, I've noticed.

"Do you have young relatives of any kind? Not children, but nieces and nephews? Second cousins maybe?"

"I do," she said.

"Are they rich?"

"They're living in a shoebox in San Francisco despite being executives in the finance sector," she said.

"Tah-dah!"

"Are you seriously going to tell me to count my blessings because I'm middle-aged with a degenerative neurological condition instead of young and healthy and strapped for cash?"

Yeah, because I'm a moron, I thought. "No, because that would be silly," I said. "I was only going to suggest that you could make a difference to your life and theirs if you reconfigured things. Get them out of the rent trap and get yourself some support."

"You're asking me to give my nephew and his wife the power of life and death over me?" she said.

"No," I said again, beginning to see why she had never found the right guy. I wasn't sure the guy existed who would meet her standards. "I was going to suggest you buy a duplex, half for them and half for you, and tell them they'll inherit the lot if you die at home. Then, when you need it, get a nurse too."

"I can't imagine that working," she said.

"Read some Agatha Christie," I told her. "They're full of rich old relatives who hold the purse strings and young hopefuls dancing attendance."

"Don't they usually get bumped off?" she asked, which was a fair point.

"In fiction," I said. "In real life, there would be a bit of a commute for them and a hell of an incentive to keep you happy if you set the will up in a wily enough way. But let's not get bogged down in a future that might never happen." She looked askance. "You might go under a bus tomorrow," I pointed out. "Or you might walk out of here and meet the love of your life who'll care for you tenderly forever."

"Or there's always Oregon," she said. "Which is why I wanted to talk to you. Because if I mention it to anyone else, they get upset and embarrassed."

"Oregon?"

"Assisted suicide."

"We can certainly discuss that," I said. "It might put your mind at rest to have procedures in place that cover all the unknowns."

Then followed twenty-five of the most depressing minutes of my life. And I've spent my professional life counselling people with lives in the toilet and hearts full of the pain that brings. She had a clipboard with her and she'd made a flowchart. Every arrow led to death no matter what boxes she put in the way.

"But promise me one thing," I said. "Speak to your nephew before I see you again. Sound him out. You might find your relatives are happy to help if it'll take some of the squeeze off them."

"Promise you?" she said. "Aren't you therapists usually telling us to stop making promises because they always get broken? My last therapist told me the only way to avoid the pain of broken promises was never to make them and never to believe them."

"I'm not your usual therapist," I said. "I think the way to avoid broken promises is never to break promises. But who's going to pay to hear that?"

∞

When I got to Todd's room, huddled into my waterproof coat with the hood tied round my face, there was a note on the door—*bring your sewing fingers to the Skweek*—and when I had splashed through the puddles and up the slippery metal steps, I found Kathi and him at the sewing machine engulfed in a sea of foaming white ruffles roughly the size of a VW Beetle. Todd was battening down about half of it with a body slam but Kathi was still in it up to her armpits.

"What's that?" I said, taking my coat off and grabbing a tissue to dry my face.

"What do you think it is?" Kathi spat. "You've got Kleenex confetti all over you, by the way."

"I honestly have no idea," I said, rubbing the bits of tissue off in balls and then carefully transferring the balls to the wastepaper basket. Kathi didn't tolerate the kind of mess some pellets of tissue would make on a pale grey floor.

"It's a quincañera dress," said Todd. "And it's getting away."

"It's a dress?" I said, rolling my sleeves up. "What are you trying to do with it?" I waded into it on the other side from Todd, slowing down to a stagger as I hit the wall of net. I put about a double duvet's worth under each arm and ploughed on another step.

"I'm trying to take it in at the waist," said Kathi, shaking away a frill that had stuck to her sweaty cheek. "Fucking childhood obesity initiative at the junior high school. It would be a hell of a lot less trouble for the kid to keep downing the donuts until after her party." She spat out a little spout of net that had foamed its way into her mouth.

"Look, let go," I said. "This is never going to work. Just let go and we'll do it methodically."

Kathi stood back and Todd stood up and I swear to God, that dress bounced out and up until it was the size of a VW camper van. It caught a draught of warm air from the heating vent and waved at us like a sea monster.

"Where's the waistband?" I said. "Roughly."

Kathi had retreated to her counter to take a long suck on a can of Coke.

"In the middle there," she said, pointing to where the sea monster's mouth parts would be.

I rolled. I started at the hem and rolled and rolled and rolled, working round in a spiral until the skirt of the thing was a giant sausage and the boned corset, sweetheart neckline and net shoulder cowl were revealed.

"How much are you taking off it?" I said, hoping it wasn't more than a couple of inches. That I could handle by folding the bones one turn over and restitching them. If it was more I'd have to cut the zip out and pull the whole thing round in both directions from the front, so the poor kid's fifteen year-old boobs would be halfway under her arms.

"From a twelve down to a ten," Kathi said. "And if her boyfriend breaks up with her and she hits the cookie jar, we'll be putting it all back on again before her birthday. What do you bet?"

Another good argument for leaving it intact and just tucking it in a bit.

"Twenty minutes," I said. "Entertain me while I do it, though."

Todd entertained me with a blow-by-blow of the streets of Cuento, where mid-century moderns with composite roofs and pools were, as I had prophesied, many and unvaried.

"They're like ..." he said.

"Shit in a field?" I suggested.

"And when you can't see the color of the siding there's nothing to go on. I zoomed in and out from map view to street view to map view so many times I swear I'm motion sick. I actually got motion sick on a virtual journey. A virtual walk!"

"But did you find it?" I said.

"Nope," said Todd. "And I'll never find it now, because I've studied so many goddam houses I've forgotten what the one on Mike's phone looked like."

"Hang on," Kathi said. She was balling sports socks at the folding table and firing them into an open laundry bag on the floor. "Why would Mike have evidence photographs on her phone? You never told me that. That's illegal. Why would she show you proof that she's done something illegal?"

"Well, she was pretty keen to convince us about all the crap she was spouting," Todd said. "She was giving more away than usual, wasn't she, Lexy?"

"Yeah, but," Kathi said. "What if they weren't evidence photos? What if they were showing up on her phone because she was logged into a—"

"Yes!" said Todd. "Oh my God. What an idiot I am." He was scrolling madly.

"Stop," said Kathi. "No fair. It was my idea. I should find them."

"Now now, children," I said. I had no idea what they were each racing to find or I would have stopped slogging through this chunk of quadrupled satin, lining, and boning that was like trying to sew a steak and joined in.

"We got so sidetracked finding the student council," said Todd, "we completely forgot about the porches in the *Voyager*!"

"Found it!" said Kathi. "'Honourable mentions in the seventh Annual Cuento Halloween Porch Decorating Competition. Witches, Tim Burton, Disney, *Silence of the Lambs*—ooooh, clever!—witches, ghosts, Mama Cuento—that's genius!—more witches, ghosts, Freddy … Here he is! *What shall we do with the drunken Scotsman?* by Mrs. Joan Lampeter of Lark Circle in north Cuento.'"

"Racists!" I said.

"And there it is," said Todd, back on his virtual map despite the travel sickness. "Sneaky bastards, putting a keyhole cul de sac under the shade trees where I couldn't see it. Yep, yep, mint green siding, pepper tree. We've got her."

"Why did we want her again?" I said, which went down like salt on a slug.

"Because she completes the set," Kathi said. "Tam is dead, Patti is missing, John Worth is unconscious, Mo Heedles is uptight enough to puke at the mention of Tam's name, Mo Tafoya either tried to sell him a parcel of land or lured him here with a promise of it. Joan could be the key that makes sense of everything."

"Hm," I said.

"Come on!" she said. "Don't tell me it's not worth leaning on Joanie. I have no idea why Mike has decided to let this drop. Suicide? Bullshit! But she *is* letting it drop and so the only way it's going to get solved is if someone else solves it."

"But if Tam's the kind of guy who can't even get the cops to care that he had lye poured down his neck, why should we?" I said. "I mean, say what you like about Mike—and I have—she's not a bent cop, is she?"

"I tell you why I want to solve it," Todd said. "Because unravelling what happened at the fiftieth reunion is the only way we'll ever solve what happened at the graduation. This is the only way we'll find Patti Ortiz."

"Find her?" said Kathi. "You think so?"

"Find the answer at least," said Todd. "Find peace for her mother after all these years. What do you say?"

Twenty-Three

"Small world," I said, as we slowed outside the mint green ranch house on Lark Circle and pulled up behind the minivan.

"Huh?" said Todd.

I nodded at the decal in the minivan's back window. It read 11-01-17 GATO. "This is the cat groomer I was tracking. Didn't I tell you? The surly one. Thank God Della lucked out in Madding."

"Huh?" said Kathi. I sighed. It used to happen every day in Cuento. I'd say something and all the eyes would go a bit flat and all the heads would go a bit quirked and I'd know that whoever I was talking to didn't have a clue what I was trying to say. Sometimes they didn't have three different clues, stacked up: they couldn't understand the sounds and, after we sorted that out, they didn't understand the words and, when that was behind us, that wasn't what they called it here anyway. The worst one ever was trying to buy curry paste in the budget supermarket, with another level: they didn't sell it.

It didn't happen absolutely every time I spoke anymore, but it had happened today. "Joan Lampeter," I said, "is the cat groomer I've been trying to get in touch with. That on the back window of her car is her business contact details."

Kathi's eyes came back to life and her head went straight again. "No, Lexy," she said, with infinite patience, "Joan Lampeter is not a cat groomer."

"Aha!" I said. "You're right. Well, it's not necessarily her anyway. It might be someone else. Whoever the cat groomer is, the pals all help by advertising on their cars too!"

"What are you talking about?" said Kathi.

"There's an advert on John Worth's El Camino," I said, "and I'm sure it wasn't *this* minivan I was behind at Swiss Sisters."

"Are you high?" said Todd. "Have you had a stroke?"

"But even that doesn't explain why, when I phoned up, they were so weird," I added.

"That's a memorial," said Todd.

"What?" My brain tried to make him be saying *That's immaterial* because at least that made sense, but it was a no go.

"That decal on Ms. Lampeter's car," said Todd, "is a memorial to her dead cat."

"*What?*"

"Use your eyes, Lexy," he said. "It's right there in white and black. Gato died on the 1st of November 2017."

"That's a date?" I said. "No, that's not a date. That's a phone number."

"Wow," said Kathi.

"Wow your bloody self!" I snapped. "Why would someone have a memorial to a dead cat on their car?"

"Why would someone have a keychain made out of its jawbone?" Todd said. "People are weird."

"Or," said Kathi, "maybe that's the car that ran it over. Maybe it's more of a *Mad Max* kind of a thing."

I knew they were laughing at me. I let them. That is to say, I flounced off up the path in a huff but I waited until they were beside me and their faces were straight again before I rang the bell.

"Com-ing!" sang a voice from inside and after a moment a woman swept the door wide open with a beaming smile on her face. It dimmed a bit when she saw the three of us. Again, I was sure I had seen her before and it wasn't the picture in the yearbook. It was the movement of her mouth fading out of a smile and then back into one again when her politeness won out over her surprise.

"Can I help you?" she said.

"Sorry to bother you at home unannounced," Todd said.

"Not at all!" Joan cried, looking as if we were all her heart desired for some weird reason.

"My name is Lexy Campbell," I went on.

"Wonderful!" Joan cried.

"And these are—" I tried to add but the rest of the introduction was lost under a racket from somewhere in the house behind her. It sounded like someone dropping a couple of bowling balls into a pyramid of cardboard boxes.

"Is everything okay?" said Todd. He flexed his muscles. They were under a raincoat, which diluted the effect a bit but I could tell what he was doing from the way his eyebrows moved. I really should train him in the ways of women; we can exercise our pelvic floors, let out silent farts, and pass old boyfriends in the street all without any eyebrow involvement. It's a skill handed down from mother to daughter, like finding stuff and remembering birthdays.

"That?" said Joan, putting a hand to her throat and glancing airily behind her. "That's just my dog going out of his pet door. He's shy."

It must be some pet door, I thought. Because that dog sounded like a Great Dane.

243

"But come in, come in," Joan was saying. "Come in out of the storm."

We all huddled into her foyer and managed to get our waterproof coats off, ask about shoe removal, wipe them lavishly on the mat when she told us not to worry and move into the house.

It was open-plan, of course, and although she led us to the bit with two sofas facing each other, the kitchen bit was in plain view. One stool was pushed back from the breakfast bar about three feet and stood at an angle. Another one was lying on its back. Either the Great Dane sat on a barstool or he slept under them. Or, and my money was on this, that was a human who had blundered out of sight as we arrived and not from shyness either.

"Poor thing," I said. "Is he missing Gato?"

There was that look again: flat eyes and quirked head.

"Your shy dog," Kathi added. "Does he miss your cat?"

"Ohhhhhh!" said Joan, just a bit too loud. "Oh yes. You saw the car, right? Yes. So sad. Such pals. I should take that off, really. It's been there long enough." Her hand was fluttering at her neck again. "But anyway," she said. "What is it I can do for you?"

We all saw the reality dawn on her. She put her hand in her lap at the very moment that she could have done with it at her neck, as the blots of colour crept up out of her collar and spread over her jaw. She had only just realised that she shouldn't know who we were and shouldn't have invited us in before we told her what we wanted.

"We are Trinity Solutions," Todd said, proffering a card. I wondered for a moment what she would say to a make-over artiste, a de-clutterer, and a counsellor descending on her and parking their bums on her couches for no reason, but then I realised that the Trinity Life Solutions business card was vague enough to fit into more than one slot.

"It's about what happened after the party," Todd went on. We had rehearsed this on the way over.

Joan's flush drained so quickly and so completely I found myself sitting forward a bit on the couch in case she fainted.

"Yes," she said. "Yes, yes, yes. I read about it in the paper. Very unfortunate." Our plan was working.

"You read about it in the paper?" I said. "I would have thought you'd have all been talking about it long before it got into the papers."

"Wh—what?" she said. There was a sheen on her top lip.

"Didn't Mrs. Ortiz speak to all of you immediately?" said Kathi.

"Mrs. Ortiz?" she said. She curled her lips inwards so she could lick the drops of sweat away without us noticing. She failed. "You mean, Patti's mom?"

"Right," I said. "Patti's mum. She said she spoke to all of you. Well, she would."

"You spoke to P—Patti's mom?" She was breathing in high light breaths, so high and so light that the individual hairs on her velour top were winking.

"We did," said Todd. "She suggested we should speak to you."

"Me?"

"You, Mo, Mo, and John," said Kathi. "And Thomas, but of course we can't talk to him."

She was going. I sat forward a bit more as she swayed from the waist like a charmed snake and her eyes started to glaze. Then, just before they rolled up in her head, she caught it. "Wait," she said. "You wanted to talk to Thomas Shatner about what happened after the party?"

"Yes," I said. "The graduation party. When Patti disappeared. Why, what did you think we were referring to?"

Would it work? It was Todd's brainwave. He had surmised that if Joan thought we were asking about the reunion, after which came a murder she might be mixed up in, and then found out we weren't, she might be so relieved she'd say more than was wise.

"I thought you meant the reunion," she said. "We had some indiscretions." She plucked a hanky out from up her sleeve and dabbed her face. "Excuse me. I'm just getting over a little stomach issue. I don't think I'm contagious anymore but I won't offer refreshments, just in case." Beside me, Kathi pressed herself back into the couch to maximise the distance between her and Joan, even though she must know Joan was lying. "Yes, undignified as it is, we reverted to our high-school selves after the reunion. There was a certain amount of hotel-room hopping amongst the out-of-towners."

"And amongst the still-in-towners?" I said.

"I'm single now," said Joan. "He's single. No one was hurt."

It didn't quite chime with what Becky Worth had said. *Drama*, she had called it. *Phone calls and tears and driving around all night.* And she had said it was the same fifty years ago.

"But about the graduation party," I said, "when everyone lived in town and no one had a hotel room? Patti set off home, we believe, and never made it."

"Never made it?" Joan said. "What makes you say that? Oh! Mrs. Ortiz, right? You said you spoke to her. And you just believed what she said?"

"We had no reason not to," I said. "As far as we knew. Is there a reason not to?"

"I should say so!" said Joan. The words sat uneasily in her mouth, too hearty for her overall demeanour. "Mr. Ortiz didn't want Patti to go to the dance. He certainly didn't want her to go on afterwards to the ... Well, if it was the Oscars you'd call it an after party, but really we just went to a quiet place and turned on all our car radios, to keep dancing. It was a magical night. Until morning came."

"But Patti didn't go to the parking place, did she?" I said. "Lover's Lane kind of thing, is it?"

"Who said that?" Joan looked genuinely surprised. "Was it Mrs. Ortiz again? Good grief, all these years later, all of us in our sixties and she still cares enough to lie!"

"So Patti *was* there?" Todd said.

"Until dawn," said Joan. "Like all of us. And then she went home. Like all of us. And I suppose a lot of us got in trouble when our parents saw us. We were hammered. And some of us were pretty dishevelled. I was pregnant! Although I didn't know it then and that worked out pretty well. Forty happy years with a good man and two lovely children."

This was a lot to take in. Kathi got on top of it all first.

"So," she said. "You think Patti Ortiz's father punished her for staying out late and coming home drunk and ... went too far?"

"Yes," Joan said. "That's what everyone thought. But no one could prove it. And Mrs. Ortiz never wavered. Either she didn't know what happened to Patti or she covered for her husband because she didn't want a husband in jail as well as a daughter in her grave. But that's what we've always believed. It makes sense of everything."

"Everything like what?" I said.

"Everything like why Tam Shatner left town in such a hurry," Joan said. "He was terrified Mr. Ortiz would come after him and kill him too."

"What for?" I said.

Joan swallowed hard. "For ... Because ... Homophobia?"

"You're saying he *was* gay?" said Todd.

"I ... don't ... know," said Joan, looking sick. "It's all rumors. I just heard things. But I do know for sure that he never came back. Never came near the place again. And this time, this last reunion ... I hope God forgives us because I'll never forgive myself." Her delivery was getting smoother again. "We said to him Joe Ortiz was dead and the old woman was ancient and no threat to anyone, and we persuaded him to come and see us all again."

"He was a friend then?" said Todd. "Not ostracized? Not cold-shouldered?"

"He was the class vice president!" Joan said.

"Only John Worth seemed to suggest that Tam was a bit of an outcast and wasn't welcome."

"John did?" said Joan. "I don't know." She looked around kind of wildly as if someone might pop up to help her. "Maybe it was their old rivalry bubbling up again," she said. "Everyone loved Tam! And John got jealous. Envious, I should say. He had selected him to be class vice-president and then didn't Tam take over and become the most popu-lar boy in school? John had the green-eyed monster. And it was just the same at the reunion, crazy as that sounds. Why, when he saw Tam arrive he went over and tried to hustle him away. Frog-marched him practically."

Finally she had said something that chimed with something else we'd heard already. "When you say John Worth tried to hustle him away," I asked her, "do you mean he was unsuccessful? Tam stayed at the party?"

"Until the end," said Joan. "I think."

"He's not in any of the pictures," I said and I must have said it far too baldly because she gave me a sharp look.

"Tam always hated having his picture taken," she said. "You should see our yearbook. The committee was at its wits' end with him. They couldn't snag him for a photograph no matter what they did. And it nearly broke the heart of Patti—not Patti Ortiz, this is another Patti, head of the yearbook drive. It's such a black mark on their record to have missing pictures. But Tam O'Shanter outwitted them."

"But what about the photobombs?" said Kathi. "That's what you'd call them now anyway. When he infiltrated the Homemakers and Nurses and Librarians?"

"What?" said Joan. "I don't know what you mean."

"Do you have a yearbook handy?" said Kathi. "We'll show you."

"No," said Joan and she kept her gaze trained on Kathi's face. She didn't so much as twitch a single neck muscle in the direction of the floor-to-ceiling bookcase just off to the right. And when Todd stood up and wandered over that way, she gripped the arm of the couch so hard that her ring squeaked against the wood.

"So ..." I said. "I'm just wondering now how much of what Mrs. Ortiz told me was true and how much was misdirection. Were Patti and Tam close? Were they boyfriend and girlfriend?"

"Yes," said Joan. "They were going steady all the way through senior year."

"Even though he was gay?" I said.

"Maybe he was ... exploring ... his ... phase?" she said. *Halting* wasn't the word for it. It was the speech equivalent of that daft wedding walk they do here, like someone's tied their bootlaces together. "He gave her his class ring at the Christmas hop and by spring break they were inseparable," Joan went on. And now it was all smooth delivery again.

"His class ring," I repeated.

Joan shut her mouth so firmly that her lips went white and disappeared. She fished around up her sleeve for the hanky again.

"You dropped it," said Kathi pointing at the floor, where the crumpled square of lace and cotton was sitting. Of course Kathi had noticed the handkerchief pulsing with fictitious stomach germs sitting there. "You should use Kleenex," she added. Of course she did. It was her biggest bugbear at the Skweeky Kleen—people who sent balled up cotton hankies full of snot for her to wash.

"Kleenex?" said Joan. "I got this set of handkerchiefs for my trousseau and forty-nine years later it's still as beautiful as the day I chose it in Gilliam's Department Store. I miss the days when you could order a set of beautiful handkerchiefs in a downtown department store and have them monogrammed, don't you?" She held it up for us to admire: a square of lawn so fine you could see the light through it, with lace in one corner and an elaborate JFL monogram intertwined with ribbons and roses.

"Me?" said Kathi. "Not really, to be honest. But I agree about supporting local businesses. I'm with you there. I'd hate to see Cuento lose its independent stores and turn into Any Town, USA."

Joan was nodding along, soothed by this anodyne chat. I ruined it.

"Did the Ortizes have a problem with you girls as well as with Thomas?" I said. "Did they want Patti to spend time with other Latinos instead of with you lot?"

It wasn't just Joan who froze this time. All three of them got a glassy look. Because that's not how you talk about it. I'd learned that pretty quickly. I should have said *with her family* or even *with people her parents knew. Her community* at a stretch. We were all supposed to be pretending we didn't know why Mr. Ortiz was angry.

"Not at all," said Joan. "Mr. and Mrs. Ortiz wanted the best for Patti." She was ruffled for sure.

"Until they killed her," I said.

Joan flushed again. "That was crime of passion, I'm sure. A moment of madness. The Ortizes didn't try to isolate Patti. They wanted her to get on the world and make friends who could help her do that. They were very happy to have Patti be our friend."

"To help her 'get on the world'?" I said.

"Yes," said Joan. "We all came from very respectable families. The Tafoyas owned a—The Heedles family had bought a—I mean, the Worths lived in that—The L—..." Realising, I reckoned, that nothing she could say in defence of the cool kids on the student council would sound like anything except monstrous snobbery, she stopped talking.

"What about the Shatners?" I said.

"The Shatners weren't part of Cuento society," Joan said, unironically as far as I could tell. "It was just Thomas and his mother and they lived at a motel on the far south edge of the town."

"Oh no," said Kathi quietly. "How shabby of them."

"And Thomas didn't have much leisure time," said Joan. "He had a job after school and on the weekends. He worked with Joe Ortiz. So when Mr. and Mrs. Ortiz said they didn't want Patti spending time with Tam Shatner, they knew what they were talking about. They—or he anyway—knew the boy. I can only assume they had his number."

"It would certainly be kind of hypocritical of Mr. Ortiz to nix him because of his job if he worked in the same place," I said. "Where was that, by the way?"

"Poor Patti," said Joan. "She loved her father but she couldn't be proud of him. He worked in the sanitation department. And so did Thomas Shatner. Every day after school and Saturdays."

"Poor kid," said Todd. "I had some crummy jobs, but I never literally swept the streets."

"Neither did Tam," Joan told us. "He worked at the roadkill disposal site. Sweeping the streets would have been a picnic compared with shovelling flattened raccoons into a lye pit."

There was a long silence after that. It was so long that the "Great Dane" must have thought we'd left. We all heard "it" shifting from foot to foot, out of sight in the bedroom corridor.

"I didn't know that's how roadkill was dealt with," said Todd at last. "Lye?"

"It's not a very savory topic for chit-chat," said Joan.

It was such an unsavoury topic that it had done for Kathi. She stood, thanked Ms. Lampeter for her time, and headed towards the front door, with Todd and me not far behind.

Twenty-Four

That wasn't a dog," said Todd. We were at one of the many frozen yoghurt shops of Cuento, the clean one that Kathi doesn't mind frequenting. And it was a good choice: the pastel colours of the walls, the shining surfaces of floor and table-top, the bright stink of sherbet and sugar over a base of pure Clorox—it all served as an antidote to the scenes we were imagining.

Kathi gave Todd a grateful look for easing into it with the dog talk. "No," she said. "There was no dog in that house. I can always spot at least a few hairs."

"And plus there was no pet door," Todd added. "She said it had gone out the pet door, but I had a clear sightline when I went over to the bookcase—and didn't that freak her! Pet door, there was none."

"What about the utility room?" I said. I was proud that I'd stopped calling it a scullery and that my friends would no longer break into fake Shakespearean English and call me a wench to take the mickey.

"The laundry room?" said Todd. So close, I thought. "It would open into the garage in that house. Kinda gross for letting a dog out to hm-hm."

"How about the yearbook?" I said. "When you went over to the bookcase."

"Oh sure, it was there. It was even wrapped in cellophane to keep it nice, like it was a treasured possession. No way she forgot she had it. She just didn't want us flicking through it and busting her."

"So who was it?" Kathi said. She had a taster pot of sprinkles and was dipping the back of her spoon into it before each mouthful; this because Todd couldn't deal with sprinkles. They looked too much like fleas.

"It was Mrs. Ortiz," I said.

"What?" said Kathi.

"Well," I began, "if Mike and the rest of the cops think Tam killed Patti Ortiz, that explains why they're shutting down the investigation of who killed Tam, doesn't it?"

"Protecting Mrs. Ortiz for avenging her daughter?" said Todd. "That's pretty maverick. For Mike. And do you really think that woman is capable of murder?"

"I meant who was in the house if it wasn't a dog," said Kathi. "But I suppose we've got to talk about it sometime."

"And if they're right," I said, "and little old Mrs. Ortiz did kill Tam for that reason, then that's kind of okay," I said. "But if they're wrong—if Joan is right—and Tam did nothing except be a bit of an old goat for the girlies and displease a heavy-handed father … and if that heavy-handed father killed his daughter and his wife kept it secret for fifty years and then killed Tam before he could bust her … then we can't just leave this. Can we?"

"But none of that's true!" said Kathi. "Joan just made it up. *She* killed Tam. She must have. She lied about the yearbook and she lied about the dog. So she probably lied about Joe Ortiz too. And she definitely lied about Tam's sexuality, like everyone is. I don't get that."

"What's her motive?" I said.

"Revenge," said Kathi. "Justice for Patti."

"It's a lot to do for a friend, fifty years later," Todd said.

Kathi rubbed her nose. "Maybe it's just that I didn't like her. Such a snob with her 'good families' and stupid monogrammed hankies."

"She lied about the hankies," I said. "Which is beyond pathetic. She said that rag was in her trousseau but it had her maiden name initials on it. Oh wait—unless her married name had the same initials. Do we know her married name? Yeah, scratch that. Talk about give a dog a bad name and hang him."

"Then cut him down and dispose of him in a tub of lye," said Todd. "No, we can't just leave it. If Joe Ortiz killed his daughter—even in a rage, even accidentally—but covered it up and blamed it on Thomas? And then when Tam finally comes back, his widow kills him to keep the story going? That's evil. And even if none of it's true and Tam did kill Patti and then years later Joan killed Tam, we still can't leave it. Where's it going to end? If John Worth dies up there in that hospital, that's three. If Joan turns on whoever was doing the Great Dane impersonation, that's four."

"What if John Worth did the killing?" I said. "He's hiding something. And he admitted to running Tam out of the reunion."

"And he's single," said Todd. "Joan just said she was with someone single, didn't she?" He thought for a moment. "But why did Mo Heedles's stomach turn over?"

"And why did Mo Tafoya pretend to list the old Armour place?" Kathi said. "Assuming Mike's right and it's not really for sale."

"And," I said, "what happened to Patti?"

"She's dead," said Todd.

There was a short silence then as we all took it in and accepted it.

"And we're all thinking the same thing about where her body ended up, aren't we?" I said, at last. Which is how I found out that we weren't. Both of them looked at me as if I'd bitten the head off a baby rabbit. "Sorry," I said. "It was the first thing that occurred to me. If Patti died, whether it was her father or her boyfriend who killed her, each of them had a great way to dispose of the body."

Kathi pushed her frozen yoghurt away from her. Todd took one last guilty spoonful and then, in solidarity, did the same. I was good because nothing in this world will ever persuade me to eat frozen yoghurt and I'd finished my bottle of water.

"What now?" Kathi said.

"I want to find out if John Worth's home from the hospital," I said after thinking for a minute. "Because if not, and if he's still feeling ill and vulnerable, he might talk to us."

"Good point," said Todd. "But I wish we'd stuck around at Joan Lampeter's house. To see if anyone snuck out. Find out who dove for cover when they heard your voice, Lexy."

"Is *that* what that was?" I said. "I'm getting pretty sick of that, to be frank."

"Why, has it happened before?" Todd said.

It had. I was almost sure it had, but I couldn't bring the incident to mind and the more I thought about it, the further away the little wisp of a memory seemed to drift. I let it go, thinking it was probably unconnected to all of this anyway.

Idiot.

∞

We thought we'd try John Worth's house first. If he was home, we could talk to him and if he wasn't, we could skedaddle right on up to the hospital and try to get past the nurses. Todd could do it, I was sure. Kathi, in her Skweeky Kleen uniform looked like some kind of maintenance person who might have legitimate business in a hospital. I'd just hope for luck. I looked down at myself and wondered if I should go down the scrubs route too. Then we had arrived at the gingerbread Victorian and were parking.

"Welp, he hasn't gone back to L.A. anyway," I said, pointing at the sacred El Camino still parked on Becky Worth's drive. "And behold the decal complete with phone number. Apologies accepted."

"Lexy, why have you got such a bug up your—Sorry, Todd—bee in your—Jesus! Sorry, Todd—hard-on for this crazy notion?" Kathi said. "That is a memorial to Coco. Not an ad. That is the date Coco died. Not a phone number."

"Oh yeah?" I said. "Well if it's not a phone number how come you can phone it?" I was dialling already and put it on speaker phone to regale them.

"Welcome to Verizon Wireless," a voice said. "Your call cannot be completed. Please check the number and dial again."

"Hmph," I said. "The lines must be busy."

Todd hit speed dial four and my phone started playing "Jolene." I answered it.

"The lines are fine, Lexy, you lunatic," he said. "That is not a phone number."

I hung up. "Let's see if John Worth's home."

As we trooped up the steps, a neighbour came out on her porch and hailed us.

"Yoo-hoo!" she said. "There's no one ho-ome!"

God, this country! Why couldn't they plant some hedges? If my neighbours yoo-hooed visitors and told them there was nobody in, I'd be ready to brain them. California's such a huge place; I would never understand why they were all so crammed into it.

"Calm down," Todd said, reading my mind. "This could be useful." He raised his voice. "Is Johnny still in the hospital?" he said. "We hoped they'd let him out today."

The neighbour woman was peering at us, hanging right over her own porch rail, and she'd moved her glasses down her nose to get us into sharp focus. "I can take in your casserole or what have you," she said. "Keep it in my refrigerator until Becky gets home from work. Of course, you'll have to tell me your names, so I can label it."

"We left it in the back of the car in a cooler," Kathi said. "Till we made sure if anyone was home."

I was glad they were here. They knew the rules. Pizza for moving house, flowers for a baby, casseroles for serious illness and death. I knew the rules too but the knowledge wasn't cemented in deep enough for me to lie smoothly.

"At least your momma raised you right," she said. "You're here at a civil hour and not just dumping gifts down on the porch any old how. So nasty! And some people don't bother at all anymore. They send Starbucks gift cards online. Can you believe it? Becky told me. There's her poor brother lying there full of tubes and she's getting text messages about credit on her Starbucks card!"

I thought that was a great idea. There was a Starbucks right beside the hospital—well, of course there was; it's in the zoning laws that there must be—and saving Becky from the hospital coffee was the work of a true friend. Sentencing Becky to eat what passes for a casserole every night until her brother recovered was a rotten trick. And if he died, it would only get worse: casseroles all the way down, madam. I had tried them before I knew better and had learned a valuable lesson. Mushroom soup is a menu item, not an ingredient. Ditto tomato.

"Have you seen him?" Todd said once he'd finished clucking about the Starbucks card. "Or is he still in the ICU? We haven't been up there since Saturday."

It could have gone either way. She might have taken the hump at us for knowing more than her. But we got lucky. I recognised the leap in her eye for what it was. If we knew John Worth was in intensive care, that leap said, then she had to show us she knew something too. Anything. Her entire body of knowledge on the Worth family was now at our disposal.

"Still no visitors except family," she said. "Are you … cousins?"

"I'm Reba's boy," said Todd. "And this is my partner, Kendra, and my sister-in-law. You remember Bradley? He used to come and stay in the summer. *His* wife. The children stayed at home with their dad. Keep your mouth shut, Lexy," he added sotto voce, being no admirer of my American accent.

The neighbour was blinking at the avalanche of names and relationships.

"I decided not to bring the children," Todd said, hitching his bum up onto the porch rail and giving Mrs. Neighbour a brilliant smile. "We didn't know what was going on here. Becky made it sound like some kind of orgy. On Saturday night? At the reunion? And we weren't sure if 'heart attack' was maybe a euphemism for, you know."

"No," said the neighbour, but her tone said she was dying to.

"Well, he works down in L.A., doesn't he?" said Kathi. "So we wondered if that was maybe a polite way of saying … "

"Drugs?" said the neighbour. "I don't think so. It was a week later he collapsed and it was the middle of the day. But you're right to say it was quite a night, the reunion night. I woke up I don't know how many times, headlights and doors slamming."

"Fighting in the street at their age!" said Kathi. "You'd think they'd know better."

"Their age!" the neighbour was scoffing. "They're young enough to be my children. But there was no fighting. Just the cars. Which was bad enough. At my age, a good night's sleep is like a good morning's bowel movement. I hate to have potential interfered with for no reason."

"Did you take plates?" Todd said. "You can complain, you know."

"Oh my old eyes aren't good enough to be taking down license plates in the middle of the night," she said. "And they were doing a good deed."

"Who was?" said Kathi. Saying nothing was killing me.

"Whoever it was. They might have watched him get passing-out drunk, but they didn't leave him to wake up on a bench frozen to the marrow. They brought him home. It took four of them to carry him, but they brought him home."

"So you're saying four people brought John Worth here, passed out drunk, after the reunion?" said Todd.

"Four," she said, nodding. "Brought him home in the small hours, carried him up the path, and left him on the porch."

"He slept on the porch?"

"What are porches for," she said, "if not to sleep off a party and not stink up the house with your breath or make messes on the rug?"

"It was a cold night for sleeping on porches, wasn't it?" Todd said.

"Well, he woke up nice and early anyways. By the time I was done in the bathroom and downstairs for my coffee, Becky had her porch decorated for Halloween."

"Well, I must say I am shocked," Todd said. "Johnny stopped drinking years ago, or so he said. I don't think I'll tell my momma what brought on this heart attack we've all been so worried over. Drinking himself unconscious again? Shocking!"

"John Worth's an alcoholic?" the neighbour said. "Well! He's leading a double life then, young man. He might be twelve-stepping down there in L.A. but he takes a glass of my eggnog every Christmas when he comes home and a beer in the yard at the Fourth of July too."

Todd and Kathi tsk-tsked and I thought it was safe to join in.

"Your momma," the old lady said. "Did you say you were Reba's boy? And Reba would be … ?"

Before she put two and two together and got IMPOSTER we smiled and waved and headed back to the Jeep.

"So that puts John Worth in the clear," Kathi said. "If he was passed out drunk. And if all the noise and drama we've been hearing about was just his friends bringing him home, maybe Tam's death is nothing to do with him."

"Are you serious?" I said. "What better way to move a body than to pretend it's a drunk?"

"Wait a minute!" said Todd. "You think John was one of the four carrying the drunk and the drunk was dead Tam?"

"No," I said. "I think John Worth is in the clear, because I think the reason his heart packed it in is that he was framed and the tension of it nearly killed him."

"Where'd you get that from?" said Todd.

"It's what that neighbour lady just said about people showing up outside polite visiting hours and dumping down presents 'all nasty.'"

Todd and Kathi looked back at me blankly.

"What's the nastiest way you could deliver a casserole?" I asked.

"Ohhhh," said Kathi. "In a garbage bag."

"Bingo. We should have seen it before now. Tam was on John Worth's porch. But not with John Worth's permission. When he realised, he dumped him in the slough. But the nightmare wasn't over. Someone kept delivering costumes. We saw Becky getting rid of one on Saturday and then another one got delivered. I really think this is the answer."

"You're right," said Todd. "I think you're right. And it clears up one question that's been bugging the snot out of us, doesn't it? Why was he left where he was for four days and then redumped? Why was he not just dumped immediately?"

"Because it wasn't the same person who killed him, dressed him, stashed him, then dumped him in the slough!" Kathi said.

"Who was it?" said Todd.

"Either Original Mo, Also-Mo, or Joan," I said. "Duh."

"Or Patti," said Todd, "coming out of hiding to dish out punishment after all these years then going home to see her mama. Hey," he added, at our looks, "I can dream."

Twenty-Five

et's check them all again," said Kathi. "You said Mo Heedles puked at the memory of Tam Shatner's gapped teeth? Maybe she put a mask on him. Maybe she has nosy neighbors too, who're willing to say she was busy all night last Saturday."

"And we know she has a nephew," Todd said. "So she has a sibling. Who might have a spouse."

"So?" said Kathi.

"I'm trying to get up to a total of four people who'd help her move a corpse," he said.

Mo Heedles's neighbours were out. And Mo Heedles was out too. However, the nephew was there. He gulped when he saw us and I wondered again if Todd was right. Did this man fancy me? He was certainly staring. And he was certainly pretty. But he was wearing cycling shorts.

"What?" he said. "Gotta do something in the off-season, don't I?"

So at least he knew it was unacceptable to be wearing cycling shorts.

I smiled at him, as bland a smile as I could muster. But it worked wonders on him. He beamed at me.

"Aunt Mo just dashed out for two minutes," he said. "You wanna come in and wait? You're the ... who are you?"

"Trinity Solutions," said Kathi. "We're exploring the possibility of a joint venture."

She was good. That was so vague that no matter what Mo Heedles's business interests might be, we could be part of it.

Inside, he stood in front of the fake fireplace bouncing on his cleats, seemingly quite at ease. But since we were all sitting in a row on a squashy sofa and eye level with the padded bit of his shorts, he was the only one.

"Could I trouble you for a glass of water," Kathi said eventually, purely to get rid of him.

Just as he came back with three little bottles of flavoured water too cold to drink—practically too cold to hold in your hand—but bogging anyway, so who cares, his aunt returned. She had a phone clamped between ear and shoulder and was listening intently as she let herself in.

"Uh-huh," she said. "Oh! Uh-huh."

Then she saw us.

"I've got to go," she said and hung up without any leave-taking. She laid the phone down in the key, glove, and pen bowl on the stand just inside the door. Actually she didn't. She shoved it so hard into the middle of the key bowl that it was submerged. It made me feel warm towards her, that she might be ashamed of her basic little flip phone. It didn't go with the cathedral ceiling and the moleskin love seats.

"Hello again," she said to Todd and me. "And hello to you too," she said to Kathi. "I see my nephew has offered refreshments. Now then, what can I do for you today?"

264

"Well, Ms. Heedles," said Todd, "it's still Tam Shatner and what happened to him after the reunion."

"Who?" said the nephew, unconvincingly. Mo moved her hand just ever so slightly to tell him to dial it down a notch. It wasn't very plausible that his aunt hadn't mentioned the sudden death of a classmate to him.

"But it's not just Tam anymore," I added. "It's Patti Ortiz now too, and what happened to her after graduation. Can you help us with any of that?"

"It's so long ago," Mo said.

"But it's still reverberating," Todd countered. "And it makes a difference. If Tam killed Patti and ran away, then what happened to him last week was rough justice. But what if Tam knew who killed Patti and that knowledge got him murdered? There's no justice in that, is there?"

"Patti's dead?" Mo's face was drawn up into stricken lines and her eyes were filling. "I always hoped she'd just gone off to have a better life somewhere."

"Talk us through it," Kathi said. "Graduation night."

"Where would I even start?" Mo said.

"Tell us about Tam Shatner," said Todd. "What kind of boy was he? You were on the senior class council with him. You must have known him well."

Mo shook her head. "I told you," she said. "He was John's friend. I didn't know him and I didn't want to."

"He certainly does seem to have caused some trouble," I said.

Mo waited to hear more, with a mildly questioning look on her face. She was being careful this time, not like our first interview when she spat his name and cheered his murder.

"The yearbook, for instance," I said.

Mo sprang to life. "Oh, that yearbook! The committee tried to pin him down to get a picture and he couldn't be pinned. They were at their wits' end. It's a black mark on a yearbook committee's record to have missing students, you know."

"We do know," said Todd. "We heard that."

He was right. We really had heard that, almost word for word, from Joan Lampeter only an hour ago.

"Did he hate having his picture taken?" said Kathi in an innocent voice that was so close to over-the-top I could feel giggles bubbling up inside me.

"No," said Mo. "He was just obstinate. Nothing delighted him more than to barge into a big group shot where he didn't belong, once it was all set up, and there was no time to retake it. I think he's in our yearbook here and there, just to stick it to the committee even more."

"What a pain in the ass," Todd said.

"And of course it all took much longer than it does now," Mo said. "It wasn't tap, tap on your iPhone and upload the best ones. Not back then."

I couldn't help looking over at the key bowl and its half-submerged flip phone. I don't know if she saw me.

"No wonder you didn't invite him to the party after graduation," Kathi said. "That's right, isn't it? He wasn't there?"

"Patti was there," said Mo Heedles, oddly. "She was there at the graduation and she was there at the—"

"—old Armour homestead," Kathi supplied.

That set her back a bit. She frowned at Kathi. "Are you from Cuento?" she said. Subtext: *How do you know where our parking place was?*

"I married into old Cuento society," said Kathi. And Mo Heedles was off, spinning her social Rolodex trying to place Kathi in her network somewhere. Her eyes rested on the *sk* logo on Kathi's polo shirt and narrowed slightly. "I own the Skweeky Kleen laundromat," Kathi explained. "Attached to the Last Ditch motel?"

Mo's nephew had been sitting quietly but he shifted in his chair then and recrossed his legs. He also put down his little bottle of disgusting orangey water and folded his arms. Which was interesting. Which bit of what Kathi had just said made him need to hug himself?

"A good business, if you get the location right," Mo said.

"But getting back to Tam?" said Todd. "Was *he* there at the party that got Patti into so much trouble?"

Mo shot a look towards the front door. Was she thinking of making a bolt for it? "I can't recall," she said. If only she had just said *I don't remember*. I mean, we still wouldn't have believed her but at least there wouldn't have been that echo of every shameless politician running down the clock at some hearing.

"I'm not surprised," Todd said. "I blacked out at my high school graduation too. And college. Medical school. Wedding. And like you said, it was different back then before smart phones. Maybe there aren't any pictures to jog your memory."

"Pictures?" said Mo. Her eyes slid to the other side, away from the front door. I guessed that the drawer in the bookcase held her photo albums. "Thankfully, no. No pictures of the four of us that night in our party dresses with our hair wrecked and our make-up running. I would have bought the negatives and destroyed them if there were."

"But I'll bet Mrs. Ortiz would have liked one," I said. "Even if Patti was dishevelled. The last photograph ever taken of her daughter?"

Mo nodded and heaved a sigh heavy with sorrow. Then she caught her breath. "Mrs. Ortiz," she said, "isn't quite the mothering angel she makes herself out to be."

"Oh, we know," said Todd. "We heard. We even wondered if she was capable of killing Tam Shatner. At her age. But then the police— Have you heard the news?"

"The police what?" said Mo.

"The police reckon it's suicide," he said.

Mo sat back in her seat. "Suicide?" she said. "Thomas, you mean?"

"Who else?" said Kathi.

"Suicide?" Mo repeated.

"Which is going to be a relief to a lot of people, I imagine," I said. "John Worth, for one." Mo sat forward in her seat again. "Did you know John was in hospital after a massive heart attack?" I added.

"Did I know?" said Mo. She sent a panicked look to her nephew. "I might have heard something. Or maybe I'm thinking of someone else."

"Yeah, I get that," said Todd. Mo couldn't crack his sarcasm code though and she merely gave him a grateful smile.

"I reckon it was the strain of an old friend dying after the reunion," Kathi said. "I mean, if John Worth persuaded Tam to come and then Tam got murdered…"

"Did he?" I asked, all innocence. "Persuade him, I mean."

"Who else would have?" said Kathi. "Everyone hated him except his friend John. Isn't that right, Ms. Heedles?"

"Ummmm," said Mo. She sucked at this game. "That's right."

"But John said he didn't know Tam was coming and he ran him out of the party as soon as he showed his face," I said. "Right, Mo?"

"Ummmm. Yes, that's right, now I remember."

"Aunt Mo," her nephew chipped in, "maybe you should go for your rest. It's been a busy day."

"Oh, of course," said Todd. "We didn't mean to detain you. We're just chatting. Although … now that I think about it again … who *was* it who said that Tam stayed at the party? Danced and visited all night long?"

"I don't recall," said Mo again, in a smaller voice.

"Wait, wait," I said, "I think, that is, I'm almost sure, it was you, Mo. Wasn't it?"

"I can't remember." Her voice was close to a whisper.

"Can't remember whether he was there?" Todd said.

"Or can't remember what you said?" added Kathi.

"I really do need to go and rest," said Mo, standing up in quite a wavering fashion and making her way towards the bedrooms.

Her nephew was left gaping at all three of us, absolutely unequal to this beyond awkward situation. "You didn't get to talk about your business venture," he said at last.

I couldn't work out if he was clever at acting dumb or too dumb to act clever.

"We can come back," Todd said. "When this current situation has died down completely. Your aunt is just the kind of investor we're looking to attract."

"Where there muck there's bras," the nephew said.

I was then, and I will for the rest of my life continue to be, proud that I didn't jump, didn't squeak, didn't even open my eyes wider or let my breath hitch.

"What?" said Todd.

"Where there's muck there's bras," the nephew said. "It's an old expression. It means women are where the money is."

"Sounds kinda disrespectful," said Kathi. "Like lipstick on a pig."

"Black don't crack," Todd added.

I said nothing. I was keeping my cool while a firework show of revelations and connections went off inside me but I couldn't do that and talk too.

269

"Well, we'll get back to you," Todd said, finally noticing that I was not in a normal state there beside him. "Or to your aunt anyway."

He stood, Kathi stood, I stood and we left.

"Omigod, omigod, omigod, omigod," I said, hustling down the path.

"What's up?" said Kathi. "You're walking like that time you drank from the irrigation hose. I'm not getting in the car with you if you're gonna—"

"This is mental not digestive," I said. "And it's going to blow your brains too when I tell you."

"Where are we going while you blow our brains?" said Todd, getting into the driving seat.

"Home," I said. "I've got a late client." I was half in the passenger door when I noticed Mo Heedles's car sitting in the drive, its 09-30-15 TABI decal as large as life in the window. I whipped out my phone and took a picture of it, hoping the Jeep was hiding me from view of the living room window.

"Shitbags, I've got a client too," Todd said.

"Don't say *shitbags*," I told him. "Or *client!*"

He ignored me. "And you, Kathi. Mel's coming to you for advice about a yard sale after I take him to the Gap."

"Melvin Ball?" I said. "Widowed Melvin Ball? Don't tell me his horrible children got to you and you've turned on him. He only wants to remember Maddy in peace. Don't bully him."

"He booked a cruise and he wants help with his wardrobe," Todd said. "Kathi's clearing his house while he's in Puerto Vallarta."

"In case he brings home a souvenir," Kathi said. "He doesn't want a new lady friend to find Maddy's teeth in the nightstand."

"They'll eat him alive!" I said. "A solvent widower on a cruise? They'll pick him clean."

"Never mind Melvin," said Todd. "I'll pick you clean if you don't tell us what's going on."

"Drumroll," I said. "It was Mo Heedles. She killed Tam."

"She was all over the place, it's true," Kathi said. "But maybe she's got early-onset."

"Nope," I said. "Todd, remember when we first met that nephew? *He* might have early-onset. Or he's just as thick as mince. Remember how he freaked out at me? And I thought he was a misogynistic queen—Don't give me that look! They do exist—and you thought he was smitten and shy? Well, we were both wrong. It was because he recognised me and was panicking that I would recognise him."

"Didn't you?" Todd said.

"I didn't recognise him until he said that mangled phrase just there. It's nothing to do with bras. The saying is 'Where there's muck there's brass.' *Muck* meaning dirt and *brass* meaning money. I said that to him, when we first met."

"On the phone?" said Kathi.

"Nope," I said. "Face to face."

"I don't get it," Todd said.

"I was discussing with him how there was good brass to be earned in dirty slough water."

"Is there?" Kathi said.

"Specifically, diving into dirty slough water to pull out corpses."

They were as stunned as I could ever have hoped for.

"He—He—He—He's the diver that went in and got Tam out?" Kathi said.

"And pocketed the class ring that would identify the corpse and incriminate his aunty," I said. "Tah-dah."

"Well, dip me in schmaltz and call me a kugel," said Todd. And since no one could put it better, we rode in silence the rest of the way.

271

Twenty-Six

"But what do we do about it?" Kathi said as we were all about to go our separate ways.

"Hand it over to the cops," I said. "Let Mo Heedles take her chances in the greatest justice system this world has ever seen."

"Are you being sarky?" said Todd.

"Don't say *sarky*," I told him. "You sound lame."

"Don't say *lame*," he shot back.

"Dude! You don't own *lame*," I called over my shoulder, walking away.

"And for God's sake, don't say *dude*," they chorused.

"Snap, jinx," I shouted.

Then I had to try to get my head back in the counselling zone, in time for the emergency appointment with Dorian who was bringing her possibly on-the-game daughter for a family therapy session. I just had time to send Todd and Kathi the photo of Mo Heedles's cat memorial decal, with the message CALL THIS NUMBER. Then I was hopping between the mounds of leaf litter Florian and Flynn had scratched up on the slough bank and climbing the stairs to my front porch.

Through the net curtain, I could see two shadows sitting on my back porch.

"Won't be a minute!" I sang out to them. I plumped a couple of cushions, turned on the soothing water feature I had turned off because of a previous client's dicky bladder, and then went to greet them.

The first thing I noticed was that Dorian was seething. She was literally pulsing with anger. Well, she was figuratively pulsing with anger because she was literally breathing hard and bright red. She had one shoe on her foot and one shoe in her hand.

"I stepped in doo-doo," she said, and I was filled with admiration for her. How anyone could stick to the word *doo-doo* while angry enough to seethe was beyond me.

"Yes," I said. "Kittens. Sorry. I'll wash it off for you." I stuck out my hand but she shook her head irritably like I was a fly. A shit-covered fly straight from a pile of kitten crap.

"*She's* already done it," she said, jerking her head at her daughter. "Didn't even blink."

I didn't see why that would be annoying, but then, when you're really at loggerheads with a loved one, you can get pissed off by anything at all they have the nerve to do.

When Todd was hauled into work for a case progress report before his status changed from long-term sick leave to whatever he was on now, he got ratty enough to insult Roger's hair. Now, Roger's hair is about half a millimetre long all over because he gets it shaved on a number one setting every Friday afternoon at the Jamaican barber. And his head is moisturised and his skull is a lovely shape and his ears sit flat and he never gets blocked pores on his neck.

And when Noleen has had too many empty rooms on too many consecutive nights, she takes aim at Kathi. Not for the obsessive neatness, which is genuinely annoying, but for the habit of giving people free services they haven't paid for at the Skweeky Kleen, such as always fluffing and folding every load and kicking in a plastic basket that's supposed to cost five bucks because it's too painful to hand back a tangle of staticky clothes in a bin bag

And when my dad stuck a fishing fly through this thumb and ignored it and went out fishing anyway and got a massive infection that meant he couldn't drive or cut up meat, he moaned at my mum so much for never getting into fifth gear and for making his mouthfuls too small "for him to feel like he was eating a proper dinner" that she bought him a bus pass, filled the freezer with ready meals, and went on a girls' trip to Morecambe.

So I smiled at the daughter and, as I did, I felt something shift inside me. I knew her. I was sure I'd met her but I couldn't remember where. Or was it that I'd seen a picture of her? No, because she knew me too. She was looking at me with exactly the same expression as the diving nephew had looked at me with. As if she knew I knew her and couldn't believe I wasn't placing her and wondered how long that could last.

"Come on through," I said. "Now then . . . ?"

"Kim," she said. I felt something else move inside me. It was like the first inkling that you didn't get away with eating three pomegranates last night after the cauliflower curry. Exactly the same as after drinking from an irrigation hose. Just a little shift. Fair warning.

"And how have things been?" I said. "Dorian? Have you managed to get a time to discuss your concerns with your daughter?"

"Did she get *time*?" Kim said. "She didn't take a single break long enough to go to the bathroom! We had discussed it plenty before she saw you last time. I told her it was none of her concern and that I wasn't doing anything illegal. But she just wouldn't drop it!"

"I know you, Kim," her mother said. "I know you're feeling guilty about something and/or hiding something."

"I'm not feeling guilty!" Kim insisted, rubbing her nose and looking away.

"Where did the money come from?" her mother demanded.

"I can't believe you were snooping on me and you haven't apologized! I told you. I got a job."

"And I told you we pay your tuition and rent and give you an allowance and cover your livery fees." That thing was shifting inside me again. "And you don't have time to study and have a job as well as look after poor Agnetha."

"Agnetha!" I said. "Aha! You're not fazed by kitten shit because you muck out horses! Aha! You're Kimberly Voorheft! Aren't you?"

Kim pressed herself against the back of the chair and said nothing.

"Aha?" Dorian said. "What do you mean aha? How do you know my daughter? You don't provide counseling for prostitutes, do you?"

"Kim is not a sex worker," I said. "She didn't do anything illegal for that money. But you're right, Dorian. She is ashamed."

"What is it? Chat lines? Drug-running? Who have you got yourself mixed up with, Kim?"

"Grandma!" the girl blurted.

"Grandma?" I blurted too. "And her name is …?"

"Maureen," said Dorian. "Why?"

"And your family name is …?"

"My mother has always been a Tafoya," said Dorian. "Why?" She turned to her daughter. "And why did Grandma give you so much money?"

"To do something for her."

"Do what?"

"Well, not really for her. Just to do something and not tell anyone I'd done it."

"Do *what?*"

"Cut off Agnetha's tail," I said. "Did she tell you why?"

Kim shook her head. Her mother's eyes widened and then narrowed and then began to fill. "Animal cruelty?" she said. "That's one of the warning signs of a schizophrenic, isn't it?"

"Sociopath," I said. "But it's not, anyway. Now, you two obviously have much to discuss. Don't shout and don't break anything. I'll be back in five. Okay?"

I ran along the side deck so quickly I could feel the houseboat dip and surge and hoped Dorian and Kimberly were good sailors.

Up in the Skweek, Kathi and Todd were fussing over Melvin, who had turned up—I noticed—in pale loafers and no socks and had left his striped suit-shirt untucked. It was as if he had done his best to look cruise-ready with what was already in his wardrobe. And, looking at him, I agreed that a trip to the Gap was something of an emergency.

"Could you … " I began, wishing I was cool enough to say *give us the room* and that it wasn't pathetic to say that about a launderette. "Melvin, could you possibly wait in the car? I need to say something in confidence to my colleagues about another client."

I saw Todd smirk and cursed him. But Melvin was already toddling towards the door, with his sta-press trousers flapping round his bare ankles. He had rolled them up a couple of times for that beachy look.

"I'm good," he said. "You take your time. I got my Clash of Clans to do." He patted his pocket and let himself out.

"Was that you?" I said to Todd. "Clash of bloody Clans? That's got you written all over it. He was quite happy with his Sunday crosswords."

"I'm juicing him up to appeal to the funnest widows," Todd said.

"Don't say *juicing* and don't say *funnest*."

"Okay," Todd said. "Make that the most super-fu—"

"And don't use *super* as an adverb! And shut up and listen. Jesus, you're annoying. I own you both, remember? Stop bugging me."

"You're the only one who ever calls those in," said Todd. "What?"

"Yeah," Kathi said. "I thought you had a client."

"I do have a client," I said. "Mo Tafoya's granddaughter." I paused. "Kimberly Voorheft." I paused again. "Who had an unexplained five hundred dollars in her bank account and whose mother thought she was turning tricks." I paused so long Todd flicked my forehead. "Ow. But who has just confirmed what we thought all along." My forehead was still stinging so I didn't pause. "The whole story about the mysterious stranger jumping out of nonexistent shrubbery at the overpass really was bogus." My forehead was better so I paused again. I paused too long.

"Her granny paid her to cut off her pony's *tail?*" said Todd.

"Yip," I said.

"Why?" said Kathi.

"To back up the story that this was a sick joke about Thomas Shatner's name," I said. "Same as the Jimmy wig and the cutty sark at the burial ground. To misdirect."

"So ... " said Todd. "You're saying it *wasn't* Mo Heedles? Despite the class ring her nephew stole?"

"Of course, it wasn't!" Kathi said. "We're idiots. Mo Tafoya is the real estate agent who faked the listing of the old Armour place to lure Tam back here. It had to be her who did that. So it had to be her who killed him."

"But it was neither Mo who tried to shift suspicion onto poor Mrs. Ortiz, was it?" said Todd. "That was Joan Lam—"

"We need to check that story with someone," Kathi said. "At least go back to Mrs. Ortiz and ask."

"Ask a woman who killed a guy with lye if she killed a guy with lye?" said Todd. "You first."

"What did you say?" I asked Todd.

"Narrow it down."

"You just said …" I closed my eyes and made a massive effort to dredge up the notion, fleeting and faint, that was tickling me. "Joan Lam—"

"—peter," said Todd. "Yeah, Kathi, stop interrupting me!"

"This is getting stupid!" I said. "I don't think it was Mo Tafoya, even if she did pay to have a horse's tail removed. And I don't think it was Mo Heedles, even if her nephew tried a cover-up. I think it was Joan."

"*What*? Why?" said Todd.

"Why? *What*?" said Kathi.

"Can you explain," said Noleen, coming in at the door, "why there's a geezer in Reception flashing his dentures at me and asking if I want to go on a cruise next week?"

"Tell him I'll be right down," said Todd. "And don't worry. He's only practicing."

Noleen turned to leave, giving us all a flash of the sweet little kitten cartoon on the back of her sweatshirt and the slogan written underneath in looping pink ribbon—*Grab this and see what happens.* "Oh, by the way, Lexy," she added. "It's getting pretty lively at your place."

But I had no brain space to worry about Kimberly and Dorian wrecking the boat in a mother-daughter brawl. I had to let my latest theory out before I burst.

"Joan Lampeter might have had her handkerchiefs re-monogrammed for her trousseau or she might not," I said. Noleen gave me a withering look and left. "And I understand now why she was so very chuffed when I first turned up."

"That *was* weird," said Kathi. "I noticed that."

"And I know who it was who dived for cover when he heard my name too."

"Who?" said Todd.

"Well, I don't know his name or what his connection to Joan is—nephew, grandson, gigolo—but I know where we met him and why he didn't want us to meet him again."

"Will you stop spinning this out before I punch you in the neck," said Todd.

"Or Noleen runs off to Mexico with Melvin," Kathi added.

"He brought her family heirloom *Lamont* tartan kilt to be dry cleaned and, when he told her where he'd taken it, she freaked out and sent him to get it back."

"And why was she so chuffed when you turned up on her doorstep?" said Kathi. "Shouldn't she have been even more freaked out?"

"When she heard my name," I said. "And she was. But when *Joan Lampeter Lamont* only heard my accent she thought maybe I'd like to sit and talk about the thrilling history of the Lamont clan with her for a couple of hours. Which, as you know, I would not. And, girl? Don't say *chuffed*."

"Don't say *girl*," Kathi replied, but her heart wasn't in it. She was thinking. Todd and I waited to hear what came of it. At last, she took a big breath and said: "What the hell's going on?"

Which was a bit of a let-down.

"Look," I said, "you need to take Mel shopping and I need to get back and finish my session. Let's get together later, Della and Roger and everyone, and hammer this out, shall we?"

As Todd and I were trotting down the exterior stairs to the car park, I asked him, "Oh by the way, did you try the number?"

"The cat death anniversary date you sent me?" said Todd. "Funnily enough, no."

"Try it," I said. "Come on, Todd, just quickly, for me. Your business partner and friend."

Todd sighed ostentatiously but he got his phone out, found his messages, opened the photo and started jabbing.

"Put it on speaker," I said and I was delighted I did. Todd's next sigh was gusty enough to make a door swing open and crash shut again, but his breath stilled in his throat when he heard, coming out of his phone, not the canned voice telling him his call could not be completed but instead, the sound of ringing.

"What da?" he said, but got no further. Because someone answered.

"Mo?" came a voice. "Stop using this number. I told you it wasn't safe anymore. Just sit tight. Mo? Is that you?" Then the line went dead.

"Can I borrow the Jeep?" I said. "To go round and snap all of them before they peel them off?"

"Sure," said Todd. "I'll take Don Juan to the Gap in Roger's car." He wiggled his key off the ring and pressed it into my hand. "Then later," he said, "we get together and make this make sense, right? Because this shit is cray-cray."

∞

"Is your grandma an animal lover usually?" I asked Kimberly when I got back to my consultation room.

"No," said Dorian, literally answering for her daughter. If she lived in Cuento, I'd have been itching to take her in hand and get her back inside her boundaries. "I think she might have had a cat briefly because she's got a memorial in the window of her minivan, but she didn't have the kitty long because the decal wasn't there at Christmas."

"Minivan?" I said. "Does she get her coffee at Swiss Sisters?"

"What kind of therapy is this?" said Kimberly. "First you leave me to be scolded by my mother then you ask a pile of weird questions about Grandma. How much are you paying for this, Mom?"

"It's a technique known as stramashing," I said. Which was a double-fried lie. *Stramashing* meant flailing about uselessly. Who knows why that word in particular sprang to mind. "It's useful to toggle between focussing attention into the room and the relationships—which is much easier in the absence of the therapist—and then focussing it out of the room away from the contentious relationship and onto shared positive areas, such as a mutually cared-for third party."

It was scary the stuff that came out of me if I was up against it.

"That makes a lot of sense," said Dorian. "And I've never heard it before. Do you do phone sessions? For after I go back home?"

"Lexy is well-known in this town for her original therapeutic thinking," Kimberly said. She was twenty and she was talking to her mother so I had no idea if she was being sarcastic about me in particular or if this was base level.

"And do you feel able to evaluate the technique?" I said. "I forgot to ask you to log your stress and upset when you came in, what with the kitten shit and all, but where is it now? Are you still angry, Dorian? And how about you Kimberly? Still feeling guilty?"

"Kind of," Kimberly said. "Because I haven't come clean about it all yet. There was more that Grandma wanted done than Agnetha's tail."

"Go on," I said. "This is a safe space, without judgement."

"Did she want you to pull tail feathers out of a rooster?" Dorian said. "Cut worms in half and Scotch tape them back together?" For a woman who believed animal cruelty was a sign of schizophrenia, she certainly had some examples all ready to hand.

"No," Kimberly said. "She wanted me to lay a nightshirt on a little hill out in the fields at the edge of town."

"Oh God," said her mother. "This is it. This is how I find out that mother has Alzheimer's and that it's in the family and I'll get it, and you'll get it, Kim."

I didn't do phone sessions as a rule but I was tempted to take Dorian on, for the challenge.

"A blood-stained nightgown," I said. "Did you provide the blood-stain or did it come that way?"

"I suppose you could say I provided it," Kimberly said. "Weird way to put it, though." She was rubbing one hand in the palm of the other, but she stopped when she saw me noticing. "I cut my finger on the shears I used for Agnetha. And I had the nightgown tucked inside my down jacket. It was the only thing to wipe the blood on. And then, when I thought about washing it, I figured it was a nice touch: blood on a shroud at a graveyard. You know, for Halloween? But after I placed it, my finger started to throb, so I went to the ER. Instead of doing the third thing Grandma wanted me to do. She's pretty angry."

I could imagine. This plan was detailed and complex and highly engineered, and Kimberly flaking out to go to the hospital to get her boo-boo kissed better had removed some essential component from it. Todd had said it—half the poem was missing—but he'd thought, wrongly, that the class of sixty-eight carousing at the market filled the gap.

Unless I was much mistaken, Kimberly was supposed to fill it. And maybe it was the key that would unravel the whole mystery. If she would only tell me.

Twenty-Seven

I was supposed to decorate the statue of that woman on Main Street," Kimberly said.

"Mama Cuento?" I said. "Decorate her how?"

"An apron and a rolling pin," she told me. "I asked Grandma what the joke was, but she wouldn't tell me. Do you know?"

"This is insane," said Dorian.

I thought hard about it for a moment. "Maybe," I said. "There's a Scottish poem where a horse crossing a bridge has her tail pulled off—"

"I didn't pull it off! I sheared it off. I was very careful not to hurt Agnetha. I ended up slicing my own finger open because I was being so careful with her."

"—by the devil," I continued. "And a witch dances in a short white dress at a lonely churchyard in the country."

"That's disturbing," said Dorian.

"It wasn't a churchyard," said Kimberly. "I wouldn't do that."

"And the first half of the poem is all about this guy's wife who's waiting for him to come home from his drinking buddies."

"Does she crack him one with a rolling pin when he finally gets in?" Dorian said.

"No, but she's very angry," I said. "She's had it with him, basically."

"But what does it mean?" Kimberly said. "Why did Grandma have me do all that?"

"I have no idea," I said. "And—if I can make a suggestion—don't ask her."

"I'm not going to ask her," Kimberly said. "She told me she'd disinherit me if I asked questions or told—Oh my God! Or told anyone."

"Your secret's safe with me," I said. "Dorian?"

"What?" Dorian said. "I'm the soul of discretion." While she paused Kimberly rolled her eyes and I worked hard at not rolling mine. "When there's an inheritance in play," she added, with a burst of self-awareness and honesty I was totally taking credit for. This was our second session after all.

∞

Della joined us after dinner, greatly increasing the chances of us making some headway and, just as I was about to launch into an update, there was a knock on the office door and Devin, the kid from Room 101, sidled in too.

"I figured we could do with a millennial," Noleen said. "Just in case." She glared at us all and the message was clear. She was not getting soft; she did not have a little warm spot for this boy; she was hardheaded and all-business and we'd better not forget it.

Anyway, she was right. It was good to have a new pair of ears in the room, forcing us to set it all out in an orderly fashion. By the time we had told Devin about Tam and the stapled-on hat, the ring and the diving nephew, the kilt on the porch and the dry-cleaning errand boy, the horse's tail and the cutty sark and the rolling pin for Mama Cuento and the obliging granddaughter, John Worth's heart attack, the uses of lye and the occupation of Patti's father and young Thomas back in the day, the yearbook and the graduation dance and the afterparty at the old Armour homestead, the bogus real estate deal, the grieving mother who might not be, and the suicide verdict that Mike was sticking to …

"I am done with RPGs!" Devin said. "This shit is awesome!"

"And don't forget the cat decals," I sang out. "Todd, did you tell them someone answered?"

"Did you get the rest?" he asked. "Did you try them all?"

"I got Joan's and Mo Tafoya's," I said. "We already had John Worth's and Mo Heedles's, so that's the set. But I haven't tried them yet."

"Well, what the hell are you waiting for?" Todd said.

"Roger?" I suggested.

"Roger's pulling a double shift. Get with the dialing, girl."

"Seriously," said Devin. "For a buncha old farts, you guys have a lotta LOLs."

Della caught my eye. "I'm twenty-eight," she said and shook her head.

I would have said something kind about how great she looked and how I wouldn't have put her a day over twenty-three but I was dialling. 09-30-15 TABI, as I had right back at the beginning of it all.

And once again the phone rang and once again someone answered with a brusque "What?"

I couldn't speak. My American accent is just about at the Dick Van Dyke chimney sweep level, I grabbed Kathi by the shoulder and pulled her into the phone. No one was breathing.

"Mo?" Kathi said. A safe bet.

"Who is this?" she spoke harshly, urgently.

"Mo, is that you?" Kathi whispered.

And then Mo—because it probably was Mo—said something that raised every hair on my head and made Kathi dink the button to kill the call.

"Patti?"

Kathi threw the phone back into my lap and sat staring at it.

"Isn't Patti the dead chick?" Devin said.

"What's going on?" Noleen said. "How come more information just makes it more confusing? It's a bullet wound! No, that's a booty suit! It's a poisoning! No, it's a suicide!"

"So ya cut off the horse's tail, Kimberly? Yeah sorry about the bloodstain. But it stopped me dressing up Mama C like June Beaver. My head's spinning." I sat back.

"Cleaver, Lexy. And mine isn't," Della said. "It's like I save up all my brain power that I don't use asking bratty kids if they want their dressing on the side and then when I do need it, I have it to spare."

"Go on," I said.

"The cutty sark, the hat, the horse tail, the scorned woman," Della said. "All of that came from the poem, right?"

"Right." It was a chorus.

"All of that pointed to the identity of the corpse, right?"

"Right." We were coordinated like a church full of Baptists.

"And yet the thing that would have positively identified the corpse to the cops was removed. The ring, I mean. Why's that?"

"Because," I said, thinking it through, "Joan's nephew, the diver, knew his aunty had just had a class reunion and here was a body with a class ring on it. He wanted a chance to warn her before the shit hit the fan. But he wasn't in on the plan. Because Tam's body was never supposed to be in the slough. It was supposed to sit rotting on a porch—John Worth's porch—until the cops came."

"John Worth wasn't in on it either," said Noleen. "And when he found the corpse, he got rid of it."

"So let's forget the class ring," said Della. Then she caught her lip in her teeth. "But if the class ring was supposed to be on the corpse and the class ring would have ID'd him, why was Kimberly running all over town planting all those other clues? It doesn't make sense."

"The class ring doesn't ID him," Devin said. "It just narrows it down. It was all the shit from the poem that pointed to his name."

"Overkill, wouldn't you say?" said Kathi.

"I would," Della agreed.

At which pregnant moment, the door to the office opened and there was Roger, a pizza box in one hand, a six-pack hanging from the other. He was still in scrubs and looked the kind of knackered a paediatrician gets after a double shift.

"Todd," he said. "Honey, this pizza and beer was meant for me and you. I'll order more."

"What happened?" Todd said. "You don't come home with carbs unless something's happened."

"I went for a cup of coffee with Maurice."

After a Sergio Leoni kind of a silence, Devin piped up: "Who's Maurice?"

"A homewrecking stalker who's going to chain my ex-husband up in his basement, which is no more than he deserves," said Todd.

"He's a pathologist at the hospital where I work," said Roger. "And he moonlights for the county. He's a weirdo all right, but he gave me some pretty hot information today."

"What's on the pizza?" said Noleen, which broke the tension.

When we all had a slice and a share of a beer, Roger swept the room with a gaze and made his announcement.

"They got Thomas Shatner's medical and dental records," he said. "They were archived in our hospital. He never sprang them when he moved to Florida. He broke his ankle when he was kid and he had his appendix removed."

"Okay," said Todd.

"The corpse in the morgue had plenty of problems," Roger said. "He drank lye, for a start. And he had cancer too. Prostate, bone, kidney, liver, pancreas ... but he had no fractures in his lifetime. And no abdominal surgery."

This silence wasn't so much spaghetti western as Buster Keaton. Della broke it.

"Of course!" she said. "Of course! Why didn't we see?"

"Right! Of course!" I said. "See what?"

"Why there was the overkill," Della said. "Why all those clues were planted to say 'Thomas Shatner'." She beamed at us. "Because it wasn't Thomas Shatner at all!"

"Bingo," Roger said. "I'm getting more pizza, Della, and you can choose what kind."

"It wasn't Thomas Shatner?" I said. "But it looks like him. The teeth. It looks exactly like him."

"So ... you knew this guy?" Devin said.

"We've got pictures of him," I said. "Todd, show Devin the yearbook. It's right behind you."

Todd opened the volume at the Future Homemakers of America and handed it over.

"Seriously?" Devin said. "This Photoshopped guy?"

It landed like a grenade. We all clustered round him to see if it could possibly be true that we'd missed something so obvious. I even put down my pizza slice. And looking at it with that idea in our heads, it was unmissable. The girls on either side weren't ignoring Tam.

They just didn't know he was there. *Because he wasn't there.* And the reason his picture wasn't in the run of senior class thumbnails was that there was no room to shoehorn him in there. And as for the portraits of the senior class council? He had never been there at all.

"What about the guy in Florida?" said Kathi, pulling up the Facebook page of Thomas O. Shatner and handing her phone to Devin.

Devin studied the blurry pictures of the motorshow and the poker game and the barbecue and shrugged. "It's the same guy," he said. "But I don't think that's Florida. The light's all wrong. I think this one is Arizona. And I think that one is Mexico. Look at the beers on the table."

"So did Thomas Shatner not exist?" I said.

Roger cleared his throat ostentatiously. "What did I tell you?" he asked. "We've got his records at the hospital. He existed. But he's not this guy Photoshopped into the yearbook, or looking like he's having such a great life on Facebook, or washed up last week in the slough."

"So we've got two questions," Noleen said. "Where'd he go? And who's that laying in the morgue?"

"So what happens now?" said Devin. "Aside from more pizza," he added, just in case Roger had forgotten.

"Now," I said, "we go and talk to Mrs. Ortiz. Of all the people we've spoken to this crazy week, she's the only one who's been straight with us. Joan hid her married name and for sure she hid her nephew. Mo Heedles hid a nephew too, and as for Mo Tafoya! She hid a fake real estate deal and a granddaughter paid to do God knows all what. And no matter what Joan said about Mr. Ortiz killing his daughter and Mrs. Ortiz covering it up, my money's on that old lady as the source of truth around here."

"Right," said Todd. "No time like the present. Devin, you stay here and order another pizza, if you like. Della, can you come? Where's Diego?"

"Chuck E. Cheeze's and a sleepover," Della said. "Try and stop me."

"I'm on the desk," said Noleen. "But I'll be with you in spirit. Rog?"

"Tuckered," said Roger. "I'd be no good to you."

"Just don't sext with Maurice," said Todd, "or I will cut you."

"I'll drive," said Kathi. "I've hardly touched my beer." I knew it was more that she loved Roger's car, but I wasn't going to argue with her.

∞

"At least she's still up," I said when we got to Mrs. Ortiz's little house on Lark Place. It was blazing with light inside and out. Fairy lights strung along the porch and every window lit it up like an advent calendar. There were a good handful of cars parked on the street too.

"You know," I said, looking at them, "if these had decals on their back windows, I'd be tempted to say they were Mo's, Mo's, and Joan's."

"But they don't," Todd said.

We could hear voices as we walked up the path and music too as we got close to the door. I rang the bell.

"*Adelante!*" a voice cried out. It sounded like Mrs. Ortiz and she sounded happy.

So we opened the door and took in the view.

Joan was in the chair that had been empty. Mo and Also-Mo were in the love seat. Little old Mrs. Ortiz was standing up halfway to the kitchen with a tray of cakes (blue), and in the other chair was a middle-aged woman I didn't know.

"Hello, everyone," I said.

Kathi was more on the ball than me though, because what she said was, "Patti. Welcome home."

Twenty-Eight

If Mrs. Ortiz's house had swinging saloon doors; if Todd, Kathi, Della, and me were wearing spurs; if Mo, Mo, Patti, and Joan were playing poker; and if the music had stopped, it still could not have been a more classic stand-off. Hoo, those things can last a long time when everyone's truly gobsmacked.

"It was the cat decals, wasn't it?" Mo Heedles said at last. "I'm sorry, girls. I should never have tried to persuade you."

"No," said Mo Tafoya. "I overdid it with the real estate listing. It's all on me."

"Oh please," said Joan. "It was me picking the wrong porch, trying to send a message. I'll never forgive myself. And wanting to clean that stupid kilt."

"It is my doing," said Mrs. Ortiz, putting down the tray of cakes and coming to squeeze Patti's shoulders. "I told the wrong story to them when they came. I couldn't do that to the memory of your father, Patti. I couldn't bring myself to say he harmed you. I spoiled everything. Old fool!"

"It was none of you," I said. "You all played a total blinder. You knocked it out of the park, I mean."

"All except Howie!" said Mrs. Ortiz.

"Oh, *Mamá*," said Patti, while the rest of us—the Last Ditch contingent anyway—were all thinking *who?*

"Is that one of the nephews?" I said. "Because it was the youngsters that blew it. Your nephew taking the class ring off, Mo. And your granddaughter cutting herself on her shears, Mo. And as for your nephew, Joan, blundering into the wrong dry cleaners! They all sucked. But none of you put a foot wrong. Mrs. Ortiz, we never doubted your story for a moment. Your story made us think Joan was lying."

"I'm sorry," said Joan.

"And your porch thing worked," Della said. "We thought John Worth was lying."

"Poor John," said Patti.

"And the real estate listing worked too," said Kathi. "We thought Mike was lying."

"Who's Mike?" said Patti.

"Sorry," Kathi said. "Molly Rankinson. Cop on the case."

"And no one busted the decals," said Todd. "I still don't know what the hell they were supposed to be for."

"Me either," said Patti.

"Excuse me," I said. "*I* busted the decals. I knew they were phone numbers. I've been saying it for days and no one believed me."

"Yeah, the cat memorials were phone numbers," Mo Heedles said. "For our burner phones. So we could stay in touch with each other without a record of it. I couldn't believe it when you started calling instead, Lexy."

"Burner phones?" I asked her. "Like the one you tried to hide in your key bowl?"

"We got carried away," Mo Heedles said.

"And why didn't John's work?" I said.

"Because his is real," said Mo Tafoya. "He must have loved that cat. He's not part of this. We just ... at the planning stage, it seemed like a good idea. To mock him. It was only ever supposed to be a private joke."

"And putting a corpse on his porch?" said Della. "Was that a joke too?"

"It was a warning," Joan said. "When the body was IDed as Thomas Shatner, John Worth was supposed to keep his mouth shut. He was supposed to find the body, call the police, and then agree that it *was* Tam Shatner."

"But he found the body, stripped it, redressed it, and dumped it in the slough," said Todd.

"Because he lives down in L.A.," I said. "And he didn't know Creek House was in the way."

"And then the missing class ring slowed down the ID," said Kathi.

"This is all very interesting," Della said, "but we're not really getting to the heart of the matter, are we? *Who is that in the morgue?* And who killed him?"

"The case is closed," said Mrs. Ortiz. "Thomas Shatner is the one in the morgue. And it was suicide."

"Except a doctor friend of ours found Thomas Shatner's medical and dental records, and it's not," I said. Todd bridled at the word *friend* but said nothing.

"What medical records?" said Joan. "I ID'd him on the slab and I loaned the cops my yearbook too."

"A doctored yearbook?" I said. "Oh yes, we're onto that."

"Was it you who stole it from the library?" Mo Heedles said. "That wasn't very helpful. We knew the cops would go there first because they need a warrant to look at the one in the high school archive. When they discovered it was missing, they were pissed. Luckily, they came to me regarding the real estate listing over the weekend so I gave them my copy—doctored, as you put it—and they IDed from that."

"Who doctored it?" I said.

"My nephew, Andy," said Joan. "He's a whiz. He's a technological genius. Of course, that can backfire. If he hadn't downloaded an app that tells him where the free first-name deals are, he wouldn't have ended up with the kilt in the wrong dry cleaner."

"I don't raise my voice much," said Della. "Even when my son put his bunny rabbit in the tank to play with his clownfish I didn't raise my voice, but if we don't stop talking about yearbooks and nephews and start talking about who is in the morgue and who killed him, I am going to blow the glass out of the WINDOWS."

And just from the decibels she reached in that one word, we believed her.

"Sit down," said Patti. "*Mamá* will make more coffee and I will tell you a tale."

It was irresistible.

Mrs. Ortiz got some extra chairs from deep in the back regions of the house and made some ferociously strong noninstant coffee that nearly cut through the sweetness of the little blue cakes.

"Graduation night, 1968," Patti said. "I went to the dance with my three girlfriends. We were ahead of our time. And then we went to the after-party at the old Armour homestead. And ..." She took a breath. "Tam Shatner raped me. And John Worth didn't stop him."

"I'm so sorry," I said.

"*I* stopped him," said Patti. "I killed him. Hit him on the back of his head with a rock and killed him stone dead. Then *Papá* put him in the lye pit at work so no one would ever find out. And I went to Florida and stayed there. The story that got around town was pretty similar."

"Except the other way round?" I said, and Patti nodded, smiling.

"If Tam had ever come back, the cops would have wanted to ask him about me; and if I had ever come back, the cops would have wanted to ask me about him. But as long as we both stayed away, it was a stalemate. *Mamá* put on a show of looking for me, but it all died down pretty quick actually."

"I see," said Della.

"And I could have stayed away," Patti said. "But two things happened. It was lovely when my mother and father came to visit, but when my father died, he died here and I wasn't beside him. And now my mother is getting older and … I don't want to say it, but I need to be here at home."

"What's the other thing?" Kathi said.

"Howie Baumgarten," Patti said. "Head of the chess club, winner of the debate team challenge, player of the bass drum in the marching band. He retired a little early due to ill health. And he moved to a small beach town in southern Florida. And I discovered that he had always carried a torch for me. He recognized me. Forty years later, he recognized me."

"*Forty* years?" said Todd.

"Yes," said Patti. "This has been ten years in the planning. Howie's cancers didn't progress as quickly as we feared. It took ten years until he was ready to go. Ten years of changing all the yearbooks."

"Did you Photoshop the smiles off the girls?" said Kathi.

"No," Patti said. "We weren't smiling. Because Tam really was there. He took the photographs and when it was just girls, he was nasty."

"So," I said. "Ten years?"

"Ten years of making a false history of Tam Shatner in Florida. He was ready a year ago, but the fiftieth reunion seemed like it was meant to be."

"So it really was suicide?" I said.

"It really was suicide," said Patti.

"He drank lye?"

Patti bowed her head and when she raised it again her eyes had filled with tears. "For me," she said. "For what I went through. To thumb his nose one final time at Thomas Shatner and so I could come home, Howie drank lye. It never occurred to him, I don't think, that it would point back to me, and to my father. He died alone in his hotel room—booked under the name of Shatner—which was what he wanted. And then we put him on John Worth's porch, as he had agreed. So far it had all gone according to plan, we thought. But then everything went wrong. Everything. Blood on the cutty sark, no costume on Mama Cuento, John putting the corpse in the slough, no class ring, Joan dry cleaning her ex-husband's family's kilt, John's heart attack, some mysterious stranger calling the cat memorial numbers. Everything. And most especially you."

"Me?" I said.

"All of you," said Della. "Investigating, interfering, working things out, getting things wrong."

"Yeah, how in the name of the Goddess did you get it into your skulls that Tam Shatner was gay?" said Mo Tafoya.

"Ummmm," I said. It was a good question. How *did* we?

"We should never have pounced on that and tried to work it into the story," said Mo Heedles.

"I panicked," said Joan. "I messed that up big-time."

"But," said Patti, glaring at me, "even though you got that wrong, you got plenty right. And you had a dose of luck. Offering cleaning to Andys on exactly the wrong day. Comparing stories, coming to speak to my mother. Even—now you're telling me—getting insider information on the autopsy."

"Are we in danger?" said Della. "Are you threatening us?"

"No," said Patti. "We're trying to persuade you. It *was* suicide. And the death of Tam Shatner was manslaughter and I'd do it again today. I'd happily take out a rapist with a rock to the back of the head. Wouldn't you?"

"But do you really think you'll get away with it?" Todd said. "Don't you think if all of this is bothering us, it's going to be bothering the cops too?"

"The case is closed," said Patti firmly. "John Worth is recovering. I'm here with my *mamá* in the twilight of her life."

"I'm not threatening you," said Todd. "I'm trying to advise you. Cases can reopen."

"I'm not worried," Patti said. Then she cocked her head.

We could all hear feet coming up the front path outside and we all saw the front door open.

"Mom?" came a voice. "I see you finally took those dumb decals off your—"

Mike stopped talking and stood in the doorway. It was bar-room stand-off time again.

"*Mom?*" I said, looking round the room and wondering.

"I'm just going to go ahead and rewind," said Mike. She held my gaze. "I didn't come here. You didn't see me. You're not going to take my badge and ruin nine lives over nothing, right?"

"Nine?" I said. I ticked them off on my fingers. "Yours, Mike. Patti and Mrs. Ortiz, Joan, Mo Heedles, Mo Tafoya, and John Worth. That's seven. Who are the other two?"

"Diego and me," Della said. "Right, Mike? ICE, ICE, baby?"

"What?" I said.

"Educate yourself, Lexy," said Mike. "If you're going to stay here, for God's sake, get a clue."

"I would," I said. "If someone would tell me to. But there's no one here telling me to. At least no one I can hear. No one I can see. The door's blown open, but maybe it'll just blow shut again."

Mike pulled the door towards her and it latched with a soft click as her footsteps began to recede back down the path.

It's what passes for a happy ending round here these days. It was going to have to do.

Facts and Fictions

Beteo County and the town of Cuento are fictional and none of the residents, streets, houses, landmarks, or businesses depicted here are real, except that: Evangeline's Costume Mansion in Old Sacramento is exactly as amazing and outlandish as I've suggested, only with much better staff; and Mo Heedles won a character name with an incredibly generous donation at Malice Domestic 30.

© Neil McRoberts

About the Author

Catriona McPherson was born in Edinburgh, Scotland, and is the author of multi-award-winning standalones for Midnight Ink, including the Edgar-shortlisted, Anthony-winning *The Day She Died* and the Mary Higgins Clark finalists *Quiet Neighbours* and *The Child Garden*. She also writes the Agatha-winning Dandy Gilver historical mystery series (Minotaur/Thomas Dunne Books). McPherson is the past president of Sisters in Crime and a member of Mystery Writers of America. You can visit her online at CatrionaMcPherson.com.

WWW.MIDNIGHTINKBOOKS.COM

From the gritty streets of New York City to sacred tombs in the Middle East, it's always midnight somewhere. Join us online at any hour for fresh new voices in mystery fiction.

At midnightinkbooks.com you'll also find our author blog, new and upcoming books, events, book club questions, excerpts, mystery resources, and more.

MIDNIGHT INK ORDERING INFORMATION

 ### Order Online:
• Visit our website www.midnightinkbooks.com, select your books, and order them on our secure server.

 ### Order by Phone:
• Call toll-free within the U.S. at
  1-888-NITE-INK (1-888-648-3465)
• We accept VISA, MasterCard, American Express, and Discover
• Canadian customers must use credit cards

Order by Mail:
Send the full price of your order (MN residents add 6.875% sales tax) in U.S. funds, plus postage & handling to:

Midnight Ink
2143 Wooddale Drive
Woodbury, MN 55125-2989

Postage & Handling:

Standard (US). If your order is:
   $30.00 and under, add $6.00
   $30.01 and over, FREE STANDARD SHIPPING

AK, HI, PR: $16.00 for one book plus $2.00 for each additional book.

International Orders: Including Canada
   $16.00 for one book plus $3.00 for each additional book

Orders are processed within 12 business days. Please allow for normal shipping time.
Postage and handling rates subject to change.